THE
SEER

LEGACY OF
STONE & SPIRIT

Front Cover and Interior Design By Rainmaker Publishing
Back Cover Photograph By D. Pepper Massey
Published by Noble Trinity Media www.nobletrinityenterprises.org
Paperback ISBN: 978-0-9789869-8-8

Publishing Support Services provided by Rainmaker Publishing.
To learn more visit: www.timetogetpublished.com

Rainmaker Publishing

THE
SEER

LEGACY OF
STONE & SPIRIT

LOVE TASHIA ASANTI

To the world-this quote from my mother is my message to you:

"True love is something that the blind can see and the deaf can hear."

—*Florence Wallace Mcgaw*

International Acclaim for The Seer: Legacy of Stone and Spirit

"THE SEER IS AN EPIC STORY ABOUT WOMEN FINDING THEIR AUTHENTIC power. It also captures the essence of unconditional romantic love. It is also a tribute to girls and women across the world who have endured the horror of trafficking and oppression. This book is Pulitzer material!"

—Sistas Love Books Book Club

"LOVE TASHIA ASANTI REIGNS AS A TRUE MASTER OF THE CRAFT OF fiction. The Seer captures the beauty of the Yoruba people and their unheralded resilience. Great storytelling!"

—GBF Media

"THE SEER IS A TESTIMONY TO THE POWER OF AFRICANS AND AFRICAN Americans. and their allies. working together to heal humanity. Lead character, Violet Brown, is a hero and woman of valor. We need more people like her to make the planet better. Bravo TaShia for another literary masterpiece."

—Urban Spectrum Media

PROLOGUE

The Seer is Born

The ancients believed in three realities. A first world where people exist to fulfill their own selfish desires. A second world, where the dead live and move as if they are still among the living. Then there is a third world, overseen by a council of Master Intuitives called The Sacred Five. The job of The Sacred Five is to keep the residents of the first world from destroying the second and third realities. Our story begins on the 400th anniversary of their birth. And on this visit, they arrive to earth on a life or death mission: Restore balance on the planet or be obliterated forever....

CHAPTER
One

Subtle. That's how they come. The same way a cool breeze brushes over your face in the early morning hours. Invisible but impossible to deny... that's how they come.

I awakened to the sound of voices. Voices without faces or bodies. They were whispering to each other. Slightly raspy but quite clear.

"Who-who are you? What you d-d-doing in my room?" My five-year-old voice shook like a California earthquake.

They—whoever they were--realized I could hear them.

"You can hear us? Do you see us too?" One of them asked.

My mouth dropped open, eyes bucked to the size of golfballs, heart pounded like a hundred drums. Then the unspeakable happened. They—the owners of the clandestine voices—materialized right before my eyes.

There was a tall, thin man leaning on a chipped wooden cane. His skin was charred like a piece of over-grilled meat. To his immediate left I saw a woman drying the tears of her children. I watched their bodies float like chiffon on the gentle wind flowing from the open window across from my bed.

Trembling, a tattered stuffed rabbit clutched to my chest, I tossed back the covers and tumbled out of bed. The tall man called out to me as I ran by.

"If you help us, we'll tell you about the necklace....and your powers. You know you've been given special powers to see and hear the dead? We'll teach you how to use them if you help us."

"You-you better leave me alone! I'm gonna tell my Mama on you!" I shouted before leaping out of bed and bolting down the hall to my parent's room to tattle on the strangers in my bedroom.

Forgetting about knocking first, I burst through the door and kid-whispered my terror to my sleeping mother.

"Mama! Mama, wake up! There's a man in my room. His wife—I can hear her crying. And the kids—they kids in there too. They got burns on 'em. Mama, I think they dead. They died in this house."

Mama rolled her full-figured frame over until she was facing me—Violet, the youngest of her two cinnamon-colored daughters. She adjusted her headscarf, wiped the sleep out of her slanted eyes and responded to my paranormal report.

"Now you listen and listen good. Ain't nothing in your room but shadows. You hear me, girl? That man you thank you seen, that's just the imprint of a jacket hanging on the ledge. And them kids you heard—that's just Puff, that scraggly ass cat you begged me for—running after Tinker, her ugly little stuffed mouse. Ain't no dead people in your room, Violet. Dead people in the ground."

"But Mama I seen them."

4

She turned over. Gave me a look that let me know the conversation was over. If I kept on talking, my behind and her hand would be making friends.

"You gon' back to bed now. You interrupting Mama's beauty rest. Keep on and you gon' wake up your daddy. Now gimme kiss." I kissed Mama's moist, salty cheek and tiptoed back down the hall. Made a beeline for my sister's room. Climbed in bed next to her. She turned over and stared me down. Shaped her irritation into an expression. I knew she was mad but I didn't care. There was no way I was going back to my room. Not that night.

"Dang, Violet! I'm tired of you waking me up over your imaginary ghosts. Why'ont you tell the truth. Ain't no spirits talking to you. You crazy!"

Instead of answering, I snuggled up against my sister's warm back, closed my eyes and drifted off to sleep.

It'd hurt that nobody believed the spirits were real. Everybody in my family thought I was making it up.

Turned out I didn't have to make Mama into a believer. Two years later, Mama became a card-carrying member of the spiritual realm. Breast cancer turned my bodacious, vibrant rose-of-a-mother into a wilted flower seven hundred and thirty days after that beast came to visit. I was seven and motherless, showing up at school with hairstyles and outfits created by a father who'd just lost his twin flame.

Despite witnessing Mama's body being lowered into that neatly dug hole, two weeks after we buried her, I sat in our living room waiting for her to walk through the door. My agony-driven denial turned into an oozing pack of lies. I told myself Mama was at *Six Doors Amusement Park* riding a roaring roller coaster and having herself a good old time. When that fantasy faded, I pictured her in Las Vegas at some fancy hotel on a lounge chair by the pool sipping on a cocktail.

Daddy sat his grief-stricken body down on my bed and lovingly but firmly, explained that Mama was on vacation in heaven, a place where the rest never ended. His brown eyes brimmed with tears as he told me the God-awful truth.

"Daddy, I don't understand. Mama said she wouldn't ever leave me. Except to go on vacation." I told him.

Daddy eased over next to me. Put his large hand over mine. Felt like a blanket of heat on my hand. His touch made me feel safe for a minute.

"Violet, your Mama ain't coming home. She's with the Lord now."

Safety left when he said that. "But Mama said...."

Daddy shushed me. "I know it's hard, baby but we got to move forward. That's what your Mama would've wanted us to do."

I'd let the tears take me. The first tears of millions to come.

Seemed like my mud-deep depression over losing Mama wouldn't go away. I loved Daddy but Mama--Mama had been my everything.

A couple of years later, the same thief that had stolen our mother slithered in through mama's sister's door. The big C had claimed two of our brown angels.

And the spirits were still coming. Coming in alarming numbers. Seemed like there were lines of dead people coming to visit me. All times of the night. Tapping me on my shoulder. Sitting on the edge of my bed. Their cool breath on my cheek. Young spirits, old spirits and everything in between.

I finally came to the conclusion that I couldn't stop them from coming. But maybe, just maybe, I could find a way to control them.

I had to.

CHAPTER

Two

Two years later, me, Daddy and my sister Diane packed up our grief in one of those slow-moving trucks and became dreamer number one million and one to migrate to the City of Angels. I fell in love with the swaying palm trees and warm California sun. My sister hated Los Angeles. City of fornication she called it. She complained almost the entire drive to our luxurious new peach-colored house.

There was one thing I had hoped to leave in the windy city—the Spirits. But they followed me. Just like the sadness my family and I were running from.

After we moved, it wasn't just the Spirits from our house in Chicago I was burdened with, there were new ones. I tried to make them go away by pretending I didn't see them but it didn't work. The voices grew louder and the Spirits materialized even clearer.

One particularly difficult day, I broke down and asked one of them where they came from and how they were able to talk to me. "Who are you? How...why're you talking to me?" Tears streamed down my face.

My bedroom took on an icy chill the way it always did when one of them came to visit. I couldn't see the Spirit's face, just the outline of its body. She had long thick braids that almost reached the floor. She wore seven strands of colorful beads around her neck. On her wrist were seven silver bracelets. As her form became more pronounced, I could see the outline of a gown with seams connected by shells. She spoke in a calm voice that reminded me of the swaying palm trees in our new home. She had a slight accent. I thought she sounded African or maybe Jamaican but I couldn't be sure.

"Be grateful you were chosen. Make peace with it and things will become easier."

How could I make peace with something I didn't understand?

I thought back to the necklace the spirit man in my bedroom had mentioned. I wondered if it was the key to my being able to control the Spirits? I was about to ask the woman about it but when I looked up the warmth had come back into the room. That familiar chill had gone and so had she.

I often wondered why my sister couldn't hear them—why the spirits talked only to me. I'll never forget the day my entire school found out I had what people called a gift—which felt more like a curse to me.

That was the day I learned my first big lesson about being psychic.

I learned the importance of knowing when to tell and when not to tell. And that was one day I should've kept my big mouth closed. On this sunny afternoon, our third-grade class was returning from lunch. I ran up to the front of the line and yanked on the bottom of my teacher's dress.

"Mrs. Evanston! Mrs. Evanston, the spirits have something to tell you."

Mrs. Evanston spun her Alabama-sun colored frame around to face me. She bent down, put her face so close I could smell the bergamot grease on her freshly pressed hair. I was standing in her shadow, completely enveloped by the light of the spirit world when my favorite teacher demanded a reason for my blatant disobedience.

"Violet, what's so important you had to disobey my directions and get out of line to tell me about it?" She motioned my nosy classmates back to the line.

Trapped by her impatient glare, lips quivering, I said, "The spirits told me to tell you don't worry. Santa's gonna bring you a new husband and you gonna get married on Christmas day."

Mrs. Evanston's red-brown complexion flushed with embarrassment.

"Violet, who told you about my divorce? I bet it was Mrs. Beasily from the art program. Always flapping her gums, telling other people's business. Doesn't matter. I'm done with that man. Now gon'and get back in line. We're late."

Becky, Mrs. Evanston's heavy-hipped assistant could tell Mrs. Evanston was irritated. She rushed over and tried to shut me up. But the spirits were on a roll. Their power was moving through me. I couldn't stop talking until they decided we were finished.

Becky pointed to the students who were already lined up. "Violet, you need to get back in line. You're making us late going back to class."

"Wait! There's something else." I closed my eyes so I could hear them better. "Mrs. Evanston, your mother says to tell you to stop crying about her because she's with the Lord. She said she'll see you in church and that she's real glad nobody ain't—I mean—nobody *hasn't* been sitting in her special seat." I said remembering to use proper English.

Up to that point, my calm, never-a-hair-out-of-place teacher hadn't let my elementary school ravings ruffle her feathers. But when I gave her a message from her dead mother—that sent her reeling.

Her mouth gaped open. Chest started heaving. Tears filled her eyes.

"Violet, what did you just say?" Mrs. Evanston turned around to face me again.

"Your mother—she said you gotta—I mean, you *have to* go on with your life. She'll see you at church. She'll be sitting in her special seat on the third row."

Shocked beyond words, Mrs. Evanston stormed toward the door of the classroom. Halfway there, she stopped dead in her tracks, turned around and came back to where I was standing.

"Violet, how'd you know about where my mama sat in church? I wasn't even working here when she passed. Nobody here knows about that. You better tell me the truth, girl!"

All I could tell her in my tiny voice was, "I don't know! I don't know how I know these things. I just do."

Unfortunately for me, the school administrators didn't think kindly of me giving my teacher psychic premonitions about her recent divorce, the new husband who the Spirits said was coming or the messages from her dead mama. Becky grabbed my elbow and marched me straight to the principal's office.

I found out later, that since the day Mrs. Evanston's mama had passed away, none of the church members would sit on the third pew, at the end of the row. That was her Mama's seat.

That was the first time a Spirit used me to get a message to their loved one but it darn sure wouldn't be the last.

Message or not, when Daddy read the note from the school principal about my little *performance*, as they called it, he promptly made an appointment to take me to see a psychiatrist. When the shrink gave her diagnosis to my daddy, I think he was somewhat disappointed.

"Violet's just a normal child with an overactive imagination. Maybe she'll grow up to be a writer." The shrink told Daddy convincingly.

"You sure? That child talkin' bout hearing voices. That ain't normal. Even I know that." My father pointed out.

"She's fine, Mr. Brown. Put her in some acting classes or something. That'll help her get more in touch with her creativity."

"Uh-huh. Creativity my ass. Something different 'bout that child." Daddy was pissed about spending darn near a hundred dollars and she hadn't found anything wrong with me.

"Completely normal." She said again as she wrote out a receipt and stuck it in his hand.

Daddy might've been off the mark a tad but he was right, there was something different about me, his baby girl. Back then, I didn't know what to call it either—my ability to know things. But I knew it wasn't my imagination or my creativity.

Bottom line was I could see and hear things that other people didn't and couldn't. And I certainly didn't imagine Mrs. Evanston's mother sitting in church, wearing her best Sunday hat, seated in her favorite seat, taking communion and reading her plaid material-covered bible.

I had never met my teacher's mother.

Never even been to their church.

Even with a stamp of mental health, I knew my search for the truth about who and what I was wasn't over. But I was thankful to Mrs. Evanston for giving me something to go on. She was the first person to tell me that I had a gift. The first among the living anyway. Couple weeks later, after she calmed down, she told me what I was like it was commonplace. Like she met people like me every day.

"You've got a gift, Violet. You're a seer. Nothing's wrong with it. Every family has one or two."

She slid her thick arm around my small shoulders while we walked to class that morning. "I had one of those grandmothers who could predict a storm long before the weatherman said a darn thing about it. She hadn't spent a day in medical school but Grandma Betty had a cure for every illness known to man."

She continued to comfort me, "No-sir-ee. Nothing wrong with being a seer at all. God chose you for this."

I ran home and told my Daddy what Mrs. Evanston had said about my having a gift. He barely looked up from the newspaper.

"You heard them people talking and put your own spin on it. That's what happened. The rest is just a crazy coincidence. You ain't no seer or prophet or none of it. Now gone in there and do your homework. See the pages in them books--that's what you need to be seeing."

Daddy was from the old school. Christianity was it, end of story. If it wasn't about Jesus, it wasn't talked about in our house. And if you wanted to grow up with lips, you had better get busy studying Psalm 91.

I did feel a sense of satisfaction when six months later, Mrs. Evanston called and told Daddy that just like I said, she'd met a wonderful man. They planned to get married on Christmas day.

"Mr. Brown, you thank little Violet for me. My Raymond is a wonderful man. We've set our wedding date on December twenty-fifth just like Mama told me to. I'm hoping you and Violet will be there."

My father just sat there at the dining room table rubbing his balding head, trying to convince her it was all just a coincidence.

She kept going on and on about how special I was and how Daddy should thank God for giving him a child with such a special gift.

"Hog wash!" That's what he said as he slammed down the phone. After Daddy hung up he called his best friend, Art Thomas, an old military buddy who had been the chef for Daddy's platoon. Told him the whole crazy story.

That's how I found out Mrs. Evanston had called. I was hiding in the kitchen listening to Daddy talk to Mr. Thomas. That conversation saved me. I had begun to wonder if I really was nuts. And my sister Diane didn't help matters any. Telling people at school I was weird. Her *weird* sister.

By the time I was twelve, the Spirits were coming every night. Then my dreams changed....

I dreamed of Africa. There were sparkling beaches, wild zebras and swaying coconut trees. Women and men dressed in colorful garb scurrying through a busy marketplace. The woman with the long locs was there. She sat perched on a huge rock telling me about my past lives.

When I asked her why she'd come, she said she was here to help me fulfill my destiny. A destiny she promised would one day determine the fate of an entire nation.

One cool summer night, as I lay gazing at the moon from my bed, she told me her name. Whispered it in my left ear.

I am Mamiwata. The mothers of all Mothers. I spit on the earth and oceans are born. I dance and mountains emerge beneath my feet. This is my world but I don't own it. I live in your dreams but I exist in your spirit. You're me and I'm you. We're one.

Mamiwata. I would never forget it.

The words that followed almost sucked the breath from my lungs.

"You must find the necklace, daughter. You can't fulfill your destiny without it."

"Everybody keeps telling me about this necklace but no one says where to find it!"

Awake and frustrated, I'd waited for Mamiwata to respond. But she was gone and I was left again with a basket of unanswered questions.

When Mamiwata returned she rewarded me for my patience. She gave me free reign in the world of Spirits but we only visited places she thought I needed to go. I traveled to Ghana, Haiti, Brazil and Cuba. The dreams always ended in what I soon learned was my ancestral beginning. A place called *Ziberia*.

As soon as I drifted off to sleep our travels began. We'd dance to the beat of ancient drums, sing ritual songs for deities I had no names for. I sauntered through the African marketplace, whisked my fingers across freshly woven baskets and thick colorful fabrics. Inhaled the enchanting aroma of sweet fruits.

My bond with the Spirits became stronger. I still didn't understand fully why they were in my life. In the years to come, they tried to show me the purpose for their arrival through my dreams.

There was a man with skin as dark as the tar they put down to make the streets smooth. He had what looked like white paint on his face. There were three stripes on each cheek. In one dream I asked him his name. He seemed to contemplate whether he would answer. When he spoke, his voice roared like thunder.

"I am Shango! Kabiosile! Obakoso! The King did not hang himself!"

The dreams showed me how Shango had won wars against thousands with only a few hundred men by his side. Sometimes a bearded woman battled alongside him. She wore a skirt the color of rainbows. Other times he came with a woman wearing a bright yellow sari with bubbling breasts and sensuous eyes. She carried a bowl of sweet honey in her left hand. She used it to sweeten his enemies.

On my thirteenth birthday I met a warrior. *Ogun*. His stomach rippled with chiseled muscles. He wore a straw skirt and had a machete strapped to his hip. As he danced, he'd run the blade across his tongue but it didn't bleed.

A few years later, during the deep slumber of my fifteenth solar return, I encountered a woman who swam up to me from the darkness of the ocean's bottom. She wore a crown of ivory sea shells and a dress covered with the same. An unborn child floated inside of her transparent belly. The baby looked like me. When I asked the child's name, the woman answered *Odu*.

I thought for sure I was losing it, that some kind of demon had attached itself to me and possessed my mind. I was so afraid that for months, every night at bedtime, I took no-doz, drank black coffee, took a cold shower and kept all the lights on to keep from going to sleep, to keep from dreaming.

I barely got four hours sleep a night for close to a year.

A few months later, the pulpit called and Daddy answered. Church became our life. If we weren't at church, we were on our way to church, coming home from church or getting ready to go to church the next morning.

One good Sunday I decided to answer the altar call. While I was kneeling and praying, I asked Jesus and his Father to take my gift away. I swore I heard Jesus say that He would take away my ability to hear the Spirits if I was a good Christian. I started going to bible study everyday after school. I joined the choir, participated in the church spelling bee. I even got baptized thinking that if I completely gave my soul to the Lord, the Spirits would stop talking.

Church and being saved helped me stay a virgin until I was seventeen and kept me from experimenting with drugs. But the Spirits didn't give a darn about my salvation. I could see them even clearer and hear them even better after being taken to the reflection pool, dunked down three times and claiming Jesus as my personal savior.

I loved the Lord but I knew there was something else out there. I had to find out what it was. If I could put a name on this thing, this *gift* I had, perhaps I could learn how to control it. Mrs. Evanston had told me I was a seer. But the God's truth was I didn't really understand what a seer was. I needed to find somebody I could talk to. I knew better than to talk to my sister. That would've been a disaster.

Diane was one of those superstitious Christians who thought anybody and anything that didn't fit into a neat little religious box was the devil. I worried she'd become a fanatic after she started attending 32nd Street Holiness Church of God & Christ No. 7. After two Sundays, Diane stopped wearing jewelry, make-up and pants. She even stopped listening to rap music. Said rappers sung the devil's lyrics.

But thank the Lord above for adolescent hormones!

When Diane discovered boys or should I say sex, suddenly those Holiness people became too extreme and according to her, *God meant for her to have a little fun every now and then.*

Still, I knew I couldn't confide in her. She spooked way too easy. Diane couldn't even watch *Stir of Echoes* all the way through without having nightmares. If I told her about my gift, the first words out her mouth would be, "That's the devil." That's what Diane said about anything she didn't understand.

I grew up thinking my gift made me a sinner in God's eyes but after Diane's dance with fundamentalism, I learned firsthand that some of those good old-fashioned Christians weren't as pure as they portrayed themselves to be.

A perfect example was Miss Shenequa, the woman who organized the bake sale every Sunday at Greater Bethlehem, the church Daddy and I attended.

It was no secret that Shenequa had shared her family jewels with just about every single man in the church—and quiet as kept, with a couple of women too.

Miss Sheneequa was always talking about how people need to repent but she was the main one sinning non-stop.

And Brother McNeily, the organ player, I'd once overheard him telling one of the deacons that he consulted a tarot card reader for the lottery numbers. I seriously considered reminding him that the good book said gambling was a sin.

Miss Sadie, the pastor's wife—oh how I wanted to tell her that those peppermint candies she ate like tic-tacs didn't quite cover up the scent of that *Johnny Walker Red* perfume on her lips.

Miss Sadie would get filled with the Holy Ghost and talk in what she called *tongues*. Nobody knew what she was saying but on some Sundays, it sounded like Miss Sadie was speaking the same language the Spirits spoke in my dreams.

With my church member's imperfections in mind, in between bible studies, I began to study everything I could about extra sensory perception and the afterlife.

I scoured Kardec's book on mediums. I immersed myself in the personal stories of famous psychics like Sylvia Brown and John Edwards. Kardec and Brown helped me understand what it meant on an intellectual level to have the gift of spiritual insight. But the spirits that walked with me had plans to introduce me to the psychic realm up close and personal...

The Spirit's plan was executed on the morning of my sixteenth birthday. I was coming back from a tennis match with my best friend, Cassandra (code name Snake because she could dance like one), at a neighborhood park. I'd won the match seven love. I was feeling on top of the world.

Snake was mad she'd lost but was trying to hide it because she didn't want to start an argument on my birthday. Whenever I won a match, Snake would argue for a whole hour saying that I did something to throw off her game.

On that day, she handed over my birthday present without a word. The shape of the present told me she'd gotten me the *Ledasi* CD I wanted.

"You got it for me! Thanks, BFF! I'll see you later at Big 10 right? And I get to pick the movie since it's my birthday." I said, offering my fist for her to give a dap too.

"Yeah, sure." Snake said dryly, smarting from the butt whooping I'd given her on the tennis court. She pounded her fist on top of mine in the official Black folks goodbye.

I gave her mine back to pound again before she darted off. Humming the Stevie Wonder version of the happy birthday song, I bounced down the road toting my birthday loot from the Snake.

I was daydreaming about the goodies I had coming later from Daddy. The birds were chirping. The sun was shining. I thought God had made it a perfect day in honor of my birthday.

Then I saw him.

The second I geared up my calves to take the hill to the broken place in the fence where I would squeeze my long, toned, brown body through the slats and take the shortcut home, I saw this tall, sweet-potato-pie colored man coming toward me.

He wore a red, black and green dashiki. Multiple strands of colorful beads were around his neck. On top of his completely shaved head was a small white cap that tilted to the right. On his feet was a pair of tattered brown leather sandals that looked like something out of a *Jesus Returns* movie.

I was a bit frightened at first but as he came closer, I found there was a peaceful energy about him. And his face—smooth as apple butter. The brother was a combination of Morris Chestnut and Blair Underwood. *Dr. Bones,* he said his name was.

I almost lost my breath when he said, "And your name is a beautiful shade of purple."

"Violet," I answered, darn near in a trance.

Dr. Bones said he was something called a *Yoruba Priest* and a doctor of herbal medicine. When I asked him what that was, he said, "One day, you'll know all about it." Then he quietly and gently invited me to join him for further conversation on a park bench.

"I have some important things to talk to you about, Miss Violet."

I was hesitant. He could see it in my eyes. I had thoughts of hillside stranglers traveling through my brain.

Dr. Bones tried to comfort me. He said he had been directed to come to the park today just to talk to me.

Concerned for my safety, I looked around and noted that there were dozens of people on the tennis courts below us within ear range of a scream. There was a lovestruck couple snuggled up on a blanket just down the path. I relaxed and positioned my tennis racket against the bench next to me. Made a mental note of how the racket could be used as a weapon. "Okay, go ahead, I'm listening."

Dr. Bones proceeded to tell me all about my life to come and the life that was behind me. It was as if Mamiwata was sitting there beside me, speaking to me through his mouth. The things he told me, she had told me many times both during dreams and when I was awake. But he knew things she hadn't told me yet.

"In the next few years, your life is going to completely change. School, work, none of it will look anything like you planned. Don't worry. You're going to be just fine."

I was speechless. Dr. Bones just looked at me and smiled like he'd happened upon a treasure chest full of gold. Then he stood up, pulled a brochure from his satchel about his holistic healing clinic and gave me his final prophecies.

"Your ancestors were great healers. You are being called by them to do powerful work in this life. One day, the fate of a people will depend upon you. This is your destiny. You must study the spiritual practices of our indigenous ancestors. Ifa. Ifa will show you the way."

I folded the brochure in half and stuffed it in my backpack. "Ifa? What's that a religion?" I asked him, now totally engrossed in what he had to say.

"Ifa is one of the oldest religions in the world. Before Christianity, before Islam, before Buddhism, there was Ifa. Do you not know that most of the Africans in the slave trade came from West Africa? When we got to America, our enslavers forced us to practice Christianity. Convinced us that the beautiful Gods of our traditional religions were barbaric and evil. Beloved, you must learn your history. You cannot go forward without knowing where you come from."

He rose to leave, then, as if someone was speaking in his ear, he paused, turned around just a bit and said, "Learn to work with your gift. Let them speak through you. Remember, you control when they come, not the other way around."

And he was gone. Like the wind he walked in on.

I sat there in a daze. A zillion questions looming in my head. We spoke by phone a few times after that but he never told me anything else about my future.

I tried to control the Spirits like Dr. Bones told me to do. They continued to come when they felt like coming. I suffered through two more years of dreams, visions, voices and Spirits. I barely slept my last year of high school.

Despite my lack of sleep, I graduated with honors and got accepted to Northpine University to study law.

Daddy was so proud he bought me a candy apple red Mustang convertible to celebrate our accomplishment. Pictures of me in my cap and gown with Daddy standing proudly beside me decorated the walls at home and at the small church he was now pastor of.

Diane was unimpressed by my accomplishments.

On the day of my graduation she sashayed into my bedroom, picked up my diploma, turned her nose up and tossed the framed certificate on my bed.

Congratulations from church members poured in. I wished Mama could've been there to see it. The Spirits said she had been. Daddy knew I was feeling a little sad that mama wasn't there so he let me have a graduation party.

Everybody came, including Terrence Richards, a jock with skin the color and texture of Hershey's chocolate kisses. Terrence was a B-ball man. A Starter. I'd had a crush on him since the 9th grade.

The adults had gone upstairs to play dominoes and drink beer. Somebody in my crew put on an Isley Brothers record. Terrence strolled over and asked me to dance.

"Can I have this dance, *Attorney* Violet Brown?"

I smiled so hard my jaw felt like it was about to crack.

We danced three records in a row. I was in heaven. It felt good being in his arms. It was nice to be the center of attention for once in my life.

Would've been a perfect evening if it weren't for the wicked witch herself—also known as my sister, Diane—showing her tail.

Diane turned off the music and quieted everyone down to make what she said was an *important announcement*. I thought finally, *finally* she was gonna break down and give me the respect I was due. I was wrong, dead wrong.

"I want to congratulate my baby sister. For a weirdo, I guess you did okay. So, tell us, what do the *spirits* say about what college you should go to? Boo-ooooo!"

Diane imitated the mythological language of ghosts. I was horrified. Everybody fell out laughing. I wanted to sock that cow dead in the mouth so she could see how weird I really was.

The truth was Diane was jealous. She was envious of my being accepted into law school. Diane was never happy about anything I accomplished.

Mama's Spirit showed up in defense of her youngest cub.

She means well. Don't pay her no attention. You hear me, Violet?

For Mama's sake, I let Diane's sarcastic comment go.

For the moment.

That night after my party, Diane and I were up late watching sci-fi movies and eating buttery popcorn. She went into a diatribe about how hard law school was and how many people dropped out after a couple semesters. "You should check out Lakewood Christian College. With your GPA, you'd do great there."

I decided right then and there that I was tired of being under her thumb. Tired of being *Diane's little sister.* That mess she pulled at my party was foul. I was through being the brunt of her psychic jokes. It was time to put Lady D in check.

"Look Diane, I'm going to *Northpine University.* Lakewood's law program didn't even make the ranks. It's important to get a degree from a school that the top firms recognize. I'm gonna miss you but I have to think about my career." I said, talking down to her on purpose.

That shut her up. But behind my back she tried to convince Daddy that I needed to go to a Christian college. Told him there were too many temptations at mainstream universities. Thankfully, Daddy supported my going to Northpine. He reminded her that sin didn't have a favorite school.

When the fall rolled around, Daddy and I packed up my room. We loaded everything in my Mustang and drove to the college dormitory I would call home for the next four years. Or so I thought...

The first night of dorm life I encountered the fancies of LaQueeta and Trunisha, my new roommates. LaQueeta was a buxom freshman with breasts like torpedoes and a butt you could bounce a quarter off. Trunisha was a tall, lanky, coffee-colored sophomore who had what looked like a thousand braids weaved onto her heart-shaped head. There were at least ten boys courting each of them at any given time. Our phone never stopped ringing. *Ever.*

The endless party life of recently freed teenagers was atrocious. I was sure that my new friends were all majoring in Party 101. I could live with the partying and the live porno on a daily basis but my real problem was the dorm where we lived seemed to be positioned over some kind of spiritual vortex.

Not only was I burdened with my own host of deities, I now had to endure the ghostly clientele of my roommates and the natives of the land that our college was built on.

Something else strange started happening. I began to hear what people were feeling and sometimes thinking. Not word for word but in bits and pieces. That worried me. I thought I might be schizophrenic, that maybe the shrink who had examined me when I was child had missed something. For the sake of my sanity and to give my mind a rest, I decided I had to find my own apartment.

I was surfing the web one night, trying to find off campus housing and waiting for my dorm mate's boyfriends to leave so I could get some sleep. Just for the heck of it, I typed the word psychic into the search engine. Nearly a million web sites came up under that heading. I'd scrolled through a twenty or so of them when I came across the *Intelligent Minds Psychic University*. IMPU had an on-line application. I took the dare, filled out the application and hit the send button. In the notes section, I'd put in a line or two about the dreams I'd been plagued with since childhood and the Spirits who visited me on a regular basis.

I was sure they'd write back with a referral to a local shrink.

In just minutes, an email invitation arrived from them inviting me to participate in a series of tests to determine the probability of my being psychic. I made an appointment for the very next day. I had no idea that I'd just scheduled a meeting with destiny.

IMPU put me through two intense hours of what the nurse called, "standard psychic tests." I had to guess words I couldn't see and describe numbers and pictures on large flash cards hidden from my sight. The results were supposed to place me in a specific percentile of those with psychic ability.

I waited in the lobby while pacing nervously, barely breathing and eager to hear my results. Not one but two counselors came out to see me.

One looked a bit shell-shocked, the other appeared to be overjoyed and that scared the crap out of me. They led me to a small sterile office with a table and four chairs and gave me what they deemed some very astonishing results. My answers, the overjoyed counselor explained excitedly, had been so accurate, that they were able to immediately confirm that I did in fact have superb psychic abilities.

"Normally," the shell-shocked one said after finding his voice, "Our clients are given a series of tests over a period of time."

"However, because there have only been three people in the history of our organization who aced every single test, we feel reasonably safe in giving you the results of your screening right away."

I was a bit confused so Mr. Joyful spoke up to clarify.

"Miss Brown, you are the fourth client in twenty-five years whose test scores came back this high. We can positively confirm that you have extremely advanced psychic abilities."

"What does it mean?"

"We'd like to recommend you to a few of our sister agencies...."

They referred me to an organization called *The California Psychic Institute* so that I could learn more about my gift. During my first visit to CPI, I discovered there was an international psychic community and that I was one of thousands of people with *the gift*.

I had found my people. Found out that I wasn't a freak nor was I crazy. I had been blessed with a talent that could either do harm or good, depending on how I used it. Finally, I was starting to understand how to use my gift and how to control the Spirits just like Dr. Bones had told me years ago. But there was still a lot I didn't get...

After I graduated, I accepted a position at a prestigious law firm in Beverly Hills. After a few months of swimming with sharks in the ocean of judiciary life, I came to the conclusion that I wasn't cut out to be a lawyer.

To be successful in the field of law, one had to abandon certain morals and idealistic values. Furthermore, it seemed to be a professional requirement that lawyers focus on one of two possible outcomes for every case, a guilty verdict or a seven-figure settlement.

The sanctuary of law was too cut and dry for me. Ruthlessness had never been my forte. But I had to eat. I had to pay the bills. That meant working somewhere. I was determined to find employment at a company that wouldn't rob me of my peace.

When I told Daddy less than a year later that I was leaving my job at the firm and enrolling in CPI's paranormal studies program, he was devastated. However, when all was said and done, to appease my father, I worked part-time at a small legal clinic for immigrants and attended CPI at night. I ended up with two totally unrelated degrees, one in corporate law and another in paranormal physics.

After my training at CPI, I merged into a pretty comfortable life as who and what I was—a psychic. Day by day, it became easier to accept the guidance of Mamiwata, the woman who claimed the main voice that spoke to me.

I started doing readings for a select group of people through an ad I placed in the yellow pages. I thought maybe I could work full-time as a psychic but quickly realized the income from spiritual work was like an elevator, up and down.

Times got even harder so I applied for and got a job doing readings at one of those psychic networks. I quit a couple of weeks later after I found out that most of the psychic hotlines were staffed with phonies. A month later, the "1-900 Call Ms. Cleo" lawsuit bankrupted the agency I'd been working for. Word in the psychic circles was that Miss Cleo was the real thing but the men she worked for let her reputation take the fall for the other phonies they'd employed.

I prayed for an answer to my dilemma. The Spirits directed me to take the test for a supervisor position at a large correctional facility. After a lengthy interview process, a generous offer letter arrived a week later. I gratefully accepted.

Diane was the first to remind me how dumb it was for someone to have two degrees and be working at a prison.

But it wasn't all that bad. I made a good salary and reported only to the Warden. My job was boring and predictable but it paid the bills. My psychic life, however, provided unlimited amounts of excitement. The lives of my clients were spicier than America's number one soap opera, *The Young and the Restless*.

I told wives about cheating husbands and husbands about their cheating wives. I diagnosed more pregnancies than the neighborhood gynecologist.

I did séances and ghost hunts. Found hidden treasures buried in walls and under basement floors.

One client even asked for guidance in selecting the right name for her new baby. When she said it was a girl, I told her Violet would be a pretty name.

The Spirits helped people get better jobs, lose weight, win lawsuits and get rid of negative energies.

At times, it could be extremely tiresome being who and what I was. I'd be eating at a restaurant with friends and upon being served our plates, the Spirits would start talking. They'd tell me which food was bad or what might make us sick because it had been sitting out too long. I'd try to come up with a way to tell my friends not to eat something.

"The coleslaw doesn't look too hot." I'd say, trying not to scare them.

They'd just laugh and say, "Violet, girl, tell those spirits to back off. You're being paranoid. There's nothing wrong with this coleslaw."

I don't think you should eat it," I'd encourage, trying to get the message across without seeming extreme. To no avail, they'd shove it in their mouth, all the while teasing me about being a hypochondriac.

Without fail, whoever I'd been dining with the night before that had been disobedient would call me the next morning to tell me they'd been throwing up all night. One day they'd learn....

Even though I had only a minute understanding of what it really meant to be a psychic, I knew and had always known that I had a mission to fulfill.

It was becoming clearer and clearer that I had been chosen for this journey even before I was born. I prayed the Spirits would give me more information. Until then, all I could do was wait for them to show me the way. And the journey ahead would be beyond anything my small mind could conjure.

Much sooner than I could imagine, I would learn more about the powers of the necklace that the first spirit who ever talked to me had told me about. And that necklace would change everything I knew about life, death and the afterworld...

CHAPTER
Three

An intensely dark dream lurked in my subconscious. I could feel it coming like the first rain after a long summer. I had come to know what kind of dreams to expect based on the energy I felt looming at bedtime. Tonight's slumber would be a haunter.

Minutes after dozing off, the dream found me. I was typing on a giant typewriter. The letters were huge, some unheard of font— like a size eighty-two. The paper I typed on stretched as wide and long as a movie theater screen.

The keys beneath my fingers were as cold as glaciers but I couldn't stop typing. I kept tapping out words that made no sense and had no relevance in my world. It was as if some force had control of my mind through my fingers. The words just kept coming and coming.

We Have Saved You. Now You Must Save The Rest.

What the hell did it mean?!

In dreamstate, I felt an icy fog float into the room and hover about like an angry ghost. The flesh under my nails turned a ghastly blue. I typed on, eventually pecking my way into a living, breathing hell. The letters on the screen melted, then shape-shifted into military men, their bodies and rifles a glimmering silhouette against a backdrop of emerging destruction. I watched the men fall like dominoes. Their tanks disintegrating into thin air.

As my nightmare continued, the scene changed. I materialized, Star Trek like, into the business section of a large city. I simultaneously heard and felt the rumble of a large engine over my head. I looked toward the sky, quickly flipped my palm upward to block out the burn of the blazing sun. I cleared my view just in time to witness the horrific sight of some sort of missile being dropped from the belly of a shiny plane on top of a skyscraper. Deafened by the explosion, all I could do was watch in silence as the horror unfolded before me.

Hot ashes floated carelessly through the air. Limp bodies landed on the cement beside where I was standing with an explosive thud.

I could hear the faint sound of desperate screams from somewhere nearby. People that had been buried beneath the heartless rubble were begging for mercy.

I dematerialized. I was back at the typewriter. My fingers danced across the keys, light as feathers, yet heavy as boulders.

Save The People and Save Yourself. Heed The Warning.

As I turned to run, an armless woman staggered toward me, her eyes silently screaming the pain ripping through her body. I shrieked when I saw a bloody bone protruding from the place where her left arm used to be. That shriek was thankfully loud enough to wake me from one of the worst nightmares of my life.

I clutched the left side of my chest as I bolted up from the sweat-soaked sheets. My heart pounded like I'd been running a marathon.

There was a glass of ice water on my night-stand. I immersed my fingers in it and brushed the refreshing moisture across my face. Images from the horrible dream flashed through my mind again. I'd had dreams like this right before the Chikawa City bombings rocked America at its core. Just like I did then, I pondered whether the Spirits expected me to do something to try to stop this catastrophe from happening. If I told the police about what I'd seen they'd think I was a crackpot. The Spirits hadn't given me any real details. What the hell was I supposed to do?

Awake but craving sleep, I decided to run myself a bath in the hope it would relax me enough to return to my slumber, minus the nightmares.

A hot, lavender salt-filled bath steamed a few feet away from me. The sensuous smell of the water mixing with the oils massaged my senses and calmed my frayed nerves. I soaked in aromatic heaven for a full thirty minutes. I rose slowly from the water and let the comforting scent of lavender seep into my pores.

After smoothing a film of vanilla-scented lotion across my legs, arms, backside and breasts, I maneuvered a pair of tweezers to remove a few unwanted hairs from my chin. The steam from my bath covered the mirror with a cloudy mist. A wet washcloth spun in a circular motion cleared a hole in the foggy haze.

I inched my face toward the glass. Chin jutting forward, I was ready to pluck the foreign invaders. Then, like the flash of a camera, a frame in a reel of movie footage, it was her face, not mine, that appeared before me.

Mamiwata.

She'd stepped out of my dreams into my bathroom mirror.

Mamiwata was here!

I dropped the tweezers in the sink, stumbled backwards a few steps, almost lost my footing.

Shocked and mildly confused, I wondered why she'd shown herself so boldly?

I knew from doing readings that when the deceased appeared in the physical it was because they'd exhausted all other methods of getting a message through. Maybe that's why she came—maybe she was trying to warn me to pay closer attention to the signs in my dreams.

After my heart's rhythm returned to normal, I returned to the image in my mirror. This time the reflection was my own.

Felt like I was looking at a stranger. And what I did know about her, I desperately wanted to forget. Forty. Still searching for a soul mate. Ten years of job experience that would be an obscure factor in four or five years.

To make matters worse, *the dead liked to hold conversations with me.*

I had to get the Spirits to give me more information. That was one lesson they didn't teach us at the California Psychic Institute. But I knew it was a lesson that, if mastered, would one day save my life....

CHAPTER
Four

America

I tapped the base of the lamp to dim the lights to a pitch comfortable for sleeping. I searched for and finally found a groove in my king-sized bed that would cup my body for the duration of my slumber.

My head felt heavy as it sank into the feathers of my rose-scented pillow. The smell of roses comforted me in my aloneness, even though I knew without a shadow of doubt that human beings are never really alone.

I lodged the thick, white, down comforter under my backside and kneecaps, insulating its tiny cushions across my body. I felt myself drifting. I was there with her again.

Mamiwata. My grandmother, four generations back.

Sometimes she spoke to me in a West African patois. Other times, she spoke perfect English. The dialect she used seemed to depend on the circumstances she was revealing. The more intense the situation, the deeper her accent.

Tonight her voice was Mother Africa one hundred percent.

She came alone on this visit. Often she came with others. Ancestors. Spirit Guides. African Gods called Orisa who the ancestors said were my Guardian angels.

Mamiwata took my hand and guided me into the birth canal of a mother in labor. As we slid into that magnificent galaxy, we became as tiny as Alice when she entered the metaphorical Wonderland.

I gazed upward and saw a baby moving into the birthing position in the mother's womb. Mamiwata summoned the baby into that dark, hollow tunnel to the light at the end of the womb. We eased out of the canal seconds before her. Our spirits rose and hovered about the small cave that served as the birthing room.

The room was filled with flickering candles. Herbs boiled in a large pot above a blazing fire. The swirling smoke of frankincense burning on a charcoal gave a pleasant scent to the musky air.

I inhaled the rich array of earthy smells surrounding us. Fixed my ears to hear the sound of fresh water flowing gently from a nearby orifice. The peace and tranquility in the cave was unlike anything I had ever known. The warm, watery floor was moist from the ocean just on the other side of its door.

My feet touched down for a brief moment to get a better view. The water seemed to baptize my feet as I moved solemnly about.

I slithered back to the ceiling of the cave and watched the large feet of those who I'd come to know as the *Sacred Five*. Serving as Midwives to the mother, they moved quietly about the rectangular platform where the child was being born.

I witnessed her shiny head erupt. Her amber-colored body slid slowly into the light. Mamiwata and I remained inches away, always in close proximity but never close enough to touch her.

One of the wives bathed her in an herbal mixture. The other caressed her writhing body with an oily balm. Another of the wives promised a name into her tiny ears. "Mamiwata," She said. And together, they chanted it, over and over, like a sweet simple song.

"Mamiwata. Mamiwata. Mamiwatahhhhh!"

It had begun. My beginning. And then there was the necklace.

The young mother sat up just a bit to greet her newborn child. The wives supported her back with their strong hands. The head wife dangled the necklace between her fingers, waiting for the perfect moment to give it to the child.

The mother nodded her head in approval. The head wife held the stones up toward the heavens and charged them with the powers of the ancient ones.

"B'ao ku ishe o tan. Ohun ori wa se. Ko man ni s'alai se eo. Ebo fin, Eru da. Where there is life, there is still hope. What Ori comes to fulfill, it cannot help but fulfill it. The offerings are accepted, evil forces depart."

The sparkling onyx and amethyst stones glowed under the moonlight. A thick silver wire held them together in a spiral embrace. The senior wife passed the necklace to each of the remaining four wives. One by one they spit on the stones and exhaled their life force into it. When the necklace was returned to the head wife, she lifted her breast, placed the necklace beneath it and let her own heartbeat infuse life into the stones.

The head wife picked the baby up, put her mouth over its tiny heart. She spoke her charge into the soul of the infant daughter.

I knew intuitively that her invocation held some key to my own path. I listened carefully, not wanting to miss a single word. The midwives joined her, speaking in perfect unison.

"Mamiwata. We bestow upon you the power to change futures. We give you and all of your descendants to come, the fruits of our gift."

"You must use your gift to save people from destruction. You must never forsake the ase' that we have placed upon your Ori. We have saved you, now you must save the others. It is done." She said tieing the necklace around the baby's plump neck.

"There will be tribulation on your path. May the colors of this stone remind you of your greatness, of the blood that runs through your veins, the power that rests in your vision. In times of struggle you must invoke the magic of the stones. We will come to you. You will be a great healer, my daughter."

When the ritual was over, the baby turned and looked up at Mamiwata and I and whispered, "Someone is in great danger. Your gift is their salvation. We will help you but you must make the sacrifice to save them. You will be told more when it is time."

Her face was that of a full-sized adult. Her face was the full-grown Spirit I knew as Mamiwata.

The alarm startled me awake. I lunged from my pillow. Slapped the button on the clock with my open palm. I tried to recall the details of my dreams as I had learned to do over the years. My mind felt like a computer hard drive that had been wiped clean of all memory.

The messages in the dream had been important. I got down on my knees and prayed, tried to force my mind to re-conjure the images.

As if they were answering my question, the spirits whispered in my ear:

Save the children and save yourself. You will be told more when it is time.

CHAPTER
Five

I washed the dishes in silence. Felt the heat of the sun as it invited me to take in its magnificent splendor. I opened the kitchen window and inhaled the morning's perfumes, let the sweet smell of dew make love to my lungs.

I carried a frosty glass of water down the hall to my altar. I stayed there long enough to witness the Spirits show themselves in tiny bubbles that floated to the rim of the glass. I lit a white candle and sprinkled a few drops of Florida Water cologne. Felt the atmosphere in the room become light and airy. The ancestors began to drift in like they always did. I left the room before they started talking.

I dressed quickly. Rushing was a way for me to avoid thinking about the things that plagued me. My thoughts often chased me down. Sometimes they caught me. Mostly it was the desire to be desired that I ran from. The hunger for kisses to light my skin on fire. For orgasms to leave me lifeless and dreaming of good things. I'd had good sex. Bedded great lovers. Been joined with what some would say were good men. But I wanted to lose myself in the soul of someone. I wanted to be completely open and vulnerable— the way the shore was when the ocean drew its foam back into her mouth.

I boarded the subway and made my way through the maze of commuters going to and from the Valley. When I sat back in my seat, I realized that even though I'd slept all night, I was still tired. The astral traveling psychics did when they slept often robbed them of that rested feeling.

I arrived at work a few minutes early and reluctantly entered the barbed-wired, cement building from the West doors. When the first prisoner came through booking, I was centered, positioned at the supervisor's desk, ready to field the energy that was part of my everyday collage. But I wasn't ready for her...

She arrived at the screening area handcuffed and feet shackled. A woman with skin as red as Arizona-mud was ushered in by two armed guards. I had never seen a human being so full of grief and hopelessness.

Incoming prisoners are always patted down, frisked and strip-searched before they're booked and assigned to a cell. After 9/11, California prisons had implemented a secondary screening. It was to ensure prisoners of violent crimes had no weapons or explosive materials in places that couldn't be seen.

Normally, I'd let one of my staff conduct these screenings. But today, something lifted me out of my chair and over to the archway. I had the wand in my hand before the woman made it to the block.

My spirit left my body the moment I touched her.

As soon as my fingertips brushed across the lower part of her left breast, at the line where the underwire lifts the flesh, the Spirits rocked my third eye with a series of scenes from the last few days of her life.

I saw everything.

Maybe it happened because I had placed my hand so close to her heart and her heart was so damn heavy. Or maybe it was destiny that she'd come to my prison, my cell block, on that particular day.

In the first scene, I saw her husband come in through the back window. Saw him shoot and kill her sister. Two shots to the head with a 357 Magnum. The sister's murder had been a mistake. She had been bundled up in the bed with her face covered. He thought he'd killed his wife.

Then I saw him go downstairs, to the children's room. He shot one baby, then two and was about to fire a round at the third child who was awake now. Sheer terror filled her twelve-year-old eyes. That's when our prisoner fired on him. Unloaded her gun into the body of her sick ass husband.

Monique Davidson. That's what the spirits said my prisoner's name was. And she was 100% innocent. One of the few prisoners who walked through my camp that really was. But the police couldn't find the husband's gun.

The spirits showed me where her husband had hidden the gun when she left him lying on the floor in a pool of blood to call the police. The gun was stashed under a loose floorboard in the children's room.

Miraculously, the husband had lived and was blaming his wife for the murder of her sister and their youngest child. Said she'd always been jealous of her sister and thought they were fooling around. The baby had been a casualty.

People were dead and somebody had to go down. The cops had arrested Monique and charged her with murder. It was her word against his.

The middle child survived the shooting but was in the hospital in critical condition. The oldest child was in a trauma-induced coma making her unable to tell the truth about the horror that happened that rainy afternoon.

From a far-off place, I heard Nancy Chavez, a short, heavyset Latina who walked with a slight limp and my second in command, calling my name. When I didn't answer, Nancy tugged on my sleeve. Her tugging brought me back from the torturous vision that had taken me into the prisoner's bloody reality.

"Miss Brown? Violet! Boss lady? You okay? Can the prisoner go on down to booking?"

I stood there in a psychic daze, right arm outstretched, four fingers under the woman's breast. I'd never been so embarrassed in all of my life. The woman probably thought I was a lesbian.

I snapped out of it like I had come back through an invisible door. The crazy thing was I didn't remember opening the door or walking through it. One minute I was there and the next I was totally gone.

"Is the prisoner approved for processing?" Nancy asked me again.

"Yeah....sure. Let her go on through. She...she looked like somebody I used to know. Somebody I went to college with."

The prisoner snapped out of the spell cast by her grief for a second or two. When our eyes met, I knew she knew that I knew.

Eyes filled with hope and grief, she said, "You know something don't you? You know what he did! If you know what happened you have to help me."

"I have no idea what you're talking about." I said, turning my eyes away.

"I'm about to go to prison for life! My kids could end up with that murdering bastard! If you know something you have to tell somebody."

I saw her eyes tear up as the guard took her elbow and nudged her toward processing. I had to think of a way to get the information about where the gun was hidden to someone who mattered. I got an idea.

I looked over at Nancy who was staring at me like I'd lost my mind. She shook her head and walked off toward her post. I called out to her. She walked back to the station.

"What you need, boss lady?"

"I need you to get me a copy of this prisoner's paperwork. Arrest reports, trial info, court appointed rep and all."

Nancy lowered her glasses and got her lips ready to ask me what for. But before she could get the question out, she thought better and said, "Sure thing, boss lady. No problem."

I thought about telling Nancy what had happened and why I needed the paperwork but quickly came to my senses.

First, if I told her the truth, she'd never believe me. Second, there was no telling what she would do with the information. I couldn't risk her blabbing her mouth to everybody.

Even though this job was just a means for me to survive, it kept the rent paid, my lights on, car note up to date.

I wanted to help Monique but not at the expense of losing my j.o.b. Plus, she knew that man was bad when she married him.

I needed somewhere quiet to finish my weekly reports and a couple of minutes to unwind from the morning's psychic journey. After the a.m. rush was over, I headed toward the break-room, poured myself a cup of tea and sat down to finish my paperwork.

My eyelids were heavy. I massaged my temples, sipped on a cup of honey-sweetened Zen tea and let the stress drain from my shoulders. An hour later, my boss came running down the hall.

"The news just announced that some kind of bomb is on its way to Los Angeles! We have to evacuate the building and..."

Before she could finish her sentence, I felt something that felt like an explosion shake the foundation of our building.

My coffee cup, along with the remainder of my morning coffee, crashed to the floor. The devastation in my dream—was this what the ancestors were trying to tell me?

I called Nancy on the walkie and told her to double the staff at the security station. I ran to the windows facing the street to check out the scene from our floor. Sure enough, something had blasted a hole into the side of our building. There was a fire burning like a raging volcano three floors down. Survivors from the lower floors galloped out of the building and down the street in an effort to get away from the lung-clogging ash. I started bawling uncontrollably. I knew we'd never make it out of there.

I felt someone tapping me on my shoulder and calling my name but I couldn't answer. I thought I had lost consciousness. I found the strength to speak and told them, "S-s-stop-stop calling me! Can't you see what has happened?"

Now they were jabbing me in my side, trying to get my attention. I was focused on getting help for the survivors.

"Stop poking me!" I said, coming out of my mid-morning slumber.

I woke up to Nancy standing over me. Embarrassed and equally mortified, I quickly wiped the tears from my cheeks and the sleep induced saliva off my chin.

I'd been sleeping on the job. Grounds for immediate termination. Nancy was on my heels for the second time.

"Jesus, I must've dozed off. What time is it?"

"Are you okay? You were crying. I could hear you from the hallway. Anyway, the boss-man is looking for you. He's waiting on your report." Nancy announced, irritated by my irritation.

I prayed Nancy hadn't told him about my on-duty slumber.

"Tell him I'll be right there." I tried to think of some excuse for my unacceptable behavior. "I didn't sleep too well last night."

Nancy wobbled down the hall back to her station, her hips and thighs weighing the rest of her body down like iron. Fortunately, she seemed to be the only one who had witnessed my inappropriate nap. The kitchen had been closed when I got there.

I dropped off my weekly reports at my supervisor's desk, drank two cups of black coffee and went back to my station. I walked down the hall in a half-stupor, still trying to make sense of the violence in my dreams.

5:00 o'clock came quickly. I was glad to leave the pandemonium behind. Between the horrors from my first incoming prisoner to my mid-morning nightmares, I'd had enough.

I packed up my thermos, the remaining items from my lunch and clocked out. My body craved sleep but my spirit was afraid of what sleep might allow to slip into my consciousness. This was one of those nights I didn't want to hear what the ancestors had to say. Tonight, I wanted to be normal. I wanted to go to sleep and wake up without a visit to the land of the paranormal.

The subway ride home was uncharacteristically quiet. My fellow riders seemed to be in a daze too.

I was relieved to be home and in the solace of my own space. I heated my vegetarian TV dinner, checked my messages and pointed the remote at the TV to see what the idiot box had to offer. I clicked on the evening news. The news at seven rattled off its regular offering of unsolved murders, raging wars, stocks crashing and missing person reports. I wasn't in the mood to watch the tragedies unveil tonight.

I was feeling my daddy. Wanted the bass in his voice to caress my heart strings. When I picked up the phone and put it to my ear he was already on the line.

"Daddy, you're gonna live a long time! I was just picking up the phone to call you. What's happening old man?"

I could see him, sitting in an old stuffed chair, curly Black hair and manicured mustache shimmering with pomade, skin the color of fresh brownies.

"You got the best hand. Told you 'bout waiting so long to call. One day you gon' call and they gon' tell you the Good Lord don' carried your daddy home. When you get my age, you never know when the Lord is gonna call in your number. How's my baby girl doing?"

"As ornery as you are, you're gonna outlive all of us. I'm fine. Had one of those bad dreams. Bombs exploding, planes crashing. It was awful."

"You still having those dreams? You know these are the last days. The Lord told us it was coming. It's all in the good book. The only thing that can save us now is salvation."

Daddy and his bible talk. Daddy thought Jesus was the answer to everything and that the answer to everything we questioned was Jesus. Maybe it was.

"Whatever you say, Daddy. Whatever you say."

"Ain't no whatever to it. I'm gon' be ready when the Savior comes. What about you, Violet? You have salvation? Did you ask the Lord to forgive your sins?"

"You know I have. At least five times just so you would be sure. Are you happy now?"

"Sure am. Cuz' when the devil comes down and that fiery pit opens up, ain't gon' be no turning back time. You got to get right with the Lord right now."

There was no sense in arguing with him. Not like he was changing his mind.

"Daddy, I'm gonna turn in now."

I couldn't take one of his hell, fire and brimstone speeches tonight. He wasn't letting me off the hook that easy.

"When you coming to see your father? I want me some of them chocolate covered raisins."

"You know you're not supposed to eat those. You have diabetes, remember?"

"Let your father enjoy the time he has left, okay?"

"You aren't going anywhere anytime soon. Being crotchety has its benefits." I said, cracking up at my own joke.

"Bring my raisins when you come."

"I'll stop by the store and pick 'em up. Love you, Daddy."

"Love you too, Slim. You ask the Lord to keep them bad dreams away."

"I….okay, Daddy. Sure."

I reclined backwards in my easy chair until my feet were high in the air. The talk with Daddy and a hearty cup of chamomile tea guided me into a peaceful sleep.

It was the phone, not my alarm clock that woke me up. I scrambled for the phone, jostling it the way sleeping people do when they're suddenly awakened.

"Yes...Hello."

I hoped it was a wrong number and not a client. I wasn't in the mood to read anybody tonight.

"Is this Violet? Deep Violet, the Psychic? I saw your ad in the phone book. I need a reading real bad. My husband is driving me crazy."

Like my mother used to say, no rest for the weary.

Six months prior, I'd put an ad in the yellow pages offering psychic readings. Calls like this one made me wonder if that had been a mistake. To my dismay, the caller continued her hysterics.

"He won't listen to me! I don't know what to do. Are you real….can you really see the future?"

Why call a psychic ad if you don't believe in psychic powers? Some of these people…I swear.

I ignored her question about the authenticity of my gift. "This is Violet. What's your husband's name?"

Glad for a distraction from my crazy life, I walked down the hall to my altar room.

I lit a candle and a fresh stick of sandalwood incense. The sweet smelling smoke swirled above the table and around the room.

"I just don't know what to do. Can you help me?"

"His name please"

"Mark."

"And his last name?"

"Devereaux."

"And your name?"

"Evelyn."

I sat quietly in my chair and meditated on their names. Mamiwata began to talk to me in a soft whisper.

"What's driving you crazy is that he won't be the man you want him to be. Either love him for the man he is or find someone else."

"I just want him to go to school and get a trade. We'll never be able to raise a family and buy a home with the pennies he makes at the factory."

"Like I said, you have to love him for the man he is. He's happy with his life. If you want financial independence, bottle and sell that salad dressing you've been making for the last ten years."

"I---how'd you know about that? Guess that was a dumb question."

It was a dumb question. And she was working my nerves big time.

"It's my mother's recipe. Everybody raves about how good it is but I just....I didn't think it would sell up against the giants."

"If you're waiting on your husband to get rich, you'll be waiting a long time. You have any other questions?"

"Will my mother's cancer go into remission?"

An answer popped into my head but for something like this I needed to be sure. I retrieved four glossy cowry shells from my altar. Spread them out in front of me. Said a quick prayer asking the ancestors to speak through their mouths.

I shook the shells between the palms of my hands and let them fall onto the straw mat in front of me. Two shells up and two face down. It wasn't her mother's time.

"Your mother will pull out of it."

"Praise God! Thank you, Jesus!" She said, crying, almost hysterical.

Sniffling and still a bit emotional, she asked, "How much do I owe you?"

"I don't charge for my services. You can give an offering if you like."

As I was getting ready to close, Mamiwata whispered something in my ear.

Tell her to tell her mother to consider ridding herself of the things and people that are driftwood in her life. I see them hanging like iron weights around her soul. Tell her to get some mud from a sacred location and have her mother rub it on her breasts. Wrap them in a white cloth and sleep in the mud overnight. Second night use a little castor oil.

"Wait. There's something else. In order for your mother to completely heal, she needs to rid herself of people that bring her down. Do you understand? This is imperative. Sometimes the negativity of people can make us sicker than any disease on earth. And tell her to go to a sacred location and get some mud. Rub the mud over her breasts and leave it on overnight. Follow up the second night with castor oil. That's all."

"I'll tell her what you said. And I know exactly what people you're talking about. Thank you so much. Thank you for everything."

CHAPTER

Six

Easy.

My being psychic made it easy to fix other people's problems, to answer the questions that plagued them and make their lives whole again. It did little to solve my own issues—issues that started with a forty-year-old wound that no medicine, spiritual or otherwise, had been able to heal.

Issues like why hadn't the Spirits shown me how to save my mother from the cancer that devoured her like a vulture feeding on unprotected prey?

Like why I couldn't find a decent man? The ones I loved didn't love me. The ones who did love me....well, let's just say they came from the reduced-for-quick-sale bin and what I was looking for was new arrivals.

I glanced under the bed at my friend Mr. V, my trusty vibrator. Thought about pleasuring myself but that cold hard plastic lost its appeal before I could plug it in and turn the power on.

I clicked off the television and melted into my bed. It wasn't long before I began to drift. Within minutes I fell into an almost hypnotic sleep.

I felt the familiar heaviness of my spirit leaving my body. Soul parted from flesh and became as light as midnight clouds. I hovered over the bed just above the fan watching myself partake in deep slumber.

She came to me. Mamiwata. She was a young woman in this dream.

I followed her down a dimly lit path into the deep forest of Africa. She sat perched atop a large rock. I stood back so that I could watch her. She was closer than she'd ever been. I could feel her heat and smell the deep musk of her amber skin.

My eyes were drawn to the glimmer of sparkling black and purple stones encased in silver hanging around her neck. I wanted to touch them, to lose myself in the coolness of the dark stones. It was the necklace the spirits had told me about. In those magical stones lay the key to mysteries my soul had been born with.

My weightless body descended to the floor. I took three, four, five steps in her direction. I expected her to turn to the sound of me approaching but she didn't budge.

I touched the hem of her dress. An electrical current rocked my body like bolt of electricity. I wailed like a hungry infant summoning its mother.

She pulled me to her. Made a river of my tears. Her embrace spoke a silent empathy for the pain I was hiding.

I laid my head across her lap. At that moment, she was all, just all.

Mamiwata's hips had a valley of gods and goddesses sleeping silently in their dips and folds. Her legs were like tree trunks. They swaggered down the dusty roads of the small village.

I remembered her better than my own mother. Remembered her sweet breath. Remembered the deep lines surrounding her eyes and the corners of her lips. I recalled her incantations. Had witnessed her fingers dancing incense across a blazing fire.

She'd been coming to me since I was a little girl but this visit was more intense than any other. I had to hold on until she revealed why she had come.

Motherless and often depressed beyond daylight hours, I sought this matriarch as if she were water. I needed to sink myself into her bosom. Drink her sweat: the salty sacred oil of woman. I journeyed deeper into the dream.

She lent me her hands. They caressed my jaw-line and eyebrows with a holy gesture. A touch only God herself could deliver. I wished I worshipped a God like her.

Our breakfast steamed in a huge black cauldron. The scent of her fruit-sweetened soup enchanted my senses. She looked at me and smiled, her teeth glowing like the logs beneath the fire she was stoking so patiently. Instantly I felt beautiful.

My thin hair transformed into shiny onyx coils that flowed from my scalp like bushels of fine fabric. It seemed Mamiwata could see the beauty in me when I felt most ugly. When I felt like my skin was oozing, begging me to slash it with a thorn-ribbed branch.

These were the visits I loved the most. In these dreams Mamiwata would speak my beauty true, strong and softly.

"Come, my beautiful child." She'd say in her velvety voice.

When I leaned into her, she drizzled a few drops of saliva between her index and middle fingers and washed the fear from my eyes. Jerked the angst from my heart. I became unafraid of looking insane to passersby.

"She left me! My mother!" I shrieked, childlike, slithering from her lap onto the dirt beneath her wide feet.

"She no leave you. She leave her body behind. Now she your light."

"I don't need no light. I need a muddah." I answered, not sure who was speaking through me.

"I'm your muddah." She said, softly caressing my face.

"But you're there and I'm here!" I screamed and bolted down the trail that led to the blue-green shadows on the foaming sea.

I sat at the shore petitioning the Water Gods for answers.

Why did mama have to die and leave me here to understand my gift?

Why had I been born in a country that didn't revere the Seers?

I wanted Mamiwata to be my mother. I wanted to travel through her bark-colored thighs into the hands of the Sacred Five.

How come I only got to follow?

CHAPTER

Seven

The sound of a blaring car alarm snatched me from my dreamstate. I remembered getting into bed but whatever happened after I slid beneath the covers was a fog. Felt like I'd been on a long trip and had gotten stuck somewhere.

I turned over and read the glowing numbers on my clock. 3:00 am.

I changed sides, wrapped my womb around a body-length pillow. My dream resumed where it had left off.

This time Mamiwata wore red. A crimson cloth framed her shiny black face. She carried a goat on her back.

"What's that for?" I asked cautiously.

I knew she discouraged questions while she was doing her spiritual work but I was worried that an animal would be slain.

She spoke perfect English this time.

"The time grows near. The path to your destiny is unfolding like a rose at sunrise. This offering will protect you from the danger the Gods have shown us through the oracle. We must make sure you arrive to the destination unharmed."

I watched intensely as she sprinkled water then a white chalky powder on the goat's eyes and around his lips. She thanked him for his willingness to take on my burdens, prayed over his body for what seemed like an eternity. When she finished, she beckoned me over to where she was working.

"Put your head to his head and pray as I pray."

I repeated after her. "Omi Tutu, Ona Tutu, Ile Tutu, Tutu Laroye…" She sprinkled water on and around the goat. "Kosi Iku, Kosi Aro…."

"What are you saying?" I asked, unable to contain my curiosity.

Her expression told me she didn't appreciate my interruption but she obliged me with a short answer just to shut me up, "I'm averting the negating energies that pursue you."

She pointed at the goat then motioned with her eyes for me to be quiet and listen.

"There is a man who will stop at nothing— not even murder— to prevent you from fulfilling what you have come to this earth to do. This goat agreed to save you. When I release him into the wild he will carry that man's malice to the Earth God. There is but one requirement for this sacrifice. Now that we have saved you, you must save the others."

The same words I'd heard in my dream.

Before the shock could register on my face, she grabbed my shoulders, twirled me around three times to the right and three times to the left. Ran her magic cloth up and down my body and held it over my heart.

She prayed to the Gods, asked them to help me get to my destiny. When she sprinkled the white chalky stuff over my head I began to shake uncontrollably. The spirits of my ancestors passed before my eyes.

Their arms were outstretched. They passed me from one to another hugging and kissing me. They made me promise not to forget them. They told me their names.

Mamiwata

Yemoja

Delores

Anna

Beezie.

The last one to come was Valentine. Valentine had been my real mother in this life. I felt them travel through my body like bolts of lightning.

Once again, I was slapped awake by the sound of a distant alarm. My spirit suctioned back into my frame as I bolted up to silence the plastic timepiece beckoning my soul back to this life.

CHAPTER
Eight

I dressed for work then remembered it was Saturday. I took off my uniform and put on a pair of white nylon sweatpants and a white t-shirt. Swathed my head in a piece of white material both because my hair was a mess and to increase my psychic connection. I needed the spirits to give me something—a sign, anything to let me know I was headed in the right direction.

A well-used set of tarot cards sat in the center of my altar. Impulsively, I shuffled the cards, pulled three from the deck and laid them out in front of me.

The first card represented my past. Elegba, the trickster in indigenous theology. His presence meant my fate had not been decided. The second card symbolized my present. It was Oshun, the Yoruba Goddess of love. That meant romance was on the horizon.

The final card spoke about my future. It was a man climbing up a palm tree to harvest his coconuts which meant my sacrifices would not be in vain.

After the tarot reading I decided to prune my plants. I needed to be close to the earth, to feel and smell the gritty, moist granules between my fingers.

I filled my watering jug with cool water. Added a bit of fertilizer and stirred the mixture with my hand. As I poured, Anna, the Geechee woman, who was also a closet Voodoo priestess and rarely came to visit me, whispered in my ear:

Your gift is not a curse, Mademoiselle. You were chosen to resurrect us. Do you understand what we gave up so that you could be our sacred one?

I spoke back to her out loud.

"I wouldn't be so damn lonely if I didn't have this gift. Men are afraid of me. Once they find out what I am, they think I'll be reading their minds day and night, that they'll never have a thought or fantasy that is secret from me. I tell them it's not like that but they don't believe me."

He who knows the secrets of the continuous circle of life will believe you. He will not be afraid of your gift, he will treasure it. And he is coming. Coming soon. He will keep your soul calm amidst the coming storms.

"Love? Not another human soul full of vacant promises and romantic ideas." I said talking out loud again in an irritable tone. "The last lover almost killed me. Don't you remember? David. I was pregnant with his child when he disappeared into thin air. My grief caused our baby to return to the ancestors. You can keep your love. Thanks but no thanks." I shouted at the ceiling.

Then I realized what I had just done. Yelled at people who weren't even here. I fell out laughing at myself.

I rose to answer the ringing summoning me from my bout of self-pity. Realized my hands were covered in earth. I rinsed them off and dashed for the phone. On the other end of the line was my sadistic sister Diane calling to torment with some of her masochistic love.

"Can't you call your sister sometimes?"

I wasn't in the mood for her drama today.

"Is your finger broken? And you know what else? It'd be nice if you brought my nephew and niece by to see me every once in a while." I shot back at her.

"Violet, don't go there. You know exactly why I don't let you keep them. I don't want to have to explain to my children about that freaky ass altar you have up in your house. You'll have my kids having nightmares. Anyway, I called to see how you're doing. Read any good minds lately?" She asked sarcastically.

I didn't have the energy to argue with her. Too much on my mind already. "I'm fine. Tired as hell. Thinking about going to the movies. Couple of new sci-fi flicks just came out."

"You always have loved that mess. I don't know how you can watch people being stabbed, killed and reincarnated without having nightmares for a month. So, what you doing for your birthday? Thought we could have dinner at that nasty vegetarian restaurant you love so much."

Diane could be a negative bitch sometimes.

"Giving up fried chicken wasn't easy. But if you knew what I knew about the journey your meat takes before it gets to your plate you wouldn't eat it either. But as you said, *let's not go there.* I'd love to go to dinner on my birthday. On one condition. Bring the kids with you. If you won't let them come over you could at least let me take them out sometimes."

"When or should I say *if* you have children of your own you'll understand. Children are very impressionable. I don't want you to get one of your visions while you're driving down the street. But yes, I'll bring them along. They talk about you all the time, especially Laney. She sleeps with the doll you gave her for Christmas every night and has to take that ugly little thing with her everywhere she goes."

"Told you before, my gift doesn't work like that. Rarely do I have visions unless what I'm being told is a matter of life or death. Usually they just talk…"

Diane interrupted me.

"Who is *they*, Violet? You sound like a psychopath talking about invisible beings that talk to you about the lives of strangers. You need to get some therapy. They have diagnoses for that kind of stuff. Anyway, let's change the subject. What time should the kids and I pick you up for dinner?"

I started to try and prove my point. But what was the use? Diane was as close-minded as a clam. Just like our father.

"Is 5:00 o'clock okay?"

"That's perfect. Sunday at five. I love you, Violet. I wish you'd get some help for your condition. You're a beautiful woman and you could find a good man if you'd just stop scaring them off with…."

"Bye, Diane. Love you too." I said, interrupting her this time and giving dial tone to her useless chatter.

CHAPTER
Nine

America

The phone rang a couple of minutes after I hung up with Diane. I almost didn't answer it because if Diane came at me with some more of her judgmental diatribe, I might just cuss her out. That would cancel my free meal and the chance to see my doll-toting niece, Laney and my video game playing nephew, Lance.

I didn't recognize the number on the caller ID so I put my attitude gage on irritation. "Yeah, hello."

"That you, Violet? It's Stanley. Stanley Grant. I met you on the rail last week. I'm calling to see what you're up to tonight? Thought we could take in a movie, have a bite to eat. If you're not already booked, that is."

Stanley worked for a large stock exchange firm in downtown Los Angeles. Wedged together on the crowded commute to the prison, he had negotiated me into giving him my phone number. I gave it to him just so he would shut up. He'd garnered a captive audience with his incessant, loud flirting. He sat so close to me on the train I thought I was going to suffocate from inhaling his funky, cheap cologne. I would've given him a fake number but he rides the subway every morning just like I do. Besides, it wasn't like I had dates knocking down my door.

Stanley looked like a cross between a white man and an African warrior. His hair had been overly processed. Looked like black straw had been glued to his scalp. His nose had to be at least three inches in diameter. His lips looked like two smashed, burnt pieces of wonder bread. But if you listened to him talk, it was obvious that he thought he was Denzel's twin.

"Well, what you say? Is it a date?"

I wasn't on the subway now. I could blow him off if I wanted to. But a free dinner and movie was a free dinner and a movie. What did I have to lose?

I didn't know him well enough to have him pick me up at home. "Dinner sounds good, Stanley. How about we meet at the Beverly Center for the flick then grab a bite to eat? How does four o'clock in front of the theater sound?"

"Anything to spend time with you and that lovely smile of yours. Hope you like *California Pizza Kitchen*." Stanley said, dropping a tired line.

After confirming Stanley's dining selection, I sunk down into a tub of my favorite *Nanina Ra* bath salts. The sweet smell of Amber made my body feel clean and serene. I adorned myself in earth-toned pants, a cream-colored halter and matching sandals. The halter showed just enough of my cleavage to tease but not give out the wrong message. My make-up and freshly twisted locks were flawless. I put just a dab of sandalwood perfumed oil on my pulse points.

When I exited the escalator at the Beverly Center, I spotted Stanley pacing back and forth in front of the box office. Even though I was only ten minutes late, he looked frantic. Like a man on the edge. I was glad I'd driven my own car.

"Hi Stanley," I said, walking up behind him, trying to sound happy to see him.

His demeanor drastically changed. He transformed into the same plastic brother that I met last week on the metro rail.

"My African Queen. You look gorgeous."

Not the African Queen line.

"Thank you, Stanley. Did you get the movie tickets?"

"Yep, got 'em right here. A slight change of plans though. I thought we'd eat first and then see the movie. Sometimes movies make me a little sleepy and I wanted to be alert during our dinner since that's where we'll probably get to know each other."

"That's fine." I said, walking toward the restaurant.

I looked over at his pronounced, overly defined features. Reminded myself that looks didn't make a man. My ex had been Boris Kodjoe fine but wasn't worth two red pennies rubbed together. At least the brother had a good head on his shoulders. And *California Pizzeria Kitchen* was one of my favorite spots. He got five cool points for his selection in restaurants.

I ordered the fettuccine with Alfredo sauce, a large caesar salad and a barbecue chicken pizza without the chicken. Made sure I ordered enough so I'd have lunch the next day.

Stanley had the Tandoori pizza and a garden salad. He ordered a bottle of white wine to go with our dinner and scored again.

Maybe he wasn't all that bad. Least he wasn't one of those brothers who asked you out to dinner then told you how broke they were. I gave him three more cool points for having a few dollars in his pocket. Already knew he wasn't my soul mate but I was hoping he could bring a little fun into my drab ass life.

"So what do you do when you're not at work?" Stanley asked after the waitress took our orders.

"I collect African art. Work out. Sometimes I go to psychic fairs. And you?"

I waited for his reaction on the psychic fair piece.

"I make millionaires on a daily basis. I'll be the first to admit my job is my life. But that's what it takes to be *the man*, right? What you said about going to psychic fairs—you a psychic or something? I never heard of a Black psychic. I always thought that was a White thing. It's all fake anyway."

"Quiet as kept, there are plenty of Blacks who have psychic abilities."

"You one of them?"

"Stanley, I thought we were talking about you."

"Oh yeah." He laughed nervously and continued, "I like football. And of course, I have to support my boys the Lakahs! Go Koby!" He cheered, sounding like a total idiot.

"What about children. Do you have any?" I asked him, already getting bored.

"As a matter of fact, I have three children. Me and my wife are separated."

That wasn't a shock.

"Boys or girls?"

"Two boys and one girl. Back to this psychic thing, I…"

Thankfully, the waitress arrived with our salads. "Can we eat first?" I asked, hoping he would drop the subject. My honesty always got me into trouble. I immediately divided my salad, pasta and pizza into two parts and asked the waitress for a to-go box for the remainder.

We crunched on the crispy lettuce in silence. Ten minutes later, as I scraped the last bit of lettuce from my plate, he picked up the conversation again.

"So you read minds?"

"No, you've been watching too many movies. I am a seer. I hear things. I have the ability to communicate with people from the other side."

"I thought so," he said excitedly, "When I read your ad…." He tried to catch himself but he was too late. The real reason for this date was out.

"Oh, so that's why we're here. How'd you know it was me?"

"When I saw the name on your badge last week, I thought it was a coincidence. Not too many people with the name Violet. I'd seen your ad in the yellow pages. When I called the number in the ad it was your voice."

"Why didn't you just call and pay the fifty bucks for a reading?"

"Well….I wanted to get to know you better."

"I see. Well, what do you think?"

The conversation halted while the waitress refilled our iced tea.

"Can you channel information about the stock market?"

"That's against the law. I think they call it insider trading and Martha Stewart went to jail for it."

"I'll pay you any amount of money you want if you can give me information about which stocks are going to hit. I have friends that'll pay too. You'll be rich overnight. No more slaving on that loser's job or wearing that ugly blue uniform and fake badge."

I wondered how much he and his friends would pay for my guidance. Probably thousands. Hell, I knew there wasn't any future in my job. Not unless I inherited the company. But *Synergy Security Systems* had paid my bills for years and he hadn't ever given me a dime. Considering the status of my bank account, his offer was a tough one to refuse. I hadn't ever done anything like what he was asking. Always saw it as abusing my powers.

Suddenly, like some magic light bulb had just been screwed in, the message in my dream came back to me. Stanley was the man Mamiwata had warned me about.

"It's obvious that you were never interested in me, Stanley. I'm sorry to have to say that this date is officially over. Please don't call me anymore."

I signaled the waitress for the check.

"What? It's like that?" Stanley asked, obviously pissed that his little scheme didn't work.

"Yes. *It's like that.* Thanks for the dinner."

"I should tell your boss about your little secret."

"I should tell your wife about your little secret. All six of them."

That shut his mouth.

Mamiwata had whispered to me when the conversation got heated that Stanley was not a man to be trusted. He'd cheated on his wife six times and was hoping to make me the seventh member of his illegitimate harem.

"So you can use your powers to tell me about my wrongs but you can't help a brother out?"

"Since when did you become my brother? First you wanna pimp me for my gift. Then you threaten to tell my boss because I'm not doing what you want. You know what? I'm outta here. Have a good life!" I told him, sashaying out of the restaurant. Stanley was a waste of a good outfit.

CHAPTER

Ten

I made my way through traffic to St. Peter's Retirement Community where my father lived with forty other lively, high-functioning senior citizens. I needed to see my flesh and blood after spending time with the likes of Stanley Grant. Stanley was the kind of man that left a woman feeling grimy after a few hours in his presence.

I signed in at the front desk. The nurse pointed me in the direction of daddy's favorite lounging place. In the lush greenness of the facility's well-manicured courtyard I spotted the back of his curly, graying mane. He was relaxing on a thick-cushioned patio recliner, reading a book and soaking up the sun.

Before I could greet him he said, "Hey there, slim. You find you a husband yet? Tuxedo's pressed and ready for your wedding day but I don't know how much longer I can hold on."

"Daddy, I just got here. Can you at least say hi before you query my marital status?"

"Come give your father a kiss, girl."

I bent down and kissed my Daddy on the forehead. "When I find the right man, I promise you'll be the first to know. Gotta find one that measures up to you."

I thought about my nightmare date with Stanley. If I hadn't paid attention, he could've destroyed my life. I'd be *in* prison instead of working at one.

"Sit down next to your old man."

I pulled a chair up and readied myself for some of his unchained wisdom.

"How's my Violet doing?"

"I'm alright. The dreams are....I wish things were different. Wish *I* was different."

"The world is changing right in front of our eyes. The end is coming. I hope you're right with God. You saying your prayers like I taught you?"

"Yes, Daddy. I recite Psalm 91 everyday. Told you, you don't have to worry about me. I'm protected by angels. Haven't I always told you that? If something bad was going to happen, I would know."

"Being a psychic won't get you into heaven, Violet. When the end comes, we won't have any warning. That's why we have to be prepared."

I had seen the end of the world in my dreams.

Every real psychic had had at least one dream about the final days. But in my dreams it was the end of the ways of the world, not the world itself. I thought about telling him that then decided against it. It was the wrong time. It wasn't like I'd been given details.

"Daddy, let's change the subject, okay? Talk about something happy."

I kissed his stubbly cheek again. The scent of Old Spice cologne rose from his freshly shaved skin. Made my heart feel safe and protected.

"You know how much I love you, old man?"

"You know how much I love you, slim? You still daddy's little girl."

His mind drifted off into space. Whenever he did that I knew he was thinking about Mama.

"I wish your Mama was alive. Darn cancer. Came up in here and stole my wife. But God has a plan in everything."

Daddy rarely talked about Mama. He hadn't been the same after she died. Never remarried. I tried to lighten up the conversation.

"You're right about that. There *is* a plan in everything. Daddy, you should go out sometimes. Lots of nice women around here."

"Ain't none of em' could hold a candle up to your Mama."

"That's true but a little heat is better than none at all."

"Ain't nothing but ice in this heart. Nothing left to love another woman with. Gave it all to her."

"Give her some of the heart you love me with."

"Not the same, Violet. I love my baby girls in a different way. Speaking of my girls, where's your sister today?"

He wanted to change the subject. I let it go.

"Somewhere between mean and evil."

"She can't help it. Diane…she acts tough. But inside she ain't nothing but a big ol' teddy bear. It's just an act to cover up how scared of life she is."

"I know what you're getting ready to say. She means well."

We both laughed at that. That was Mama's saying.

"I gotta run, Daddy. A bunch of shopping to do before sundown. I wish you'd come home with me. Told you a thousand times, you don't have to live at a senior citizen's home."

"I know, baby girl. But you can't meet no husband with your daddy hanging around like a watchdog. And your sister's busy with my grandkids. I don't need to be no burden to my children. I'm just fine here. There's people my own age with the same aches, pains and bad memory. I'll be over on Thanksgiving. Gon' now. You know I don't like you to be out after dark."

"Daddy, I'm grown."

"But you're still my baby. Gon' now. Get outta here."

CHAPTER
Eleven

California clouds were pregnant with rain, ready to give life to the earth and all that dwelled upon it.

Whenever a storm was on the way, Mama used to say that *the sky had the blues*. Mama believed storms—real and metaphorical—came to spiritually cleanse God's people. I prayed the storm was here to free me from everything and everybody that didn't fit who I was becoming.

The rain carried my thoughts to Dr. Bones, the prophet of my youth. I ran into him a week ago. It had been years since I'd seen him. I was at the gas station pumping gas when he drove up and parked behind me. I watched him jog up to the cashier window to pay for his petrol. I didn't say anything until he came back.

I walked up behind him and tapped him on the shoulder "Hello stranger."

He spun around. "So you're the reason they had me come out."

Dr. Bones was still Denzel fine. He had that brand of manliness that got better with time. Found out he worked at a holistic healing clinic in South Central L.A., just minutes away from where I lived. After we caught up a bit he told me about him relocating to the Big Apple.

"New York? That's a long way from California. Any way I can get a reading before you move?"

"Call me. I'll squeeze you in."

The following Tuesday I was sitting in Dr. Bone's office listening to his spiritual counsel and gazing into his amber-colored eyes.

He read me with the shells. Not four like I used but sixteen.

Dr. Bones told me all was well in my body. Recommended I take a little Dong Quai to keep my feminine parts in good working order and that I should pop a tab of Valerian Root to help me sleep at night.

"It's here." Dr. Bones told me looking down at the way the shells had fallen on his large wooden tray.

"What's here?"

"Your destiny."

"How can you tell?"

"Shango, the God of justice, speaks through the oracle. He's prepared to fight for justice on your behalf but there's a few things we have to do to ensure your victory. Number one, you gotta learn to trust your intuition."

He got a hit on the case of Monique Davis, the prisoner I'd saved from life in prison, came up in the reading.

"The oracle says you helped someone. A stranger. You risked a lot to stand up for this person. The deities recognize your sacrifice. They say a major blessing is coming your way as a result. The oracle speaks of great change coming to your life. When it's time, don't be afraid to let go. Remember, Shango battles at your side. He will protect you and those you love."

He threw the shells again. Five out of sixteen shells were face up on the mat.

"Oshun speaks in this wisdom. Love is coming. Be ready. It's time to live, Violet. There's a lot more that I could tell you but you know what you need to know and what you don't, they'll show you in due time."

"You know you're leaving me hanging right? That's some pretty heavy stuff to drop on somebody without details."

I slid a love offering across the table. He didn't want the money but I insisted.

"You know I don't charge you."

"It's just a little something. Can we keep in touch?" I asked him hopefully.

He handed me a business card. "Here's my contact info in New York. If I were you I wouldn't worry about our keeping in touch. We'll be together soon."

"What are you talking about?"

He didn't answer. Just smiled, gave me a light embrace and nudged me out of the door.

I hoped the shells were right. I couldn't take much more of the loneliness that had become my life.

On the way home from meeting with Dr. Bones, I thought about the job I was chained to. Working for people that didn't give a damn about what our institution was supposed to stand for. *Rehabilitation.* They didn't even know how to spell it. If it weren't for that reading from Dr. Bones, don't think I could've gone home that night to sleep in a bed void of a man's muscular body and woody scent.

Before he moved to New York, Dr. Bones and I met one last time. Over lunch he told me more about Shango, the West African thunder God. Dr. Bones said Shango was my father in the spiritual realm. Told me our struggles were the same.

"Just like Shango, you're a fighter. Always seeking justice and balance for God's people. Remember, Shango's powers are based in uprightness. Shango can alter a situation for the better or he can let justice be served in the case of a person who did wrong."

Shango's story made me think once again about Monique, the woman who walked through my station at the prison that day. Maybe it wasn't a coincidence. The powers that be had tried to lock that woman up. Wanted to make her their sacrificial lamb. They didn't care if she was innocent or not. Didn't care that she'd lost a child or if her other two children ended up in foster homes.

Something lit a fire beneath me that day at the prison. I'd sent Monique's defense attorney an anonymous letter. Some woman by the name of Myah Wellbrook. Her investigators searched the house and found the gun. Had Monique's husband's prints all over it. Monique was exonerated. Shango brought down his gavel of justice and freed that lamb.

My talk with Dr. Bones that day was also the first time I really felt religion. Felt it all in my bones.

Dr. Bones hugged me on the way out of his office. When he touched me, my skin tingled like somebody had run a feather across it. I wondered if he felt it?

We agreed to meet one more time before he moved. We met at the park, the same park where we met. Dr. Bones stood waiting under a tree puffing on a cigar and sipping a bottle of juice. He wore the same multi-colored beads he did on my sixteenth birthday but I noticed he'd added a few more over the years. I sat down on the grass and asked him to tell me more about the spiritual traditions of our ancestors.

"Before slavery, every nation and every people had their own Gods and their own religion. The Orisa were our deities until our enslavers brainwashed us. A lot of us have re-embraced our ancestral spiritualities. But most are still afraid. Even though the African Gods are a reflection of us, we prefer to worship a God that looks like the man who enslaved us. But you can't get mad at the student for doing what the teacher taught them."

"Jesus got our people through a lot of rough times. Maybe it doesn't matter what we call God as long He answers when we call Him."

Dr. Bones nodded his agreement.

"I gotta a lot to do before I get out of here. I want you to take care of yourself, Violet. I'll see you soon."

"What do you mean by soon?"

He winked his eye before taking off down the path toward the parking lot.

On the way home I was caught by a red light. Mama started whispering to me. Mama rarely came. When she came, I knew it was something serious.

Violet, it me, Mama. We see a man standing on the playground at Laney and Lance's school. He's a bad man, Violet. Tell your sister to pick those kids up early, by four o'clock. He wants to hurt them. Save them, Violet. It's up to you.

A cold sweat broke out on my forehead. I floored the gas pedal, ran the red light, made a sharp right turn cutting off a delivery truck. Felt like life had switched speeds and was moving faster than fast, like one of those clocks they use in high-speed chess games. I zoomed up Crenshaw at top speed.

How in God's name was I supposed to convince Diane that some strange man was gonna hurt Laney and Lance? Diane didn't believe in psychics and darn sure didn't believe people could see things that hadn't happened yet. But I couldn't let something bad happen to those kids. I had to face the wicked witch.

I voice dialed her number on my cell. Her voicemail chimed in.

"Diane, call me as soon as you get this. It's an emergency."

I burned rubber into the parking lot of my complex, ran up the steps to the door and tore through my closet looking for my gun. In the midst of snatching open boxes trying to find the one that stored my Smith & Wesson, I dialed Diane's number again.

"Diane, I need to talk to you *now*," was the message I left her.

CHAPTER
Twelve

C ouldn't remember which shoebox I'd hidden my gun in. I was on box number twelve when the phone started ringing. My cell was on the bed which was now covered up with clothes and boxes. Scared I'd miss the call I started hurling clothes and shoes off the bed until I found it. I clicked the talk button right before the call rolled into voicemail. Diane greeted me with her usual rudeness.

"I'm on the way to the nail shop so make it quick. You said it was an emergency—is Daddy okay?"

I glanced at my watch. 3:15 p.m. Time was running out.

"Daddy's fine. How long will it take you to get to the kid's school?"

I went back to searching for my gun. Found it in a box on the bottom of the closet floor. Where in the heck did I put that box of bullets?

"I can be there in thirty minutes if the traffic's good but I don't have to pick them up until 5:00. What's going on?"

"Diane, you have to pick them up before 4 p.m. It's really important. I need you to trust me on this."

"What's going on, Violet? Don't mess with me. Those are my children."

I was trying hard to hide how afraid I was but I knew Diane had picked on it.

Tell her. The voice spoke loudly into my right ear.

"Diane, I saw….I saw something happening to them."

She exhaled. "Is this about one of your crazy psychic visions? The kids are fine, Violet. I would've known if something was wrong with my children. I just talked with Susie—the woman that does Saturday day care at the school—a little while ago. The kids were outside on the playground playing in the sand box."

I ignored her doubting words. "Diane, Mama told me that a man is at their school and that he wants to hurt them. You have to get there by four."

"What man? Violet, stop it. You're starting to scare me."

I felt bad for stressing her out. What if Mama had been wrong? What if there was no man?

"Are you sure it's Laney and Lance?"

"You wanna take a chance I'm wrong? Look, get your ass to that school right now. I'll meet you there. And call the police."

"What the hell am I gonna tell them? That my sister had a psychic vision?"

"Just tell them that your sister drove by the school and saw a strange man loitering near the playground and you're worried about your children's safety."

Tell her he's wearing a black and green sweat suit and a black baseball cap.

"Mama said he's wearing a black and green sweat suit and a black baseball cap. Now get off the phone and drive!" I said taking a box of bullets from the nightstand.

I slammed down the phone. Stuck the gun and the bullets in my jacket pocket. I was heading toward the door when Mama spoke again.

Leave the gun at home. You won't need it.

"Mama, are you sure?"

No answer. Mama never did like to repeat herself.

I tossed the gun and bullets on the bed, bolted down the stairs, jumped in the car and headed north along Alvarado toward Sunset Blvd. The kids went to a private school just off of La Brea and Wilshire. I drove like a maniac down Sunset. Ran a red light as I turned left onto La Brea. I took the right turning lane, darted in and out of slow traffic. When I got to the school, the police were out front. Whatever Diane said must've worked.

I jumped out of the car, dashed toward the playground. I saw a man with a black baseball cap standing by the slide holding two kids tightly to his legs.

Laney and Lance were crying out for help. My heart almost stopped beating.

Laney clutched the doll I had given her against her stomach. Diane didn't know that Laney's doll was a protection doll filled with herbs and crystals. Mamiwata told me to make it six months ago. The spirits were always thinking ahead.

"I'll kill these brats if you come any closer." The crazy man shouted at the police officers.

"Let the children go and we'll go easy on you." The policeman shouted back.

Where the hell was Diane?

I scurried over to the officers and introduced myself. My insides were bubbling. It took every bit of strength I had to calmly talk to one of the officers.

I noted the name on his badge. "Officer Jacobs, I'm their aunt. Their mother's on the way."

"You say you're their aunt?"

"Yes. My name is Violet. Violet Brown. Think your guys'll be able to get them away from him?"

"Well, when we got here the perp was sitting with the kids in the sandbox. When he saw us walking up, he grabbed them and headed for his vehicle. Our cars blocked him in. He took the kids back to the sandbox where we surrounded him. We're trying to get him to surrender. It's not looking good."

I shuddered at the thought of what could happen if they didn't get him to surrender. "Maybe I could talk to him."

"And say what? I'm sorry, lady but this is a police matter. He might be armed."

"He doesn't have a gun." I said quietly.

The officer looked at me with a puzzled glare. "How do you know what he has? Look, we're gonna need you to step back. What's your name again?"

"I just know. The name is Violet."

Go get those babies, Violet. Tell that crazy man that you know about Rochelle. Tell him that Rochelle is in heaven now, with their baby.

"No problem, Officer." I said backing away from the growing crowd.

I waited until their attention was off of me then I walked almost invisibly through the maze of cops. I inched my way slowly around the back of the crowd toward the man who held my family captive. I walked along the fence that surrounded the playground. I was almost to the sandbox when the police noticed me. The officers shouted over the bull horn for me to come back. I heard one of the cops tell another that I was going to get myself killed.

I started praying out loud. Mama's favorite prayer.

"And though I walk through the valley of death I will fear no evil."

I paused, swallowed the nervous saliva on my tongue.

"Thy rod and thy staff shall comfort me."

Another voice prayed in unison with me.

"You prepare a table for me in the presence of my enemies."

I was almost to them. The man hadn't noticed me yet. His head was down.

"You anoint my head with oil."

He was stroking Laney's face. A few more steps, I could grab them and run. A scream from behind us got his attention. It was Diane.

"Violet, what are you doing? You're gonna get my children killed! Come back, Violet! Come back right now!"

The man lifted his head slowly. We locked eyes. I wanted to tell Diane everything was going to be okay if she would just shut-up but I instinctively knew I couldn't take my eyes off of him. Diane's mouth had always been her downfall and today it might cause both her children and me to lose our lives.

The ancestors didn't warn you about something unless they could prevent it. That's what the books said. I hoped to God they were right.

There was hatred and violence in the man's eyes. I needed to keep him focused on me and avert his attention away from the kids.

"Bitch, you better take your ass back over there. I will kill these kids. Snap their necks like a pretzel. Ain't got nothing to lose. My wife is dead. My son killed her. I don't feel nothing about these goddamn babies."

"Who....your wife Rochelle?" I said, my voice trembling.

His face contorted, darn near turned purple when I said her name.

"How you know my wife's name? Oh, those pigs told you, huh?"

"She's in heaven. Rochelle wants you to know that she's in heaven with the baby."

"What the fuck.....who are you?"

I saw his grip loosen on Laney.

Tell him it wasn't the baby's fault. Rochelle had a tumor. The doctors didn't find it 'til the last minute. That's what killed her, not the baby.

"The cops didn't tell me anything. I have a gift.

Tell him Rochelle loved the yellow roses he left on her grave on Mother's Day.

"Rochelle…wants you to know that she loved the yellow roses you left at her grave. And it wasn't the baby's fault. She had a tumor on her brain."

"What tumor? No! Rochelle died while giving birth. The baby killed her."

He started bawling. He let go of Lance for a minute. He was still holding Laney but Lance was completely free. I beckoned Lance to me. He inched away from the man and ran into my arms. The man doubled over crying like a baby.

Tell him that Laney wants to give him something. Something that will make the voices stop.

"Sir, my niece needs to come home with me. She's going to give you something. Something that will make the voices stop.

"I can't let her go. Somebody has to pay! These babies have to pay for what happened to my Rochelle! I let you have one of them but this one has to die just like my child and my wife died." The man yelled.

Tell Laney to give him the doll.

"Give him the doll, Laney."

Laney shook her head crying.

"Auntie will make you another one. I promise. Now give him the doll so we can go home."

Laney tearfully passed him the doll. He took the doll in his hands, pulled it to his chest and slumped down into the sand crying. She ran into my arms.

I grabbed Laney and Lance's hand and ran like a track star over to Diane. Put my sister's babies in her arms. The three of them embraced. Diane was crying so hard—I think she scared the children.

The police advanced toward the playground, guns drawn, poised on the man in the sand box. He didn't resist, just kept sobbing and saying he didn't know about the tumor, that he thought the baby had killed her. They handcuffed him and led him off the playground. Before the officer closed the door to the squad car, the kidnapper spoke to me.

"I didn't mean to hurt them. I thought the baby took my wife away. I'm really sorry."

"It's…okay, mister. It's….okay."

One of the officers approached me.

"That was a brave stunt but it could've gotten you killed. If you ever find yourself in a situation like this again, do us all a favor. Let the professionals handle it."

He took me by the elbow. "Step over here to the car, we'll need your name for the report."

"Told you two times already. My name is Violet. Violet Brown. And that man needs counseling not prison."

"Rest assured the judge will get him all the help he needs. Hey, are you a psychic or something?" The officer asked me with a smirk.

"No. I'm a seer. That's what I am. A seer." I said proudly.

CHAPTER
Thirteen

I decided to leave my car at the school and ride with Diane and the children. They needed my support after an atrocity like that.

On the way home, Diane did something that in the forty years I had been her sister she had never done. She apologized.

"Violet, I...I'm so sorry. I always thought you were....well... crazy and you know--weird. I still don't understand how you knew...and I'm not sure that I want to...but I'll never doubt you again. From here on out you can see your niece and nephew whenever you want."

That one privilege made the day's horror worth every heart-stopping moment.

I had forgotten all about my birthday until Diane popped the trunk and announced that she and the kids had something special for me. Laney shoved a huge oblong box with a purple bow into my hands.

"Open it up, Auntie Violet!"

I wasn't in a present opening mood.

"Aunt Violet's really tired. I promise to call you guys while I'm opening it up tomorrow."

Diane took my hand and squeezed it one last time as a show of gratitude for saving her children's lives. I squeezed her hand back. Let her know I was glad everything turned out okay.

I dropped my keys on the kitchen counter. The answering machine blinked with a glowing red number letting me know there had been two callers. One was Daddy who'd heard about the scene at the school on the local news. That must've been him blowing up Diane's and my cell phone on the way home. The other caller was some guy named Darryl Collins. Said we had met a club. I didn't remember him but his voice sounded like Black satin and hot cocoa mixed into one smooth drink. I decided I'd call Mr. Collins back in the morning.

I dialed the number to the senior citizen home. The nurse said that my father had told her to get him up when I called regardless of what time it was.

Daddy came to the phone in record time.

"Are y'all okay?"

"We're okay, Daddy."

"What's this about you hearing voices? I thought you stopped all that crap."

"Daddy, my gift isn't crap. I don't know why or how but God allows me to see things in the future and from the past. What I have comes directly from the Creator. So please don't...just don't call it crap."

Daddy was as quiet as a church mouse after the last Sunday service.

"Daddy, I didn't mean to....didnt' mean to disrespect you. I...."

"No need to apologize, Violet. Some days your father gets a little crass as your Mama used to call it. If your gift saved my grandchildren then we should all thank the Lord above for what He gave you."

He got quiet again. Nothing but air on the waves between us. His next few words would heal a lifetime of confusion about who and what I was.

"I've always known you were….*special*, Violet. I just didn't want anyone to call my child a freak or something."

As raw as he'd said it, this was the birthday present I'd been waiting for the last four decades. Daddy acknowledging my gift was worth more than anything he could ever buy me. I changed the subject before he said something that would ruin it.

"I appreciate those words more than you'll ever, ever know. I'm gonna make you real proud of me one day."

"I already am, Violet. Don't tell Diane but you're my favorite."

"That's what you tell all your children."

We both cracked up at that one. I was glad the call was ending on a good note.

"I'm gonna turn in old man. I'll see you on Sunday for our regular visit."

"You ain't getting off this phone without telling me what happened to my grandchildren today!"

I really didn't want to relive today's trauma. "Daddy, I'm trying to calm down. Can't handle too much stress right now. Some sick man tried to kidnap Lance and Laney. I stopped him."

He wouldn't be satisfied until I told him the whole story.

"I had a vision about it before it happened and tried to warn Diane. She didn't believe me because she thought I was…well, you know, nuts. So I went to the school and look…the kids are okay. Isn't that what's important?"

"Crazy sons-a-bitches! I ought to get my pistol out of storage and take that bastard out of his misery. You and Diane need to find a husband. I wouldn't worry so much about you if I knew you had decent men in your lives."

When Daddy cussed, it meant he was really mad.

"Daddy, calm down. You'll make your blood pressure go up. It's over now. They're okay. The man is in jail, probably for a long time. He lost his wife and child and that pushed him over the deep end. We need to pray for him. I'm going to bed now and you should too."

"Wait a minute. Diane reminded me that tomorrow's your birthday. I knew it was coming up but I couldn't remember what day it was on. Happy Birthday, baby. I got something for you. Something that belonged to your Mama. You did good today. Real good." He said softly.

"I'll come by in a couple of hours. Forgot I won't be able to come tomorrow. I'm heading out to Malibu for my annual birthday retreat."

After I took a nap and showered, I drove over to see Daddy and pick up my birthday present.

I followed Daddy back to his small one bedroom cottage. I was speechless when he handed me my mother's most prized possession. A string of pearls that my mother's mother had given her and my grandmother's mother had passed down from her mother. The pearls had been in our family over a hundred years.

"Daddy, these are beautiful. You know Diane's gonna be mad you didn't give them to her."

"You let me worry about Diane."

"Thank you, Daddy. I love you."

"I love you too, Slim."

"Daddy?"

"Yes, baby?"

"Thanks for calling me slim."

CHAPTER
Fourteen

I was pillow-deep in some Sunday sleep. Housework done. Groceries for the week stacked up in the refrigerator. My favorite foods--oatmeal raisin cookies, vanilla pudding and teriyaki tofu—were on the shelf. Life was in order. I could relax.

I was sleeping so soundly it took me a minute to realize the ringing I heard was the phone. I fumbled it to my ear and uttered a raspy hello. The perky, caffeine-driven voice of a female caller broke my slumber.

"This is Amy Rodgers from the J.B. Good talk show. We're doing a show on psychics and the Chikawa City bombing. We're wondering if you'd consider being a guest for this segment?"

I looked at the clock. 8:36am. This had to be a joke. Somebody's bad idea of a prank. I played along with it just for the hell of it.

"How'd you get my number?" I said, trying to come to life. "J.B. Good….wait, that the guy on channel 13?"

"Yep, that's the show. Your sister called. Told us about your gift. She heard an announcement we made on one of our shows about our search for psychics."

Diane was one of the few people that knew that I had dreamed about the Chikawa City bombing before it happened. The morning I woke up from that horror movie I'd called her crying. I had to talk to somebody and she was the only person I could think of who wouldn't offer me a key to a sanitarium. As usual, calling Diane in my time of crisis was a bad choice. She told me to get a hot cup of tea or a stiff drink and go back to sleep. After the bombing, I was tormented for months with dreams about the victims. But just like the dreams I was having now, I didn't have enough information to put it all together until it was too late.

Amy continued her hard sell. Meanwhile, Mama started talking.

They must be out of their mind. You'd have to wear a coat of sage and a skirt made of crystal to go to that place. You can't do this, Violet. Don't know why Diane gave them your number. Them people crazy.

"Amy, I'll have to get back to you. What's the best number to reach you?"

I wrote down the number, got up, peed, brushed my teeth, ate a bowl of granola and soy milk and went to my altar. As I was shuffling the Tarot cards, Cassandra, my best friend from high school, called to wish me a happy birthday. I told her about Diane referring me for the J.B. Good Show.

"I think you should do it. Your boring ass life needs some excitement in it. Hurry up and call 'em back before they change their mind."

"Cassandra, lemme get back to you."

She got on my damn nerves.

I put the cards down and picked up my shells. I was getting ready to cast them on the mat when I thought about what I was asking. The opportunity to be on television was bittersweet. I'd read stories about psychics who'd gone on TV. Their lives were never the same after a public appearance. I did a quick libation and went right to my questions.

"Should I—no—is it in my best interest to be a guest on the J.B. Good Show?"

All of the shells fell white side up. A strong yes. The ancestors had spoken. I put my fingers to my lips and touched them to the floor.

In African divination systems, there was one answer that the sages considered to be a message coming directly from God. When all the shells fell white side up, it meant that the issue being asked about was not only blessed by the Gods, it had something to do with one's destiny. The Spirits had given me a firm answer but there were still things that could go wrong.

"Should I talk about my dream?" I cast the shells again.

All of the shells fell white side up.

I threw one more time to complete the reading. Two white side up and two dark fell to the mat. Perfect balance. The ancestors had spoken.

My mind went back to the reading Dr. Bones had given me before he left for New York. He'd read me right before a grieving man tried to kidnap my niece and nephew. A few days before my Daddy and sister embraced my gift for the first time. Then I got the call from the J.B. Good Show. This was what Dr. Bones was talking about. Change had come. Change was here. I couldn't stop it if I wanted to.

I looked for the paper I'd written J.B. Good's producer's phone number on. I'd cuss Diane every which way but up when I talked to her. She could've at least asked me before she gave them my number.

But maybe, just maybe, doing this show was my fate. My *sacrifice* as Dr. Bones would call it. And the shells never lied. Diane might've gotten the ball rolling but fate pushed it through the door.

On that note, I picked up the phone and called destiny back. It answered on the first ring.

"Hi, Amy. This is Violet Brown. I spoke with you earlier this morning. I thought about your invitation and I've made a decision. Yes, I'll be a guest on your show."

After a long interview with Amy, I was approved to be a guest on one of the upcoming episodes of the J.B Good Show, one of the hottest talk shows in the country.

The show had been tentatively titled, "Chikawa City Bombing: Psychics Speak Out," and was scheduled for taping in three weeks. I would fly to Chicago for the filming.

I hated flying with a passion. Up there in those clouds—it was too close to the other side for me. Felt like I was dancing on the winds of another world.

Amy told me that there would be three guests, two women and one man. They wanted us to talk about our premonitions of the bombing. That meant reliving the dream. That meant coming out to my co-workers. I would enjoy no more anonymity. Why in the hell would the ancestors want me to do this? How could a stupid talk show be connected to my destiny?

I informed Amy that I had a few stipulations. I would not under any circumstances go to the bomb site. She said her producers had already thought of what to do in case the psychics didn't want to go to the site. They were going to bring personal objects from some of the families who'd lost loved ones to the set and have us work from there.

I told her, too, that I would not under any circumstance make a circus act of neither my gift nor those who had lost their lives in this terrible incident. Death is a sacred stage of life and I would not defile it for Hollywood or anyone else. Lastly, I told her I wanted to be referred to as a Seer, not a psychic. Before we hung up, Amy had agreed to all my stipulations. I told her to put it in writing.

Daddy taught me that. Nothing was for sure until you had it in writing.

CHAPTER
Fifteen

O n days off I like to sit and daydream that I'm normal. Like to pretend I can't see through the thin veil of this world into other dimensions.

Instead of daydreaming, today I watched the neighborhood children play outside my complex. Watched them jump, roll, dance and eat popsicles. As I looked on I realized how free humans are at that age. Free to be exactly who they are, whenever and wherever they are. Too bad most of us give up that freedom when we grow up.

As I observed their kiddy games I prepared for work on Monday. Starched and ironed my uniforms. Cooked a week's worth of food. Thought about my insane life and what I'd just agreed to do in front of millions of TV viewers.

I must be out of my damn mind agreeing to do some TV show.

Then I saw their faces.

Their eyes had haunted me for years after the Chikawa City bombing. I'd driven myself mad wondering if I could've done something to stop it. Took me fourteen months of therapy to get over the guilt.

Even now I wonder if I hadn't let fear stop me could I have prevented that horrible day from happening? Mama interceded on my pity party.

Get a grip, Violet. You didn't kill those people. Prejudice and intolerance did.

The phone jingled. I thanked God for that merciful interruption.

"Happy Birthday, big sis."

"Thanks. But, um, excuse me missie, have you lost your entire mind giving those J.B. Good people my phone number without talking to me first? First you don't even believe I have the gift then you want me to tell the world about it."

"Calm down, Violet. I thought I was doing you a favor. I'm grateful for...I wanted you to know how grateful I am for what you did for the kids. You're always complaining about how sick of your job you are. How you can't meet anybody cuz' all you do is work and sleep. Maybe this'll open up some other avenues for you. Besides, what else do you have happening in your boring ass life?"

"Yeah but I want to be in control of what avenues open up. In another ten years that boring ass job is gonna give me three thousand dollars a month for my retirement pension. Anyway, let's change the subject. How're the kids?"

"They're fine."

I thought she might just let it go but she had to prove her point as usual.

"So, that's what you're living for? Retirement? Bitch please. To do what? Play with yourself? You're scared, Violet. I can't believe it. The same woman who walked up on an armed psycho to save my children is afraid of a little old TV camera."

"I'm not scared, Diane. Well…maybe I am a little afraid. But how are you gonna compare the two? My niece and nephew's life was at stake. And I've been hearing and seeing things all of my life. I've never been on TV before."

"The fact that you've never done it before is what makes it interesting and fun. You need some fun in your life, Violet. When's the last time you got laid?"

"None of your business. When's the last time you had a date that didn't end with a Barney cartoon?"

That got a laugh out of her. "That was low. You got me on that one. But I have news for you. I met someone."

"When did he retire?"

"Go to hell, Violet. Anyway, when are you going to Chicago? I wanna be there. Brandon—that's *my* new man's name—has an office there. He agreed to fly me and the kids up for your show. Of course, it's just a ploy to get me up there so he can get some. But a free airline ticket is a free airline ticket."

"How come I'm just finding out about this Brandon? Wait a minute, how'd you know I'd do the show? You know what.....forget it. Fine. I leave in three weeks. We tape on Friday but they want me to come in on Thursday morning. I'm staying at the Crowne Plaza. You want me to book your room too?"

"Hell yeah I want you to book us a room. I was waiting for you to invite me. This is so exciting!! My sister's gonna be a star. Wait until I tell Daddy."

Invite her? She invited her damn self.

"Diane, do me a favor, let me tell Daddy, okay?"

"Okay, don't get all huffy. I guess that's only fair. But don't wait too long. You know I never could keep a secret. Soooo, what you doing for your birthday? We still going to dinner? We're up for it if you want to go. I'm keeping the kids home from church. The doctor said I should watch for signs of delayed shock."

"I'm treating myself to a massage and a suite at the Malibu Beach Inn. You know that place I go every year for my birthday. About dinner—think I need to chill out after yesterday but I'll call you if I change my mind."

"Did you open your present?"

"No, hold on a minute. I'll do it with you on the phone."

I slid the huge box on my bed, pulled the bow apart, tore the wrapper off and lifted the lid. Inside was a lovely lavender-colored robe with slippers to match. Beneath it was a matching camisole and underwear. It was gorgeous.

I hope somebody besides me gets to see me in it.

"It's beautiful, Diane. Thank you. I love you. Even if you do get on my damn nerves."

SINCE IT WAS MY BIRTHDAY, I WORE AN OUTFIT THAT MADE ME FEEL super sexy. An espresso-colored, lycra wrap around dress with a low-cut v-neck front. Shoes and bag to match. Tortoise-shell earrings and sunglasses. I changed my shoes at the last minute. Wore my leopard-print leather sandals with the straps that wrapped around my ankles and criss-crossed up the lower part of my legs. I put my hair up in a french roll and let a few locks crown my face. My hair stylist called them African bangs.

I went for a massage—two hours long with two therapists kneading and rubbing my tight, sore muscles. Afterwards I took a dip in the spa's huge marble jacuzzi. I had a deluxe pedicure, manicure and an herbal facial. Felt like a millionaire when I left there.

I drove over to Santa Monica and had a fabulous raw food lunch at *Juliano's*. Didn't care about the cost. The amazing flavor of food in its natural, uncooked state was worth every dollar.

I checked my voicemail messages from the restaurant. Darryl Collins had called again. I started to delete his message then remembered it was my birthday. I remembered, too, Diane's painfully true comments about my lonely, boring personal life and the fact that nobody had tasted my cookies in what had to be eons.

It wouldn't hurt to call the man and see what he was all about. I dialed his number and hoped for an answering machine. He picked up on the second ring.

"Talk to me." A sexy voice answered, stroking me in all the right places.

"This is…this is Violet Brown returning your call."

"You called back." He said it like he didn't believe it. "Hold on a minute, let me clear the other line."

He was gone in two seconds at the most. Got some cool points for not keeping me on hold.

"You probably don't remember me. We met a while back over drinks at *Champions Nightclub*. I misplaced your number. The other day I bought a new briefcase and when I cleaned out the old one, there you were in the side pocket, under my calculator, in between two business cards."

I couldn't remember what he looked like. But if he looked half as good as he sounded…

"Just so happens my girlfriend canceled on me tonight. We were supposed to go out dancing. I'd love to have dinner with you, Darryl."

Let him be free tonight. Please.

"Tonight? Yeah, that works for me like a mofo. Gods must be smiling down on a brother. What about eight? That work for you?"

It was four now, that would give me enough time to run to the mall.

"Eight o-clock it is. If you're into seafood, there's a nice restaurant in…."

"Thanks Violet but I got this. Text me your location. I'll pick you up at eight."

After I hung up, for no reason at all or at least so I thought, Mamiwata's words echoed in my mind.

He who knows the secrets of the continuous circle of life will believe you. He will not be afraid of your gift. He will treasure you. And he is coming. Coming soon.

Was Darryl the man Mamiwata was talking about?

I went on a search for the perfect black dress. Hit the jackpot at Nordies.

Found a spaghetti strap number that pimped out my cleavage and showcased my firm arms. Slingback pumps with rhinestone trim made it all sparkle and bling.

Darryl Rollins turned out to be a handsome Black attorney who worked for a large firm on Wilshire, west of La Cienga i.e. *Beverly Hills*. The ride to the restaurant reintroduced me to an intelligent brother with a healthy sense of humor.

He scored at least twenty points and one future coochie coupon for his taste in restaurants. *The Fish Company* on the Marina. One of my favorite Seafood joints.

After the valet took his vehicle, he took my elbow and guided me toward the restaurant. I checked out his body as he rushed ahead of me to get the door. Liked what I saw. Wide shoulders. Long thick arms. Firm butt. *Big feet.*

We were seated in a booth overlooking the boats parked on the Marina. Our waiter took our food order and rushed off to get our drinks. Minutes later we were sipping on sparkling water and exchanging light conversation. Darryl took things to the next level when he inquired about my relationship status.

"This isn't a line but I just have to know. How come a beautiful sistah, with a good head on her shoulders, is still single?"

I pretended I had a mouthful of food so I could think of a good response. He was right, I should have a man. I was rapidly approaching cougar status but I had the body of a gazelle. My butt was a little wide but it was still firm and round. My face didn't reveal anything about my age—thanks to Mama and Daddy having some good genes.

"Well, you know how it goes, I've met a lot of frogs but I haven't met my prince. And there's no rush." I told him, fibbing for the second time tonight.

I didn't tell him it was my birthday until we were ordering dessert. I didn't want the man to feel obligated to do anything special on our first date. The Spirits were being quiet about this one. Maybe they were undecided, just like me.

"It's your *birthday?* Happy Birthday, Violet. Must be my lucky day."

He summoned the waiter. "Bring the lady a bottle of your best champagne."

"Right away, sir."

I was the lucky one. I felt like I was starring in a movie about a woman who might be meeting her soul mate after a long life of despair.

There you go being melodramatic. It's just dinner. That was Mama.

Couple glasses of champagne later, I got a little lightheaded. There was a tall piece of birthday cake in front of me and there was no way it was going down my throat anytime soon. I needed some air.

"Darryl, would you mind terribly if we boxed this dessert up and went for a stroll on the beach? There's a place just up PCH I love."

"Pacific Coast Highway, here we come." He said, in his seductive, baritone voice.

After a short but scenic drive, we found a spot along the beachfront just steps from my hotel.

We parked, paid our fee to one of those staffless parking booths and strolled down the beach arm in arm like two teenagers, our laughter decorating the shore.

Any place near the ocean in Los Angeles got chilly at night. My nipples stood at attention, hard as bullets, not just because it was cold but because Darryl was waking up something in me that had been asleep longer than Rip Van Winkle.

We sat and talked for hours. I wasn't bored for a single minute. Darryl's strong arms around my shoulders kept me nice and warm.

A patrol car cruised the parking lot where we had left the car. I figured that was a signal it was time to end our little party. Darryl walked me back to the room I'd reserved for my solo birthday celebration. When we got to the door, he leaned over and planted a light kiss on my cheek.

"Violet, tonight was…it was special. I really enjoyed talking with you. I really hope we can do this again real soon. You enjoy the rest of your evening. And happy birthday again."

We both wanted him to come in but Darryl was a gentleman hands down.

He waved his goodbye and headed for the elevator. Mama spoke up before I blew the opportunity to have some worthy companionship on my birthday.

Invite the man in, Violet. Stop being such a damn prude. Enjoy yourself for a change. If you don't stop being so fickle, you ain't ever gonna have no man.

I called out to him before he got on the elevator.

"Darryl, would you care to join me for a cup of coffee? It's the instant kind but at least it'll warm you up before you take the drive in."

"I'd love to." He answered without hesitation.

We sat on the balcony, hand in hand, listening to the blue-green surf wash over the shore. We talked and laughed until darn near three in the morning.

Talked like we'd known each other all of our lives. He told me about his family, his estranged daughter who he hadn't seen for ten years because his ex-wife's abusive husband forced her into hiding.

He told me how hard it had been for him as Black man to make it in the field of law.

His eyes became misty with tears when he talked about his parents who'd been found dead near the swamps of Louisiana, victims of a racially motivated crime. His father still had the rope around his neck. His mother's neck had rope burns. The police never found the people that did it.

He shared the worst day of his life, the day his baby brother had been killed by a drunk driver. He let go of my hand for a minute to deal with the emotions.

"That was a heavy one. Even harder than losing my parents. Everybody knew Little Ray was on his way to the NBA. He was on the top ten list of most valuable players in college. An honor student, president of the Black student union—all the stuff that puts a brother on the road to fame. Dang drunk driver stole him from us when he drove through a red light."

I told him about me. Losing Mama and Auntie Anne to cancer. Being raised by a single father. Moving to Los Angeles from Chicago. Going to law school. Hating being a lawyer. Taking a job in law enforcement. Seeing Black people being railroaded into America's prisons. My love of African history and culture. My crazy sister. Told him darn near everything with the exception of my being a seer. That part of my life was always difficult to share.

"There's something about me I didn't tell you. I'm afraid it's going to change how you see me."

Darryl's mouth expanded into one of his hypnotic smiles and I felt my stomach quiver.

"Unless you're going to tell me you robbed a bank, there's isn't much you can say that'll change my mind about the respect I feel for you already. Losing your mother when you were so young. Choosing a career in law enforcement. You're a brave sister. But go ahead. I'm listening." He said, inching closer to me.

"I'm a seer. I see…I see things in the future and the past."

I watched him closely for a reaction.

"Woman, please. My grandmother had the gift. She was always telling us stuff before it happened."

"You don't think I'm a freak?"

"It depends on what kind of freak you're talking about." Darryl whispered with a sly grin.

He leaned over and kissed me. His tongue explored every crevice of my mouth. My insides felt like butter melting on a hot stove.

His large, manly hands caressed my face. It had been so long since a man touched me like that. That pearl between my legs started throbbing.

He kissed his way down my face to my neck. When he ran his silky tongue across my adam's apple, I let out a soft moan. A pang of guilt shot through me. I remembered I had just met this man.

But it was my birthday. I deserved this.

We were romancing each other in one of the most seductive hotels in the city. I knew there was a chance that he wasn't what I thought he was. But if I was wrong, the ancestors would've told me. This might be his lucky night. And mine.

I took him inside, sat him down on the small couch in the suite's living room. Still fully clothed, I straddled him. Planted light kisses along the bridge of his chin and across his cheekbone.

He kissed me deep enough to taste all my secrets. I smelled the intoxicating cologne behind his ears and along his collarbone. I nibbled playfully on his neck. Pressed my groin into his. I felt his manhood poking me through his pants.

His body became unexpectedly rigid. He put our passion on pause for a sec, lifted my chin and asked my soul for permission to love me.

"Violet, I'm a respectable man but I'm still a man. Don't misunderstand, I want you. Want you in a bad way. Just don't want this to move faster than you want it to. You ready to take it *there*?"

His hot breath massaged my skin. His voice grew increasingly husky with each word.

"Make love to me, Darryl. Make me never forget this birthday."

His lips grazed my forehead as he leaned across me and retrieved the bottle of jasmine scented body oil I had on the nightstand.

He got up, poured a generous amount of the oil in a coffee cup and stuck in the miniature microwave.

While Darryl nuked the oil, I made a dash for the shower. Realized my body hadn't seen soap and water since early that morning. Had a thing about not playing house unless my body was squeaky clean. I'd just gotten the water to my ideal temperature, stepped in and let the spray hit me, when the shower curtain slid back.

Darryl stood in front of me naked and smiling. I tried not to look down but the size of it drew my eyes downward like a magnet.

"You mind if I join you?" Darryl asked, a grin stretching across his fine face.

"Uh...No, I guess not. Come on in. I like my water kind of hot. That okay?"

He stepped into the shower in front of me. His firm buttocks brushed my thigh as he moved to the side.

"Perfect. Just like I like it." Darryl said soaping up with my *Nanina Ra Mango-Tangerine* scented bath gel.

I felt a little insecure about him seeing my imperfect body but after he rinsed off, he sponged me down with such tenderness. Made me feel like I had a Halle Berry body, well, okay....maybe Angela Bassett, with an extra pound or two.

We took our excursion back to the bedroom. I put on the new robe Diane bought me for my birthday. Left the front open for easy access. Darryl extended his left hand toward the bed. I was as nervous as a virgin when I slid onto the bed. Darryl requested that

I turn over on my stomach so he could massage my back with the oil. I turned over without saying a word.

He slid my robe off my shoulders and laid it on the other side of the bed. He started with my feet. Worked the warm oil through my toes, over my ankles and up my calves in long relaxing strokes. I spread my legs just a tiny bit so he could massage my thighs. He took full advantage of that opportunity. Inched his fingers up to my ass and kneaded and caressed it like he was certified. No, let me correct that, *licensed.* I became ice cream in ninety-degree sun kind of wet. And he wasn't done stirring yet.

Slowly and sensually, he tongue-dried my back. Licked away all the tiny, fragrant, drops of water. He laid his body across mine, let his hardness sit between the smooth slit at the center of my ass. Rode me until I was begging. He slid off me and turned me over on my back. Did a repeat performance on the front. Darryl licked and kissed my nipples like they were chocolate-covered bon-bons. I could feel the juices trickling down my thighs.

He spread me wide. I let his skillful tongue take me to Jamaica in California.

I became a sinner. A sinner that didn't want to be saved.

"Oh shit….Darryl. Damn baby, don't….oh please…shit, don't stop. I'm about to….I can't hold it. Baby…it's so good. You're making me. Come too fa…."

An orgasm rocked me so hard I thought California was having another six- pointer. I rolled over, let myself slither off the bed onto the floor, clamped my legs together, let the aftershocks comfort me, crawled to a corner and let the tears come.

Brother man was proud but not arrogant about the job he'd just done on me.

"Come here, baby. Come back to bed. I'm not done."

"Oh yes. Yes you are." I said, out of breath, embarrassed by my vulnerability.

"Violet. Come on. Get back in the bed." He muffled a chuckle.

The way he talked to me. Did something to me. Made me feel crazy. When I got up my legs started trembling. I was barely able to walk. I went over to him.

"What am I going to do about this?" He pointed to his manhood.

His manhood was a meal I needed to cook. A story I knew the end of. A memory I had to make. I got my second wind. Positioned myself between his legs. Licked his thighs, his hips, up and down his side, everywhere but there. When he was damn near begging, I let the warm wetness in my mouth massage just the tip. Tasted like hot cocoa. I flicked my tongue across it. Slid my lips down on it. Watched his back arch. Had a moment of clarity. Thought about AIDS and that I didn't make him get tested before we did the do. I had been tested six months ago and hadn't done anything to jeopardize my status in way too long. But that didn't mean anything.

There was an empty sandwich bag that had the remnants of a few pieces of sliced mango I brought from home. Not 100% safe but better than nothing. I turned it inside out, put some oil from the bowl on it and slid it over him.

He got the side with jasmine oil and I got the side with the leftover mango juice. The scent of the oil and the sweet juice of the mango made me suck that bag like my life depended on it.

He gave the encore to my earlier performance.

"Damn. Violet. Ummm…Baby…..That's good. Shit…. come here."

He turned me on my side. Got on his knees. He put my leg over his shoulder, draped it around his neck. His index finger played with my pearl while he stroked. Kept the sandwich bag around his cocoa with his other hand. I started screaming.

"Oh God. I'm…. I'm coming again." I was gone, in another world.

Darryl countered my sentiments. Stroked even harder and longer.

"Take this. Take… all…this."

So I did.

Then I challenged him.

"Take it….take it then!" I slid into him fast then slow. My juices ran all down his fingers.

He took all of it, every last ounce.

And I would never, ever, forget that birthday.

CHAPTER
Sixteen

A wave of sentimentalism washed over me. Darryl and I sat up in bed, backs propped against a mess of pillows, sharing a tasty breakfast. Blueberry scones, fruit salad, scrambled eggs and fresh squeezed orange juice. Delicious. Just like him.

It seemed only yesterday I was sitting in bed wallowing in my self-pity about how drab my life was and now, I was sitting here with this amazing man. He seemed perfect. The question was, was he for real? I had been burned by enough men to know that they were all perfect in the beginning.

After breakfast, Darryl told me he had to finish up some cases he had to have ready for court the following morning. Before he left, he dropped a little more of his dark, sweet chocolate on me. I covered it with some of my personal whipped cream. There's nothing as good as love-making in the early morning hours, especially when your body is still humming from the night before.

Hallelujahs and amens bounced off the walls. I was sure our neighbors got an ear full.

When the room was quiet again, he eased out of the bed to attend to his business. On the way out, he wrote down his cell phone, office and his home number and left it on the mantel over the fireplace. I was so drained by our lovemaking I laid in the bed watching him move about. He leaned over and kissed me on the forehead. We promised to email each other throughout the week, call when we could and get together over the weekend. When I asked him what we'd do on our second date, he said it was a surprise.

I slept like sleeping beauty and awoke totally renewed. I packed my overnight bag, felt slightly sad to leave a place that had brought me such joy. There were two beautiful shells lying on the counter in the bathroom that we'd found on the beach the night before. I put them in my purse. When I wanted to feel Darryl's energy, I would take out the shells and inhale the smell of the ocean and sand that had brought us together.

I hadn't been this happy in years. Had forgotten what happiness felt like. Fear slithered in like a snake through tall grass and tried to steal the spirit of joy right from underneath my nose.

Like a spot on a floor that wouldn't come clean, I flashed back to the trust I'd given another man.

David. A caramel-colored brother with bewitching eyes. I came to him innocent and open. He tossed me back bitter and closed.

David lied to me over and over again. Even after I caught him and forced him to admit he'd been seeing someone else, he begged me to take him back and like a fool I did.

He promised things were over between him and his mistress. Asked me to spend the rest of my life with him. Fast forward four weeks, I found out I was pregnant with our child. David said he was thrilled. We agreed to marry a few months later. A week before the wedding he left town on a business trip.

I didn't hear from him for over a month.

The punk had the nerve to call me and apologize. Said he'd met someone on a cruise ship. He didn't know what happened, they just fell in love. I was devastated. Didn't get out of bed for two days. Grief caused me to lose the baby. I was sure of it. That was the day I promised myself I'd never be that vulnerable again.

I could easily fall in love with Darryl. I knew that the first time he kissed me. I didn't want to fool myself. We had a good time with each other. Shared some great sex. But the man hadn't said anything about a picket fence. I needed to stop thinking about weddings and children. If we saw each other again, it would be great. If we didn't, oh well. The spirits had promised someone was coming. I just needed to stay ready.

I called into work. Let them know I was taking the rest of the day off. Hell, I had enough sick days and vacation time to take off a month without missing a quarter from my paycheck.

Back at home, I put aside the erotic flashbacks of my passionate night with Darryl to focus on what I was going to say on the J.B. Good Show. I purposely hadn't told Darryl about my being on the show. If he didn't run when I told him I was a psychic, I darn sure wasn't going to make matters worse by telling him I was going on national TV to talk about my *other* life.

I wrote a dictionary-style definition of what it meant to be a seer. Tried to make it so a novice to the spirit world would understand. I made a list of the questions I assumed they would ask about me about the day of the bombing and about my being intuitive.

Did I tell anybody about my dream of the bombings before it happened?

What did they say when I told them?

What went through my mind the day the bombing happened?

How long had I been able to read minds?

Could I see people's future?

Could I really communicate with the dead?

Was there anyone else in my family that had or has the gift?

They weren't gonna catch Violet Brown off guard. I had to be sharp, on point, speak with clarity.

After I finished the list, I turned on my computer. Planted a steaming cup of green tea next to me and typed J.B. Good's name in the Google search engine.

J.B. Good had 232,000 web links about him and his show. His one and only official web site had an extensive bio about his background and history in show business. I clicked the link to his press photos.

J.B was a looker. He had amber skin and naturally wavy black hair. His manicured beard and mustache was so perfect he looked like a ceramic sculpture.

I scrolled down to read his bio. Found out J.B. had attended nothing but Ivy League schools. Those same people had positioned him to climb the Hollywood ladder. His recipe for success had worked like a mofo.

There was a picture of J.B. posed on the beach wearing scuba wear. His solid arms, wide chest and rippling stomach were intoxicating enough to make a woman give up all her presents. I could see why he'd become an overnight sensation weeks after his show hit the big screen.

J.B. had more than looks—the man clearly had talent and brains too. From rape victims, survivors of hurricanes and tsunami's to abused children, J.B.'s compassion had touched millions. His bio described him as happily unmarried. I was sure that was code for his being a gay man.

The next few days dragged by. My daily rituals became a rhythm—work, home, dinner, two or three psychic readings, talk to Darryl for a couple of hours, watch my DVR recording of the J.B. Good Show and go to sleep.

J.B. Good was a pro. I checked out his moves, the way he made his guests feel safe enough to tell it all on national TV. The man was as charismatic as Bill Clinton, passionate as Al Sharpton and as suave as Blair Underwood .

When Friday came, I called Darryl at his office to see what time we were getting together. He was having a bad day.

"Afraid I'm gonna have to cancel. My boss assigned me to a big case and I'll be here until the rooster crows. Sorry, baby but I gotta run."

"Okay, I'll talk to you---."

He hung up before I could finish my sentence!

I sat there thinking about how stupid I'd been once again. The bastard could've told me all he wanted was sex. Going on and on about how this was the beginning of something beautiful. It was nice while it lasted and brother man darn sure did break me off something nice before he jetted. That's what I got for hoping.

Violet, stop jumping to conclusions. Have a little confidence in yourself for a change. Don't let your low self esteem mess up a good thing.

That was the spirit of Anna, my great aunt. Anna had been one of the first female real estate brokers in Tuscaloosa, Alabama. A shrewd businesswoman, she'd married two doctors, one dentist and a lawyer. Collected high end property on the back end of every divorce. Maybe Anna was right. Darryl was just busy. We'd get together as soon as his schedule opened up.

Unfortunately, Darryl's schedule didn't have an opening for two weeks. I'd written him off by then even though he managed to call me every other day to say hi and let me know how busy he was. I wanted to tell him to stop calling, that I was fine with parting ways and celebrating what we shared, which was some good ass—no scratch that—some *phenomenal* sex.

113

This was precisely why I kept my heart closed. Every time I opened it, even just a little, pain seemed to seep in through the cracks.

I threw myself into preparing for the J.B. Good Show, which I still hadn't told Darryl anything about. I didn't want to tell him about it over the phone.

Finally and mercifully, it was two days before I was to fly out for the show. I was at the mall, trying to find the perfect outfit for my big debut. My spirit guides had been quiet lately. Hell, now I wanted them to talk. I was as nervous as a teenage girl on prom night. But I had to go through with it. The ancestors had deemed it so.

Diane made plans to meet me at the Studio in Chicago. We were going to our birthplace after nearly thirty years of being gone. Diane and the kids were coming in early so the children could meet her new flame and see if the family chemistry was as strong as the energy between her and her new beau.

I was glad Diane would be there. I needed to see a familiar face in the audience. I needed her to be her controlling self so I wouldn't mess things up.

Daddy called early Wednesday morning to give me a pep-talk. As usual, Diane had blabbed the big news. Her mouth was like a safe with no combination.

"Your sister told me you going on TV. I know you'll make me proud. You always been a good speaker. I remember that time you gave the graduation speech for your sixth grade class. Tell you the same thing I told you back then. Don't break no verbs, sit with your back straight and cross your legs like a lady. The rest'll take care of itself."

My friend Cassandra called me too. Cassandra was a flight attendant and was hardly ever home long enough to call her own mama.

When Cassandra wasn't flying, she was staying at five star hotels, having wild, untamed sex with one of her rich passengers.

Cassandra worked what I called the RFS section of the plane or in laymen's terms, the "rich folk's section." That's where she recruited her financiers—which was code for *sugar daddies*. She'd become so spoiled by their first class treatment I doubted she'd ever meet a guy that could meet her high standards. When I told her to *keep hope alive* on meeting a good brotha, she told me Bob Hope died a long time ago and she was staying alive for either Kevin Costner or Sean Connery. That made me laugh.

"You ready?" Cassandra queried about my foray into the world of television.

I could see her sitting on her black leather couch, wearing those mink slippers one of her investors had given her, sipping some ridiculously expensive wine from a crystal goblet.

"Girl, I'm so nervous I can't breathe. I know I'm not going to sleep tonight. I don't want to be tired for the show."

"Sleep on the plane. I upgraded your airline ticket to first class so you'd have a good meal and sit in a comfortable seat. Just remember to study your notes. I know your anal ass made some. And dress conservative. Novices always make the mistake of dressing fancy for TV appearances. Wear a nice two-piece suit in one solid color. Drape an expensive scarf over the suit and put your locks up in a French-roll. Wear a pair of fake diamond studs. No one will know the difference. You'll be a hit, I know you will."

"How do you know so much about the TV world?"

"I dated a television producer a while back."

"I should've known."

I made my way through traffic, back to the Beverly Center and put together an outfit that Cassandra would've been proud of. And she was so right. I looked like a million bucks. Thank God for snobby, well-traveled friends.

CHAPTER
Seventeen

It was almost midnight when the phone started jingling. The only reason I was awake was because I was doing the last-minute packing for my trip to Chicago. I started not to answer but picked it up figuring it was probably Diane checking on me. I was wrong. The caller ID had Darryl's number on it. It was too late to put the receiver down without exposing my anger.

I wasn't interested in a word he had to say. I was done with him. In fact, maybe I'd tell him just that.

"Yeah, hello." I said nastily.

"Violet, it's Darryl. I won, baby! I beat a multi-million dollar corporation at their own game."

"Great. Wonderful."

"I got an award today. Firm gave me special recognition for all the hard work I did on this one. I told them nothing would make up for the time I missed spending with my lady. But you know I took the check." He laughed like everything was fine between us.

Did he call me his lady? *Bullshit artist.* That's what he was. All attorneys were liars and all men were dogs. Everybody knows that. Why I thought he was different from the rest is beyond me. The truth is I barely know this man.

"Good. I'm glad for you. Listen, I'm really busy. I have a lot to do before I…" He interrupted my banter.

"Can I come by? I have something I want to show you."

Oh, hell no. I know his ass wasn't trying to make a booty call on me after all this time. I fought the urge to cuss him out. Don't know why I resisted it.

"Darryl, I'm tired. I was just about to go to sleep when you called."

"Look, it'll just be for a minute. I promise not to keep you up too long."

He had some nerve calling here acting like nothing was wrong. I dropped my anger on him full force. "It's been two weeks since our little romp in the hay and you haven't had the time or decency to come by, send a girl some flowers, nothing. I barely heard from you this week. Now that your schedule has an opening, you wanna come hit this again? I don't think so. It was nice while it lasted but it's over. I'm going to bed."

I was about to slam the phone down but that damn sexy ass voice of his voice froze my hand to my ear.

"Violet, I need to talk to you. There's a reason this case was so important to me. I'm on my way over. If you don't want to see me anymore after I explain things, I'll leave and never bother you again."

I gave him dial tone. After I hung up, Mama had to put in her two cents.

Violet, get your behind up and do something to your hair. A woman's hair is her crown and glory. Put some lotion on your knees and elbows too. There's nothing worse than an ashy woman. And stop acting stupid and give the man a chance to explain.

Mama was a fusser by nature.

Twenty minutes later he was knocking on my door. I smelled him before I saw him. I was scared I'd cave in if I opened the door so I cracked it just a bit.

"Open the door, Violet. I have something to show you and tell you."

I wouldn't look at him. If I looked at him it'd be over.

"Give me one good reason why I should let you in."

I felt him put light pressure on the other side of the door.

"Because I need to make you understand something. And I can't do it from out here. Open the door woman."

I opened up just enough for him to slither through. His shirt got caught on the lock and ripped. I was glad. Served him right.

"That's what you get."

He ignored my sarcasm and his ripped shirt. When I saw him my heart quickened, legs trembled, fingers spread. I wanted to touch him so bad. Had missed him so much. He looked even better than I remembered.

"I'm sorry, baby. This was a really important case to me. The plaintiff was a drunk driver who killed a little boy in the crosswalk. D.A. was trying to get him off cuz' he was a big shot. CFO for one of those mega dot.com companies. He would've walked if I hadn't land-blasted him. And that boy's mother, you know she wouldn't have gotten a dime."

"And why couldn't you call and tell me this?"

"Everything happened so fast. Another attorney had to drop the case because of a family emergency. It was assigned to me two weeks before the trial. You're right, I should've told you. I didn't think you'd understand."

"Next time don't assume."

"The good news is with the chunk of cash we got the boy's Mama, old girl and at least two of her generations to come won't ever have to worry about money. And get this, the company has to sponsor a *don't drink and drive* campaign. Won't take the place of that boy's life but at least his mama can buy a nice home with a view and go on a vacation somewhere pretty while she grieves."

He did it for his little brother. I told you. He's telling the truth, Violet. Now get off your high-horse and forgive the man. Besides, he has some more good news.

"Oh shut-up." I accidentally said out loud to Mama.

Darryl looked hurt.

"Not you....I-I would've understood that, Darryl. I wish you would've called."

"I've been working eighteen, sometimes twenty-hour days. Barely sleeping."

He wasn't getting off that easy.

"Congratulations. I know it must have meant a lot to you. I hate to rush you but like I told you on the phone, I've got a lot to do. I'm leaving tomorrow. Why don't you call me in about a week?"

He acted like he hadn't heard a word I'd said.

He took my hand. I felt his warmth envelop my fingers.

"Remember when I told you our next date would be a surprise? Well, after they honored me at the meeting for getting more billable hours than any other senior partner, as a special bonus, I got keys to the firm's waterfront condominium. And that's not all. I have passes for an entire season of Broadway theater debuts. Box seats. I know how much you love the theater. And I'm not finished, open this up."

Bastard. He knew I loved the heck out of some Broadway plays. He handed me an envelope.

I slid the flap open and peaked inside at a check whose zeros kept going until the paper ran out.

"Yep, after all of that, the firm dropped an envelope in my hand that had a bonus so fat….well, lets just say this—my woman and I are going to live a little. No, I take that back. We're going to live a lot. Well, what do you say? You wanna walk the acres and talk about it?"

Smart ass. Coining a phrase from Martin Lawrence's stand-up routine. Did he just call me his woman?

"It sounds wonderful and I'd love to go but I have some news for you too. I'm leaving tomorrow night for Chicago. I've been trying to tell you but you've been so busy I didn't have a chance." I said, still mad about his absence.

"Chicago! You're kidding right? What are you doing in Chicago? Is it business or pleasure?"

So he thought he had the right to question my whereabouts.

"It's a bit of both. I've been asked to be on television. They want me to be a guest on the J.B. Good Show."

"That's…wow. That's huge news. I can't believe you're going to Chicago. That's where the condo is."

What was he talking about? Didn't matter. This, *us*, was over.

"Anyway. As I was saying, I leave tomorrow. We tape on Friday. Maybe we can get together when I get back."

"How would it look if your man missed your big moment? How about this? Pack some extra clothes and we'll stay over a few days after you finish taping. I need a vacation right about now and I bet you could use some down time too. I better jet so I can pack. What time does our flight leave? You book first class?"

I just stood there staring at him in disbelief, love filling my heart. I hated myself for falling in love with him so soon. I was afraid. Terrified of being hurt again. This was going way too fast for my comfort level.

After he was gone I went right to sleep. A familiar dream came to visit me in slumberland. The explosions.

They were getting closer. I didn't know when or where they were going to hit but when I woke up the next morning, I had a feeling the bombs in my nightmare were coming to America. I didn't have a clue on how to stop them.

CHAPTER
Eighteen

Airport was packed. Seemed like representatives from every ethnic community in the world were traveling through LAX.

Darryl walked through the security screening without incident. When I walked under the square dome, the red light blinked on. A tall, lanky man pointed to the pre-painted footprints on the floor, told me to spread my arms and legs so his female counterpart could make sure I wasn't carrying any weapons of mass destruction.

I was irritated. Hoping like hell they'd leave well enough alone but no, one of America's worst had the gall to ask me to remove my belt, shoes, watch and all of my jewelry. Had the nerve to take everything out of my neatly packed carry-on and line it up like police evidence for the entire world to see.

After confiscating my tweezers and toenail clippers, the female officer opened the small pouch I kept my cowry shells in. She bounced them around in her plump hands and asked me what they were for. I started to tell her to be careful, that the shells might explode any minute but thought better of it. Wasn't worth a federal case. Instead I told her that I had found the shells on the beach and was planning to make my mother a pair of earrings. By the time she released me to Gate 37, I was so mad I snatched up my carry-on, left her with a look that I'm surprised didn't ignite her plastic badge on fire.

We took our seats in first class. Darryl let the tray down and started reviewing the briefs for a couple of cases he had to handle when he got back to L.A. I glanced over at the fine brother sitting next to me. The corners of my lips curled upward into a thankful smile.

It was hard to believe *he* was my man. *Mine.* Intellectual and handsome. Spiritually grounded. Works out and eats healthy. Exactly what I prayed for. Sitting over there looking like a young version of Billy Dee. He could have any woman he wanted. Could've easily pulled one of those size two, age twenty-two, synthetic from head-to-toe kind of sisters. But he chose me.

Mamiwata painted her wisdom over the canvas of my shallow question.

America falls in love with what it sees. Africa falls in love with what it feels.

For the first time in my life, I disagreed with Spirit. I was in love with what I saw *and* what I felt. I'd never been so happy and scared at the same time.

I popped a couple of herbal relaxers in my mouth and curled up on Darryl's shoulder. I was asleep in minutes. The Spirits had a party in my dreams. I had no idea what they were celebrating, only that the event was in my honor.

The dream took me to the entrance of what looked like an African village. Mamiwata stood at the gate with two men who wore some kind of royal regalia.

"Who are they?" I asked her cautiously.

She pointed to the man on the left. "He was your fadah in a past life. Now, he my husband."

She was speaking patois. That meant she was here in a spiritual capacity.

"What's his name?"

"Babaluaye."

"Who is the other man?" I inquired about the man with hair the color of snow.

"Obatala. My uddah husband. Your fadah in dis' life."

A woman with two husbands. Worked for me.

"Why are they here?" I asked, feeling like I was beginning to levitate.

She ignored that question. Instead Mamiwata began to spin. She spun faster and faster until the colorful skirt she wore became a giant rainbow in motion. She stopped spinning abruptly, never losing her footing. She began to dance. Her hands flailed about like she was gathering power from an unseen source. The intensity of her dance increased with every movement. To the beat of ancient drum rhythms, she erected her fist up in the air and brought it down with a fiery energy.

"Mo-fo-re-bo-re-re! Sango Tokan Oyade!" She sang in a high pitched voice.

She was preparing me ready for something big. I could feel it. At the same time, I felt she was summoning something or *someone*. Maybe it was one of the deities she spoke of. Suddenly, I wasn't just having a dream I was inside the dream watching everything take place. I danced next to her. Twisted and jerked my body in a fashion I had never seen or known. I touched my face. When I pulled my hand back, my fingertips were coated in that white chalky substance that Mamiwata told me protected the living as they communed with the dead.

Mamiwata snatched a large white piece of cloth from her waistband. She ran the cloth up and down my body, spiritually cleansed me with a snap of her wrist.

She shook the cloth over a large bowl of water. Picked up the bowl, drank its contents and spit out my fire.

Babaluaye joined her in the ritual. They sang together, sung with rage and passion.

"Kai, Kai, Kai, Yemoja Olodu. Kai, Kai, Kai. Asesu Olodu!"

Babaluaye blew the smoke of a large, sweet-smelling cigar in my face. He brushed me from head to foot with a bushel of fresh herbs.

Babaluaye wrapped me in a large piece of burlap then spun me out of it. Called out to my spirit once again. My eyes rolled back in my head. Body shook like I was having a grand mal seizure.

"Kai, Kai, Kai, Yemoja Olodu. Come! Spirit come down!" He commanded.

My soul answered.

I closed my eyes for a brief second. When I opened them I was no longer in my street clothes. I was now wearing a pearl-colored dress covered in translucent blue beads.

Mamiwata shouted, "It is Yemoja who has claimed her head!"

Babaluaye shook his rattle over my head. His voice became calm, calm as a pond at sunrise. He prayed to the Gods on my behalf.

"Yemoja. We salute great Mother. You have claimed your daughter. She is ready to walk with you. Today she gives you her mind, body and soul."

The rhythms of the drums reverberated through my feet and up through my spine. The Violet I knew was gone. I had no idea if she would ever return.

Mamiwata placed a shell-encrusted mirror in my right hand. "See yourself as the divine you are."

I peered at my reflection in the mirror. On my head was a crown made out of luminous blue net and tiny sea shells. From the net hung seven strings of sky-colored beads. They swung back and forth across my forehead, just above my eyes.

The man with bleached white hair and skin the color of onyx stepped forward to pray for me. It was the man Mamiwata called *Obatala*. He placed his hands around the crown of my head, reached down to pick up a calabash of warm, fragrant liquid that smelled like sweet coconuts. I closed my eyes and let the soothing water rain over my scalp.

When I opened my eyes, I was knee deep in a blue-green ocean with waves crashing all around me.

Obatala prayed for me. He spoke to me in a foreign language but my spirit heard him in English.

"I, your Fadah in the spirit world, hereby bestow you with the protection and powers of the Gods of our ancestors. Remember my daughter, giving birth can be painful. There are places on the earth where the ground has never been broken. Even your own children will forsake you. You must forgive them for their ignorance. Follow the wind and you will always find your way home. Ayoola Omikunle is your new name. It means: the joy of restoring the Mother's crown. You must go now."

I felt myself being energetically pulled somewhere. "I don't want to go back...Obatala please....I want to stay with you and Mamiwata and Babaluaye."

When I turned around to look for Mamiwata, I felt a blow to my gut. Felt like the air was being drained from my lungs. I had been sucked out of the spirit world back into the world of the living.

When I came to, I heard the announcer say, "Welcome to Chicago."

I felt the plane bounce down on the runway.

"We're here, baby." Darryl said, kissing me on my forehead.

I must've looked a bit frazzled.

"Violet, you alright?"

127

"I…I don't know. My name isn't….name isn't Violet anymore. It's Ayoola Omikunle."

I spoke the name like it was already mine, like I had been born with it.

"Huh?"

"Nothing. Grab my bag from the overhead. It's time to get out of here."

As I gathered my things, I had a flashback of my dream. I remembered enough to know something monumental had just happened.

A voice spoke to me from the other side. It was Mama.

You have your powers now. All you need is the necklace. I love you, Violet. Live. Life is yours…

"Love you too, Mama."

"Violet, you keep talking to yourself. Wait a minute….are you talking to the Spirits?" Darryl asked.

"Like I said, it's nothing. Nothing at all."

CHAPTER
Nineteen

O ur hotel room looked like a photo spread in Architectural Digest magazine. I assumed the J.B. Good Show had splurged on our accommodations but it was Darryl who upgraded our standard room to hotel paradise.

Two huge, overstuffed, white-linen chairs with matching ottomans were positioned in front of ceiling-to-floor windows looking out over Lake Michigan. A cherry-wood entertainment center was layered with a host of modern electronic toys bearing their identifying initials—DVD, CD, HD and XBOX. A lavish bar stocked with gourmet treats, exquisite liqueurs, aged wines and a state-of-the-art espresso machine was just steps away from the door. A refrigerator full of juice, sandwich fixings and more made this Chicago haven feel better than home.

Darryl and I drifted to the bedroom where a thick, peach-colored down-comforter invited us to sink our bodies into a king-sized mattress. Tired from our commute we ordered dinner in. While we waited for the food, we soaked in a tub of lavender bath salts.

After the bath and a scrumptious dinner, we got ready for bed. Darryl was calling hogs the minute his head hit the pillow. Unfortunately, our heavenly quarters didn't have the sleeping pill effect on me. My nervousness about the show had me tossing and turning half the night. Around four in the morning I slid out of bed, took a tarot deck from my overnight bag and went to a quiet corner of the suite. I needed to know what the Spirits had to say about my big day.

I laid three cards face down. When I turned the first card over it made my heart skip. It was the female Eshu, the symbol of marriage. After a long, deep breath, I turned over the second card. The Guardian Angel. This meant the prediction of the first card was in agreement with and supported by the spirits that watched over me. I slowly turned over the third card. The moon. Travel, major change and destiny.

Drained from his hectic work schedule, Darryl slept on his stomach, right leg extended, left one pulled up toward his chest. I moved quietly around the room so as not to wake him.

I lit a stick of Frankincense and Myrrh, ran another hot bath, sprinkled a few drops of lemon verbena oil in the water and tried to relax. Mamiwata came almost immediately. She spoke the King's English tonight.

Everyone comes to earth with a mission to fulfill. We promise our fate to the universe when we are but a soul spinning in the womb of God. You are at a bend in the road. There will be many things you will have to leave behind. But he is not one of them. We brought him to you. Like you, his heart has danced with the demons of life. But he is ready to love now. Step forward and claim your place. There is no more time.

I lifted the silver lever at the front of the tub. Let my fears and self-doubt go down the drain with the lemon I'd scrubbed off with. I patted myself dry with a luscious bath sheet. Saturated my skin with Nanina's almond-scented lotion and my own mixture of jasmine and coconut essences.

I laid out the attire I had selected for my psychic debut. Poured myself a glass of orange juice in one of the champagne flutes.

As I sipped my OJ, Beezy, my great aunt, surprised me with a rare visit.

You been waitin'yo' whole life for dis' day. Shine Vi-let. Be what God made you to be. Don't worry 'bout nuthin'. The Good Lord gon' take car-ah-you. Don't let nobody steal yo' thundah. We gon' be watching o'er you. We's proud a you chile'.

I understood what Beezy was trying to tell me. To be in the moment. To enjoy an experience that few had the opportunity to know.

I was about to share my gifts on national television. This was, in part, what I came into the world to do. I went back to getting ready for my moment in the sun.

The second I had my make-up on the way I liked it, I remembered I had been instructed to wear only the basics to the set. The folks at J. B. Good had their own make-up artists. Since it was already done, I let my face stay like it was. Plus it was way too early in the relationship for Darryl to see me without my face on.

I called room service, ordered myself a light breakfast and ordered a big breakfast for Darryl. I didn't know how things would flow when we got to the studio. I didn't want him sitting around hungry.

I was in the bathroom pinning my locks up when he came up behind me and wrapped his thick, manly arms around my waist. He planted a tender kiss on my cheek. I pushed my butt into him, felt him rock hard.

"Better be glad we have somewhere to be." I threatened.

He laughed, poked me in the side. "You better be glad. You mind?" He pointed at the toilet.

I nodded. Moved my party to the breakfast nook. Reviewed my notes for the show. Heard the shower crank up.

Minutes later I got hit with the musky aroma of his Lagerfield shower gel seeping from the door in a steamy, erotic mist. He emerged from his morning ritual. Fragrant water drops covered the upper half of his body. The lower half of his body was wrapped in one of the hotel's double-thick towels.

He smoothed a fragrant balm over his face, neck and hair. I licked my lips and remembered his flavor. Better than Mama's Thanksgiving Day peach cobbler. If I had more time and didn't need all my energy for the day's activities, we wouldn't have ever seen the outside of our hotel room.

"Violet, how should I dress for this thing? Should I wear a suit?"

"Dress to impress but be comfortable. Amy warned me that sometimes the taping can go on hours after the schedule."

He looked down at the counter where I had laid out the tarot cards. I quickly tried to gather them up. He stopped me. Put his warm hand over mine.

"Wait. I want to look at them. Tell me what they mean."

I swallowed hard.

"This…this card is a symbol of marriage and love. It means that…"

He interrupted me.

"You don't need to tell me anymore. I already know the rest."

I looked at him confused.

"I have dreams too, Violet. I knew you were going to be my wife the day you walked into that restaurant."

Did he just say what I think he did?

A bucket of butterflies started flapping their wings inside my belly. I made a conscious decision to let them fly free for the time being. Couldn't afford to let my guards down before I went on TV.

Darryl came back into the bedroom with the same rhythmic step, slid a pair of stiffly starched pants over his firm behind. I watched him, damn near hypnotized by his every move, mouth watering as he zipped his fly and fastened his belt around his firm waist.

"I made reservations for dinner at Gino's. Seven sharp. It's an Italian joint in Downtown Chicago. One of the best. You think we can make it?"

He kissed me on my lips hard enough to make my insides ache but soft enough not to mess up my lipstick. He pushed his long feet into shiny leather shoes, fastened his blazer at the center.

"Don't forget, I had you before you were famous. You ready to go to our destiny?" He asked me with a sexy chuckle.

"What did you say?"

"Get your coat woman and let's go."

As we walked out of the door, I remembered I hadn't told Darryl the details about my being on the show. He hadn't ever seen me in psychic action. I'd managed to keep that part of my life somewhat hidden. He said my abilities didn't scare him but that was when we first started dating. He was about to be fully exposed to the reality of what our life together would really be like.

Stop worrying about nothing. How many times we got to tell you that?

That was Anna, my Grandmother's sister. The bossy one.

The limousine driver waited for us in the valet parking area with a sign that read, VIOLET BROWN. Chauffeur did the door opening thing, told us where the water and drinks were, made us feel like royalty.

We were almost to the studio when I told Darryl, "I'm sorry. But we have to make a stop. Do you mind?"

"I'm on your clock. Where we going?"

"I gotta stop by Mama's grave and leave some flowers."

I knocked on the window that separated us from the chauffeur.

"Driver, pull over at the next flower shop."

Mama couldn't be physically present for my big day but going to her grave would put me as close to her as I could come as a resident of the living....

CHAPTER
Twenty

A bumpy-face security guard escorted us to the production area. The three of us walked in silence through bustling halls painted in that boring eggshell-color, decorated with pictures of the station's historical moments and iconic visitors.

After I had my face done, Darryl and I were scooped up at the door by yet another of the show's producers. Cindy, a buxom blonde with eyes the color of sapphire, passed us off to Alana, a too-damn-thin twenty-something-year-old woman with Gothic-black hair. Alana whisked us to the yellow room where the guests were prepped for the show. Darryl sat on a big pink couch watching me as they tried to figure out what to do with my hair. Obviously they'd never styled Black hair in its natural state.

I glanced over at Darryl. He winked at me and flashed one of his sexy smiles.

"We could blow dry it," The hair stylist said, looking confused.

I quickly intervened. "I think it's fine just the way it is. Why don't we just leave it?"

"I agree." The frazzled stylist said, glad to be off the hook.

Half-hour before taping, Amy, the show's senior producer introduced herself. Amy's rhinestone encrusted horn rims and sixties flip hairdo made her look like Annette Funicello.

I introduced Amy to Darryl. She had one of her assistants take him to the room where the studio audience was seated. I was taken to the green room where the star of the show, J.B. Good himself, was getting his hair trimmed. He shook my hand, TV style, and welcomed me to his show.

The other two psychics came in and sat down across the room. There was a short, plump older woman with freshly dyed burgundy hair. The other psychic was a middle-aged, tall, wiry man who had a long white beard. He looked like a wizard. Beneath his piercing eyes were bags the size of suitcases. But his spirit was good. I liked him immediately.

Amy began the introductions and explained to us how the show would go.

"J.B., you've met Violet Brown. I'm pleased to introduce you to Thomas Walkingbear and Margaret Stanfield. I'd like to review how the show will flow beforehand so that we can keep things running smooth. Each of you will be introduced with a short bio about you and your experience as a psychic. You'll be seated from left to right and J.B. will address you in that same order. Violet is number one, Thomas you're two and Margaret, you're number three."

"Why do I have to be third?" Margaret complained in a rickety old voice.

Amy ignored her question. "J.B. will ask each of you about your premonitions of the Chikawa City bombing. We want as many details as possible as you recount what you saw. He'll also ask a few questions about your psychic ability. When you see the yellow light, it means two minutes to commercial break. The red light means filming has stopped. J.B. will take the viewers to commercial break and bring them back in when we come back live."

Amy was on a roll now.

"Re-mem-ber, when the light turns red, you're off the camera and can take a drink of water or whatever. When the light is yellow we're going back up—you have about thirty seconds to get it together. When the light is green, we're live again. The second half of the show, we'll bring in the property and belongings of some of the victims. Each of you will be given a piece and asked to relay what you pick up from the items. During the last part of the show, we'll allow the family members to ask you questions. They'll be seated in the audience. J.B. will always start the conversation off and will moderate throughout. Got it? Any questions?"

The three of us nodded our heads yes then no.

A tech appeared at the door to escort us to the set. J.B. Good went in another direction.

"Amy, where'd they take Darryl?" I asked her on the way out.

"We've seated him in the audience in the front row. Okay, look sharp people! We're about to go live!"

I heard the theme music to the show begin. Heard the applause when J.B. Good stepped on the stage. It felt like I was in a dream. I heard him mention our names. I remembered being led to a door that opened to the stage. It wasn't until I saw the lights and cameras that I realized I was in front of forty-six million J.B. Good viewers.

As I walked onto the stage, I peered out into the audience, blinking my eyes to field the blinding lights. I saw Darryl in the front row, and Diane and the kids sitting right behind him. I exhaled a breath of relief.

You gon'be fine. Just breev, baby, breev, Beezy told me.

Everything went like clockwork until it was time for us to work with the property of the victims. J.B. Good mistakenly addressed us in reverse. He started with Margaret Stanfield instead of me. Margaret lost it in the first few seconds.

She was holding the sweater of a woman who died in the building. I couldn't tell if her hysterical display of emotion was an act or not.

It wasn't like psychics couldn't feel the pain of someone who crossed over, especially the ones who died tragically. Professionals knew how to contain their emotions until the reading was over. Kind of like how a doctor keeps his emotions in check when delivering bad news to a patient. Not the place or the time to lose it.

Margaret was minutes away from rolling around the floor screaming. J.B. moved on to Thomas while Margaret tried to pull herself together.

Thomas was given a day planner that belonged to one of the victims. Its owner was a business man who'd recently moved from Toronto to Oklahoma. He left the planner home the day of the explosion. Thomas ran his hand over the leather exterior, closed his eyes for a minute and began to channel in a serene, controlled fashion.

"He was on his way home to get this when it happened. He was in the elevator with three other people. He tried to call his family but his cell phone wouldn't work in the elevator. He wants his family to know about an insurance policy. They should check in the third drawer of a file cabinet in the garage. He says to tell his children he loves them. There's a message for his wife.....he wants her to move on. He's okay now. He says he's with the Lord. That's all."

Audience members were openly weeping. It was now my turn. The big moment had come.

I was given the rosary of a cleaning lady. When I touched it, I felt a surge of energy flow through my body. The woman's daughter and husband were in the audience.

"She almost got out. A cabinet fell down and locked her in a utility closet. It wasn't the explosion that killed her. It was the fumes from the gas. She didn't suffer long. Her message is for her daughter. She says move forward with the wedding. She'll be there in spirit. She's….she's bringing someone else through. It's a younger man. I think it's her son."

The daughter started sobbing loudly. "Oh my God! It's my brother! He was killed in a car accident."

The dead woman's husband did the Catholic cross over his heart and mouthed the words, "Thank you, Father."

"Your brother wants to remind you to send your photographs to National Geographic. Especially the picture you and him took of the Zebra. He says…he says you're gonna get the job you applied for. And…he loves you."

The daughter was beside herself. "How could you have known that? Nobody has seen that picture. Not even my husband."

The audience went nuts. Started clapping and cheering. Next thing I knew they were standing, giving us an ovation.

We went through the question and answer period with little effort. Old lady Margaret came through with some pretty accurate predictions. Thomas channeled the spirits of two families. I had more messages for the man from Toronto and from the cleaning lady. Finally, the yellow light came on followed by the red indicating we were off air. I was relieved it was over. But there was a part of the show that they hadn't told us about. After the show, the cameras went live with the audience.

One of the cameramen walked up to Diane and the kids. Laney's words, spoken in her little innocent voice, would forever change my life.

"That's my Aunt Violet. She saved me and my brother's life. A bad man was coming to get us at school. The spirit people told her about it and she shaved us. She whelly did. God taught her how to do it. That's what Mommy told us."

I don't know if it was the innocence of her voice or the sincerity of her words. Whatever it was, five minutes later Amy came running into the dressing room frantic as ever. She was talking so fast I almost couldn't make out what she was saying.

"Slow down, Amy. What are you saying?"

"The switchboard is blowing up. The callers, they all want to talk to you!"

"What? Why?"

"You were a hit, Violet. Our producers want to have you back on the show. It's unreal. Our ratings shot right through the roof."

"I-I need to think about this. I have a job back in California. I have a family to consider. We…"

She cut me off. "We'll pay you. The exposure you'll get from being on the show'll take your business to a new level. You'll be rich and famous in no time."

"You don't understand, Amy. I didn't get into this to be rich or famous. It was never going to be my whole life. I tell you what. Let me call you next week. Is that okay?"

"Sure, we'll be in touch."

The executive producer of the show met me at the door as I was leaving. An old showbiz geezer, his starched haircut and pasty skin made it clear he'd been in Hollywood all of his professional life.

"You were ahh-mazing, young lady. We have a spot for youuuu. Amy will be in touch with you soon. I hope you'll come back and see usssss."

"Thanks I…I better go. Think the limo driver is waiting for us downstairs. Thank you so much for having me. Give my best to J.B. Good."

140

"Take care, Vi-o-lett." He pumped my hand like there was oil under my feet. Maybe there was. Some green oil. Oil with money stuck to it.

Diane, Darryl and the children were waiting for me in the lounge. Darryl sat in one of the director's chairs sipping a bottle of juice. Laney and Lance ran up to me and hugged my legs tightly.

"Are you going to be a movie star, Auntie Violet?" Laney asked me.

"No, baby. No, I'm not."

Diane grabbed the kids, made them stand back. "Okay, stop treating your Aunt like she's a human jungle gym. Violet, you were good. *Really* good. And by the way, there's a fine ass man over there who says he's with you. You keep secrets from your sister or what?"

I blushed. "No, I'm not keeping secrets. I just haven't had a chance to introduce you."

Darryl walked over and kissed me on the lips. Looked at me like I was some kind of enigma. "Wow. You were amazing. I had no idea."

Laney and Lance started chanting, "Auntie Violet has a boyfriend!"

Darryl smiled and said, "They're right you know.

The butterflies were dancing in my tummy again.

"Darryl, this is my sister Diane. Diane, this is Darryl."

"It's nice to meet you, Darryl. Violet told me so much about you." Diane said sarcastically.

"So what are you two up to tonight?" Diane asked, trying to clean up her little stab.

I let that one go. I'd cuss her out later.

"We have a dinner date. Then we're gonna be out of reach for two, long, glorious days. How about you?"

"The kids and I are meeting Brandon for dinner. When you come up for air give me a call on my cell. I'd like you to meet him. Maybe we can have breakfast on Sunday."

"That sounds good. You know how to reach me if you need to. But don't call me unless you need a kidney."

Diane pinched my arm and said, "Remember this. You ain't no star to me. It was nice meeting you, Darryl. Take good care of Count Dracula."

"You too, Diane." Darryl said, cracking up.

I could tell she liked him. And that was monumental. Diane didn't like anybody. And she had never liked any of my boyfriends.

CHAPTER
Twenty-One

After dinner we went back to the hotel and had dessert. I had deliciously daring Darryl. He partook in vivaciously, vanilla Violet. I gave him every inch of me from head to toe.

Darryl made me climax so many times I lost count. In return, I slid my lips up and down his manhood, built the intensity in measured doses until he exploded, cursed and blessed me at the same time. He turned me over on my back, spread my legs and lapped me up like I was a bowl of chocolate pudding. I cried religious tears. Thanked him over and over for finally making me a free woman.

Thoroughly satisfied, we stretched out on the bed and took in the beauty of Chicago's night view from our eighteenth-floor suite. Darryl pulled me close to him. We stayed that way—glued together—for hours.

Around midnight I got up and ran us a steaming bath in the suite's huge Jacuzzi tub. Added a few granules of Nanina's Eucalyptus salts to relax our bodies. We sunk down into it, interlocked our thighs and feet. After we'd been soaking for a few minutes Darryl dunked his entire head under water. When he came up he had something lodged between his teeth. It was a diamond ring.

"Violet, I want you to marry me." He said through clenched teeth.

Words got stuck in my throat. I couldn't believe it was happening. Nothing in my life happened like this. Him and that big ass diamond he was holding between his juicy lips were simply too good to be true. Thoughts of David's betrayal, how he'd shattered my faith in love haunted our special moment.

"The ring...the ring is beautiful. You know I love you baby but....I'm just not ready. We've only known each other for a few months. Marriage is a big step. What if I'm an ogre to live with? You should see how I look when I wake up. You'll probably run for the hills. And you know I'll be going through menopause in a few years. Sorry. It's not the right time."

Violet, shut-up and tell the man yes. That was Anna, my great aunt.

He dropped the ring into the palm of his hand. "Where's all this fear coming from? Just say yes, Violet. We can figure the rest out as we go. Not like we're getting married tomorrow."

"I can't, Darryl."

He slid the engagement ring on my finger and for the second time that night, I cried. "Okay, fine. Just hold on to the ring until you're ready. Can you do that for me? Damn, woman, why you have to make things so difficult?"

CHAPTER
Twenty-Two

A glorious week later, I picked up my car from Darryl's place, pecked him on the lips and hopped on the freeway toward home. Hadn't been gone thirty minutes and I was already missing him. I'd gotten used to being close to his warm body and breathing his manly scent. For the next few days all I had was his voice on the other end of a cold phone. And a beautiful diamond ring that came with a promise of forever…

I dropped my suitcases by the front door and ran for the bathroom. My bladder thanked me for making it a priority.

There were twenty-six messages on my answering machine. Ten of them were from the J.B. Good show. Fourteen were from people who'd seen the show and wanted readings. One call was from Cassandra telling me how good I looked on the J.B. Good show and that she was glad I had listened to her about what to wear. The other call was from Daddy.

When I agreed to do the show I had no idea it would air a week later. I thought I'd have a little time to prepare people so it wouldn't be so much of a shock. By the time we made it back to Los Angeles, millions of J.B. Good viewers had experienced my psychic abilities. So had a few of my neighbors and co-workers....

I unpacked my clothes. As I got ready for bed, fears of facing people who didn't understand who and what God had made when he crafted me filled my brain. Darryl was the sweetness that would get me through. I tried to keep my mind on him.

I drifted off to a fitful but thankfully dreamless sleep. The phone jarred me from my land-strip of heaven. The clock said ten-thirty. Who was calling on a Sunday night at this hour? It had to be one of three people-Daddy, Diane or Darryl. My psychic ad specified that I didn't take calls after 10 P.M.

I answered without looking at the caller ID. Later I would be sorry I did that. It was the head honcho at the prison where I worked.

"Violet, this is Warden Peters. I'm sorry to call you at this hour, but I have to talk to you about something."

"No problem, Warden. What's going on?"

"Lemme cut right to the chase. We saw the show."

I wondered who *we* was? Guess old J.B. Good had more fans than I realized.

"I thought....I didn't know they were going to air it so soon."

"Would've been nice to get a little warning. You planning on coming back to work?"

"Why wouldn't I be?"

"Well...there's been a lot of talk here. Your staff and colleagues.... I hate to be the one to tell you this but you've become the focal point of a lot of bad jokes."

"They won't say it to my face."

"We'll see you tomorrow, Violet."

"Yeah, I guess you will. Good night, Warden."

I'd acted like I didn't care but the truth was, I was worried. What had I gotten myself into? Had the good I'd tried to do for the distraught families caused the downfall of my career?

Who was I kidding? I didn't have a career. I had a *job*. And the way things were going, I didn't know how much longer that was gonna last. I got up, turned on the light and headed toward the kitchen. Thanks to the Warden, I could forget about sleeping.

The next morning, when I walked through the entrance to the prison I realized things were a lot worse than the Warden made out. It was never quiet in the front area. For the first time in the years I'd worked there, it was so quiet you could hear a mouse pee on cotton. Everybody stopped talking when I walked in.

Nancy walked over to me to issue her own warning. Her pants were hugging her tree trunk size legs so tight they looked like latex gloves.

"I wouldn't go in the breakroom if I was you."

"Why?"

"Somebody did something mean to your picture."

I went into the break room and sure enough, on the bulletin board where the director's pictures were tacked up, some idiot had glued antennas to my picture.

There was a balloon tied to the antenna. It had a message written across it in purple marker. The message read: "Beam me up Scottie."

Warden Peters walked in to get his morning cup of coffee. He immediately noticed the sick display created in my honor.

"I'm sorry, Violet. This is the third exhibit since you made your TV debut. Guess stardom has its drawbacks. Guess some people can be a little close-minded about these kinds of things. We'll investigate the incident thoroughly."

"It shouldn't be hard to find out who is doing this. We're in a prison. There's cameras everywhere. Did security review footage from the other incidents?"

"No, they haven't. I put in an order to have it done immediately. Unfortunately, I think these pranks are gonna go on for a while. I can see if there's somewhere we can transfer you but don't be surprised if your reputation follows you wherever you go."

Tell him you're resigning. You have much bigger things to do.

That was Mama. I ignored her guidance and pressed on.

"I'm not giving up my job over some stupid prank. I worked hard to get where I am. I paid my dues—put in years in this department."

"Look, it's your choice. But I'd give a transfer some serious thought. The things they've been saying around here are....well... you have a good day, Violet."

DARRYL AND I MET DOWNTOWN FOR LUNCH. HE LOOKED HANDSOME in his blue pinstriped suit, ocean green tie, starched white shirt and black loafers. In contrast, I wore an ugly blue uniform. I'd left my gun in the glove compartment.

The waiter seated us and took our orders. We sipped on iced tea and caught each other up on our day at work. I went first.

"My boss asked me to resign today."

I told him the sordid details of the incident at work this morning.

"You sure you don't want to sue them for harassment? I'll gladly take the case, pro bono of course. But you'd have to find a way to pay me for my services."

"I think I have a currency you'd be interested in." I said playfully.

Our food arrived. The vegetable fried rice was delicious. I fed Darryl off my fork like he was Osiris and I was his Isis.

I loved feeding him. Not just food either. I would've loved to give him a piece of me right there on the table.

"That's some straight up bull. Oops, sorry, baby." He said, apologetically, after a piece of rice flew out of his month and across the table.

"What I was saying, Violet, is you don't have to work there if you don't want to. I make more than enough to support both of us comfortably."

"I can't let you take care of me. I've always worked. Worked somewhere since the day I graduated from college."

"I just want you to know you have options. Speaking of options, I have a little something for you."

He pulled out a small manila envelope.

"Look inside."

Inside the envelope was a set of keys.

"So you can come and go as you please."

"Darryl.....baby, this is...this is a sweet of you. But I...I'm not ready to move in with you yet."

"July 4th. That's the day I want you to marry me. Independence Day Will make a great wedding anniversary won't it?"

"Darryl, are you listening to me? July 4th is two months away."

"I was thinking, July 4th of next year. But I just want you to be Mrs. Rollins. I don't care when we do it."

"Darryl, I told you I'm not…"

He leaned in close to me. "Violet, what are you afraid of? Leave the past in the past. This--we, us, together--that's your future."

"You're saying that now but as soon as things get a little tough, you'll change your mind."

"What do your Spirits tell you about me? About us?"

I stared at him. I was shocked he would mention spiritual guidance in the same sentence as our relationship.

"Nothing really. Couple of times they confirmed your story."

I was lying. Didn't even know why. The Spirits had given our relationship their blessings a thousand times.

I was protecting myself. Scared of having my heart robbed again.

You's plain ol' dumb, chile. Dis man luv you. He wont you, girl. You bettah make dat man's home your own. If I's alive I slap sum sense into yo' head. Jus dumb.

Beezy could make me madder than any of them.

But she was right. I knew he loved me. And I loved him. But my heart couldn't take being hurt again. I thought of a compromise.

"Okay, I tell you what. We'll try living together for a while. If that works out, we'll talk about the marriage thing."

"Woman, you drive a hard bargain. Guess it's the lawyer in you. Once it's born, it never dies."

We both laughed at that. Law school *had* taught me a few things.

"You just made me one happy man. When are you moving in?"

I made plans to move in with Darryl in two weeks. I'd have to pay my manager to get out of my lease but it was a small price to pay to be with the man I loved.

The day I moved in with Darryl, I played hooky from work so we could christen my new dwelling. I'd visited him many times, spent the night on numerous occasions but now this was going to my house. Well, it was a little larger than a house....

Darryl had a six-bedroom estate in West Los Angeles. He had a weekly maid service, a part-time chef and a grocery shopper. His house was eloquently decorated. There were marble countertops in the kitchen and bathrooms, an indoor pool and a whirlpool. On the second floor there was a state of the art workout facility. The bedrooms and den were done in cultural motifs, mostly modern African and Native American. I loved it. Violet Brown had fooled around and hit the lottery.

Darryl was a Buddhist. A small room next to the master bedroom housed his Gohonzun and a ton of reading materials written by Nicheren Daishonin and President Ikeda, the leaders of the Soka Gakkai Buddhist movement.

The space felt good, like prayers were bouncing off the walls. Spiritually clean and calm.

As happy and excited as I was, fear threatened to rob me of the joy I should've felt. I asked myself why a man like Darryl would want a woman like me when he could have a fashion model with a twenty-two inch waistline?

*Africa falls in love with what it feels, America falls in love with what it sees.....*the spirits reminded me once again.

I put my fears on the backburner and started unpacking boxes. There were other things to worry about....

I still hadn't called Amy back. I was intentionally avoiding her until I could figure things out. There was so much to consider in a decision of this magnitude. I'd already talked to Darryl. He not only supported the idea a hundred percent, he said he could work out of his firm's Chicago office and we could live in one of the company's corporate apartments. That meant we already had a place to stay. I was worried about Diane being in Los Angeles all by herself. And there was no way I was leaving Daddy behind.

I could tell Brandon, Diane's new boyfriend, was a good man but only time would tell where that relationship was going. From what I learned about him during breakfast, Brandon would make an excellent father for Laney and Lance. If he could put up with Diane's moods, he had to be a spiritual man. A man had to have religion to love my sister.

Even if Diane and Brandon's relationship worked out there was still Daddy to consider. I couldn't leave Daddy in California alone. Diane would be here but she was always so busy with the kids. She barely had time to visit Daddy as it was. The only way things would work with us moving was if Daddy came with us. I decided I would talk to Darryl about it when he came home.

It was a sun-filled Saturday. Perfect day for staying in and getting some early morning loving. Unfortunately, Darryl had to go to the office and review some briefs for a case he was working on. Darryl had given me one of the guestrooms for my spiritual space. It was more than enough room, way bigger than the small altar space at my old apartment.

Moving to Chicago was one of those decisions I needed input from the ancestors to make. After Darryl left, I sat down at the makeshift altar I'd put up at Darryl's place, lit some incense, sprinkled Florida Water perfume around the table and lit the candle that sat in the middle of the altar. I shook the shells over my head and petitioned my ancestors for guidance.

"Is it in my best interest to become a regular guest on the J.B. Good TV show?

I dropped the shells on the straw mat in front of me.

All four shells were turned light side up. Alafia. Destiny had spoken again.

I took a deep breath and threw again. "Should I take Daddy with me to Chicago?"

Two dark and two light shells fell this time. *Ejife*. Yes and balance.

Everything was in perfect balance with the universal energies for me to move to Chicago. But I had this funny feeling I'd be coming back to California sooner than I thought.

My last question was a difficult one to ask. If the spirits gave me a negative answer, it could change everything.

"Will Darryl and I be happy together?"

Alafia fell to the mat once again.

I called Amy from work the next day and told her I would do the show.

"I knew you'd say yes! You're gonna be huge, Violet. Hey, you think I could get a reading before you're a household name?"

We both laughed at that.

"Sure. Give me a call and we'll get something scheduled. Gonna cost you though. My prices have gone up since I became a TV celebrity."

We laughed at that one until our sides ached.

I made up my mind about something else too. I called the Warden at home.

"Warden Peters, this is Violet Brown. I'm sorry to call you on the weekend but I have some news for you."

"Yes, Violet, go ahead."

"I'm turning in my two week resignation on Monday. I hope you understand."

"You know we wish you nothing but the best?"

Mamiwata countered his sweet remarks.

He's glad he doesn't have to find a way to fire you. Already talked to that woman Nancy about your job.

"I guess Nancy will take my place." It was a statement, not a question. I wanted him to know that I knew. He got a little nervous.

"Uh…well….she'll be a good candidate but we have to make the announcement, post the position and all that. You know how it goes."

"Yeah, sure I do."

"There will be a going away party of course."

"No thanks. I'm fine. Thanks, though."

After I hung up the phone, I got up, walked into the living room and stared into space. I was in awe of what I'd just done.

"I quit my job!"

I did the happy dance around the room and shouted, "I'm free!"

Yes, Violet. Yes you are. That was Mama.

On Sunday I went to see Daddy to tell him the news and talk to him about moving to Chicago. When I got there Diane was just leaving.

"Hey TV Star." She teased. "Now that I've told Daddy, I guess I can tell you. Brandon and I are getting married."

"Oh my God! That's great news." I hugged her tightly. Felt the happiness oozing from her heart for the first time in a long time.

I grabbed her elbow and pulled her over to the reception area. "I have some news for you too. I had been holding off on telling you until I decided what I was going to do."

"Tell me, girl. You know I can't stand secrets. Daddy's eating his dinner so we have a few minutes to talk."

We moved two chairs next to each other. The reception area was virtually empty so we had plenty of privacy.

"I'm thinking seriously about...no, I've *decided* to take a job in Chicago. The J.B. Good show offered me a weekly slot on their show. It's a one-year contract. After that I'll decide what I want to do."

"Wow. Violet's finally got a life."

"And, there's something else. I've moved in with Darryl. He proposed to me but I turned him down. I'm not ready for marriage but I don't see any harm in us seeing if we can live together. It'll give me a chance to see what he's really all about."

Somehow she missed the part about the job in Chicago. Didn't even return the warm congratulations I'd just given her.

"Dayum, Violet. You *are* stupid aren't you? You know how many women would die to be Darryl's wife? And you just up and quit your job? What about your retirement? You only had a few years before you got your full pay. How you gonna pay your bills? And what about Daddy?"

"Diane, for once can you support me instead of judging me? This is hard enough as it is. Things weren't exactly cool when I went back to work after the show aired but it worked out. I can cash out my 401k if I need to but I have enough saved to carry me for a while. The J.B. Good Show is paying me quite well so I'll also have that coming in too. As far as Daddy's concerned, I'm still trying to figure that one out. But he does have more than one daughter. You're just going to have to make more time for him. Have you and Brandon set a date?"

I chose not to tell her about asking Daddy to move to Chicago with Darryl and I. I wanted to talk to Daddy first.

"No, not yet. Hey, wouldn't it be cool if we had a double wedding? Daddy would jump for joy."

"Just told you I'm not ready."

"That man loves you, Violet. Damn, what a brother gotta do? You're gonna fool around and lose the best man you ever had."

"There's nothing wrong with me taking my time, Diane. I'm not taking a chance on a David situation happening again." I said, proud of how firm I was being with her.

"Whatever—its your life and you have the right to fuck it up just when its finally going good. I still don't know about you quitting your job. What about health benefits? You know that Hollywood stuff isn't reliable. Stars rise and fall everyday."

"I'll do Cobra or something. Maybe by then President Obama's healthcare act will be in place. I'll worry about that when the time comes."

She glanced at her watch. "I gotta run. I'm meeting Brandon at the airport."

"I'll have more details after I talk to the producers."

"Call me later, Beanhead." She whispered, hugging me tightly around the neck and heading toward the door.

"Bye, Beanpole." I said, thumping her in the back of the head. *Beanhead and Beanpole.* Our childhood nicknames.

Childhood. It seemed so very long ago. Too damn long ago. Wouldn't mind being there now. But time only moves forward, never backwards. Or so they say...

CHAPTER
Twenty-Three

It was the last night in my apartment. I had purposely left the core of my altar up to the very last day.

I prayed quietly as I packed up the pictures of my deceased relatives. I invited them to join me on this new chapter in my life. I wrapped my tarot cards up inside of a large white cloth and washed all of my crystals in salt water before packing them in a small cedar case. I wanted their energy to be fresh and clean when we arrived to our new dwelling.

It was dark by the time I finished packing. Darryl and I had planned to have dinner at the Tex-Mex Diner but he'd called and canceled due to a last minute work project. I was disappointed but I had grown used to his late nights at the office.

I decided to sleep at my apartment. It was my final night as a single woman and while I was glad to give up my status, I thought it would be good to have a little alone time before I took the big leap.

I ordered in from a local Chinese restaurant and prepared to retire early. The movers were scheduled for the ungodly hour of six a.m.

I curled up in my bed, nestled my head into the soft feathers and spooned the second pillow against my belly. I relished the thought that after tonight I'd be spooning my man instead of a bag of feathers.

I turned over on my side and pulled the pillow close. Just as I started to relax a sharp pain shot through the left, upper side of my body. A breath-stopping fear surfaced from my gut and covered my body like a dark cloud.

"Mamiwata! Mamiwata, please come. Something's wrong!"

He's in trouble, Violet. Your husband is in serious trouble. There are two men wearing masks. One of them has a weapon. You must go to him. Go to him now! He is at the tall building. Hurry!

She was talking about Darryl! I could see him in my mind's eye lying on the asphalt in the empty parking structure at his office. I called the police. Told them that a robbery was taking place and where.

Please God. Please don't let anything happen to him, I prayed as I slid into my pants and shoes, yanked on a T-Shirt, grabbed my keys and headed for the door.

I raced down the stairs, jumped in my car and sped down the street to the freeway entrance. Twenty minutes later I drove up to the building where Darryl worked. I saw an ambulance parked outside of the parking lot.

Its overhead lights twirled and flashed signaling a deathride was about to begin. I hopped out the car, ran up to the ambulance and banged on the door before it took off. A police officer stopped me when I tried to open the door.

"I…I'm his wife. Is he….is he okay?"

It was the hardest question I'd ever asked in my life. Part of me didn't want to know. My heart couldn't take it if something happened to Darryl. Tears streamed down my face. I was about to lose it when the spirits started talking to me.

Iku has come for him. You must do an offering to the Gods to save his life. He is still with you, for now.

"Open the door! I'm his wife!" I demanded, banging hard on the door.

The door to the ambulance popped opened. I saw Darryl lying there lifeless, an oxygen mask over his mouth and nose. An IV bag hung over him pumping hope into his veins. While one paramedic took his vitals, the other radioed them in to the hospital dispatch. I climbed in, shut the door and we spun off to the hospital.

My husband-to-be had been shot in the side. Blood was everywhere. The medic tried to stop the bleeding by applying pressure to the wound. Darryl flicked his eyes open, grabbed my hand and squeezed it right before he lost consciousness. The second we arrived at the hospital he flatlined. They raced him into surgery.

This wasn't real. This could not be happening.

Maybe I was dreaming. No—this had to be a nightmare. I'd wake up any minute and Darryl and I would be home, eating dinner and making love.

Somebody led me to the family waiting room. Gave me a pill or two for my nerves. Two hours later the nurse came out to inform me that Darryl had pulled through but he wasn't out of the woods. The bullet had punctured his right lung. The doctors were doing everything they could but he was bleeding internally. I went to the bathroom and dropped to my knees.

"God! Please don't take him from me. Mamiwata, tell me what to do. Tell me right now!" I cried desperately.

It wasn't Mamiwata that spoke to me. It was Oya, one of the African spirits Dr. Bones told me about. I remembered Dr. Bones telling me that Oya was the one that ruled over the cemetery.

I called out to her and she came. She was dressed in a multi-colored skirt, just like the one Mamiwata had worn during my dream journey.

She wore a brass crown on her head. Her eyes were like fire. She had a whisk that favored the wispy tail on a horse's ass.

I was wide awake but I could see Oya as if she was standing right there next to me in the bathroom stall. She told me exactly what I needed to do.

Get three eggplants and cut them into nine pieces each. Buy nine different colors of ribbon and place them across the eggplant on a white plate. Buy a bottle of red wine and pour it into the earth as you pray for his life to be spared. You must go now. Time is running out.

I raced out of the emergency room and realized that I'd left my car at Darryl's office. There was a taxi parked in the lot where the ambulances drove in. I ran over to it.

"Please--please take me to the nearest grocery store!" I threw twenty dollars in his lap and jumped in the backseat.

When we got to the store, I begged the driver to wait. "Can you wait for me? My husband's been shot. I have to get…have to get something for him."

"Sure, no problem, lady. Have to charge you though."

I ran through the aisles of the store like a mad woman. It was one of those superstores with at least a hundred lanes that sold everything known to man. I found almost everything I needed but I could only find eight different colors of ribbon and Oya had told me to get nine. What was I going to do?

Mamiwata spoke to me. *Go to the checkout counter.*

I ran to the checkout counter. On the lapel of the cashier was a purple ribbon. "Miss, I know this is going to sound crazy but my husband just got shot and I need that ribbon to make him something. I'll pay you for it. Please, it's an emergency."

"This ribbon is a prayer ribbon from my church. It was prayed over by my Pastor. I normally never wear it to work but tonight I was led to pin it on my collar. Here take it. I'll pray for you and your husband."

I was almost in tears. "Thank you....thank you so much and please, keep the change." I tossed two twenties on the counter and ran back to the cab.

"Take me to the nearest park."

The park was two blocks from the hospital and around the corner from the store.

When we got there I jumped—half fell, out of the car. I ran to a tree and prepared the offering. I had to tear the eggplant into pieces with my bare hands. When I laid the ribbons over the eggplant, Darryl's spirit came to me.

I love you, Violet. I'm...sorry. I never should've stayed at the office so late.

"Go back, Darryl! It's not your time. Turn away from the light!" I screamed out.

I saw a vision of an older woman beckoning Darryl toward her.

Pour the wine! Mamiwata screamed.

I popped the cap on the wine and poured it into the earth. In my mind's eye again, I saw blood pouring into his lungs.

"Stop the bleeding Oya! Stop it!"

The cab driver was obviously freaked out by the whole scene. He sped away without looking back. When the last drop of wine was out of the bottle, a peace crept over me. I wasn't sure if it was because Darryl had died or because his life had been spared. I walked toward the hospital in a daze.

When I got back to the emergency room, the nurse was calling my name.

"There you are! We've been looking for you. They're bringing him out of surgery. You can see him for just a few minutes in the recovery room."

"Is he…is he gonna be alright?"

"Your husband is very fortunate. The doctors were able to stop the bleeding. He'll have to do some work to get back to where he was but he has a good shot at a full recovery."

"Thank you, Oya."

"Huh?" The nurse asked, looking at me like I was crazy.

"Nothing. Take me to him. Please."

We walked and she talked.

"Like I said, he's not totally out of the woods but they're moving him from critical to serious condition. If all goes well, we should have an update sometime tomorrow. Follow me."

She glanced at me, my wild hair and wine-stained T-Shirt.

"Would you like something else for your nerves? I can give you Valium."

"Sure, just hurry, please. I need to see him."

I tossed the valium back with a small cup of water and followed her into the recovery room. When I saw him, I noticed immediately that the color had come back into his face and that his breathing had steadied.

"Thank you, Oya." I said out loud again as I took the chair by his side.

CHAPTER
Twenty-Four

Twenty-four hours later, Darryl sat up in the hospital bed. I thanked Oya and Mamiwata again for sparing his life. The surgeon said it was nothing short of a miracle that the bullet hadn't caused any permanent damage to his lung.

Darryl tried to talk me into bringing his briefcase to the hospital so he could work on some files. I told him not even if Jesus asked would I bring those files.

After two and a half weeks of painful physical therapy, a shitload of x-rays and breathing treatments, Darryl started to get better. Dr. Jamerson, a short, stocky doctor with a British accent told us that if Darryl promised to keep up with his physical therapy and made every single one of his doctor's appointments, she'd let him go back to work in three to four weeks.

"Doc, there's no way I can stay off work that long. I have cases that need to be filed, deadlines that can't be missed. If my work gets too far behind, I won't be able to catch up. What I need is...."

"What you need is to let that lung heal. If you get an infection, you may not ever make it back." Dr. Jamerson said, her thick frame moving around the bed to check his vitals.

"If you do what we tell you, we just might let you go home in a few days under the care of a day nurse, one of our physical therapists and this pretty lady sitting next to you. But if anybody tells me that you're doing too much, I won't hesitate to re-admit you to our fancy resort. And don't even think about going into the office."

"I think I need to have one of my attorneys look at these papers because I..."

"Put your John Hancock on that paper before I send it back."

"You can do that?"

She didn't answer. Just smiled at him, tossed her shiny braids back on her shoulders and hurried out the door to see her next patient.

Diane scurried in for her daily visit. She sat down on a folding chair next to Darryl's bed complaining about something or somebody like she always did. I sat on the edge of the bed feeding my man his lunch. He scrunched up his nose, wrinkled his lips and spit that gourmet hospital meal back onto the plate.

"Baby, go get me some real food. This stuff is tasteless."

Diane laughed, "Darryl, next time if you want a vacation, just take one."

"You might be on to something. If I hadn't stood your sister up for dinner, I'd be at work right now."

I smiled at him, scooped some mashed potatoes onto his fork and held it in front of his mouth.

"That's right. Now stop talking and eat, Mister. You need your strength."

An hour later Diane gathered her things and headed for the door. "I've gotta run. Have to pick up the kids from school. Hey, how'd the talk with Daddy go? Have you thought about what we're going to do with him while you're in Chicago? I was thinking, maybe you and Darryl should take him with you."

Diane and her flapping gums were at it again. Thank God I'd told Darryl about taking the job. Darryl jumped into the conversation.

"I'm all for it. We have plenty room and...."

"Call me and we'll talk about it. You have the new number right? I'm at Darryl's now. He's going home tomorrow." I leaned over and gave him a kiss.

Darryl shot me a mean look, "She won't be at *Darryl's* house, she'll be at *our* house. You can reach Violet at home." My man said, correcting me.

Diane giggled and said, "You're perfect for my sister. Yeah, I have the number. I'll call you later, beaney."

I threw an empty bedpan at her. She dodged it, laughed her way down the hall to the elevator.

"What'd she call you?" Darryl said, chomping on a piece of bread with butter smeared on top.

"Nothing. Ignore her, baby. Here, finish your food."

After Diane was gone and Darryl finished his flavorless food, he stretched out on the bed and stared contemplatively up at the ceiling.

"What's wrong, honey? You in pain?"

I propped the pillow up behind his head and tucked the corners of his blanket in around his feet.

"I'm aught. Was thinking about something that happened after I was shot. I had this crazy dream or maybe it was vision. I saw you in a park with a bottle of wine and a plate of food. My grandmother was there. There was this beautiful light and I wanted to go to it.'

A lone tear escaped from his right eye. I kissed it away.

"What you had was a near death experience. The image you saw in your dream was me giving offerings to the deities on your behalf. In the Ifa tradition, they say there's nothing a person can't change in life except for the day they're supposed to be born and the day they're supposed to die. I knew it wasn't your time but I was told that you weren't going to make it unless I did the sacrifice."

"Are you telling me that you saved my life, Violet?"

"No, I'm telling you that the spirits spared your life. It wasn't your time to go but death saw a window and tried to jump through it."

Darryl looked confused.

I walked over to the sink and filled his carafe with cold water from the faucet with the filtered water. I poured him a glass, handed him his medication.

"I still don't understand but thank you. One more reason to marry your fine ass. Come kiss your husband."

"Who said I'm marrying you?"

"I did. Now come here. Don't make me get up and come get you."

"Well, since you put it that way, I'll guess I have to marry you. Somebody needs to."

"Now you're talking some sense. Close that door for a minute. Come lay down next to me. Have you ever done it in the hospital?"

Darryl came home a couple of days later. In between doting on him like a mother hen, which I loved doing, I planned our wedding.

After Darryl started getting his strength back, we took an early honeymoon in the comfort of our beautiful home. Our private paradise included early morning walks on the beach, quiet meals on the balcony of the master suite, black and white movie marathons. One evening, on the way back from a leisurely drive to the mountains, we pulled into a parking lot by a State Park.

We hopped in the backseat like two teenagers and teased each other until we were too hot to stop the foreplay. I sat on his lap, hiked my skirt up over my hips and rode him until our passion exploded like fireworks. When we finished, I used my scarf to wipe the beads of love's perspiration from his forehead. He kissed and licked the salty perfume on my neck while moaning his satisfaction.

When Darryl was strong enough to make it on his own, I flew to Chicago to meet with the executive producers of the J.B. Good show. They'd received a ton of mail about the segment on the Chikawa City bombings. Half of it was addressed to me. Amy had received invitations for me to speak at national psychic fairs, metaphysical bookstores and to be a guest on other talk shows. A Hollywood literary agent had even written offering to represent me.

With Darryl well, my focus returned to what to do with Daddy when I went to Chicago to film the show. Daddy had jumped for joy when I told him about my plans to marry Darryl but I hadn't had the courage to tell him about the move to Chicago. I was actually hoping Diane would tell him. For once she kept her big mouth under control.

When Sunday rolled around—the day I always went to visit Daddy—I knew I couldn't keep it from him any longer. Diane was pressuring me to tell him because she and Brandon were thinking about relocating as well. She always left the ugly tasks to me.

I cooked Darryl some cheese eggs, grits and whole grain toast and left it on the top of the oven for him to warm up when he got out of bed. I tiptoed out the house and drove toward the retirement community.

Daddy was in his favorite spot out in the courtyard in a lounge chair, overlooking the rose garden, reading the bible. He looked so tranquil I hated to disturb him.

"Hey old man."

"Hey slim. Come on over here and hug your old man's neck."

I bent down and hugged him. Smelled the familiar scent of sandalwood and amber in his Old Spice Cologne. Loved his strong fatherly arms around me. "How you feeling today, old man?"

"I'm feeling righteous in His name. The good Lord has blessed me above and beyond. I'm breathing, that means I'm alive. As long as I'm alive I can keep spreading His good word."

I sat down next to him on a patio chair. He pulled a cold bottle of lemonade out of his mini-cooler. Handed one to me, then pulled out another and popped the lid.

"Thanks, Daddy. You still take good care of your girls."

"I know what my babies like. How's that fella treating you? He feeling better?"

"He's doing much better. And he's treating me like a queen, Daddy. Like a real queen. I can't wait for you to meet him. The doctor is releasing him to go back to work next week. Daddy, you already know about my plans to marry Darryl. Well, there's something else I need to tell you. It's really important. I need you to let me tell you everything before you make a decision."

He stood up and threw his hands up in the air.

"You pregnant? Praise the Lord! Thank you, Jesus! Come give your Daddy another hug. I done already put my tux in the cleaners. You and your sister made my heart happy, both of y'all finding good men at the same time. Now I can go to my grave in peace."

"Daddy, don't start talking about going to your grave. Ain't nobody dying no time soon. And no, I'm not pregnant and don't you go jinxing me. I'm glad you approve but that's not what I came to talk to you about."

"Go 'head chile! I don't have all day." He sat back down in his chair.

"The TV show that I was on, you remember right? The J.B. Good Show? They offered me a job, Daddy. It pays really good money but there's a catch. I have to move to Chicago for a while.

Darryl and I discussed it and we want you to come with us. Before you say no, let me finish."

"I don't think it's gonna work. Plus it's too dang cold in Chicago."

"With the kind of money I'll be making, I think we can afford a heater. We'll get you a full-time nurse too. Please Daddy. I can't do this without you. I need you to be there so I won't worry."

He looked up at the sky, patted the bible sitting on the TV stand next to where he was sitting. "I never could say no to my baby girl."

"You'll come? You'll come to Chicago with us, Daddy?" I jumped up out the patio chair and squeezed my father as hard as I could.

"Every man has to return to where he started. Can't go forward if we don't."

"And guess what else? Diane and the kids might be coming too. Her fiancé has offices there. If everything goes okay, we'll all be together, one big happy family."

He stood up and stretched. His long arms and tall body reached toward the sky.

"One big happy family? That'll be the day. You know you and your sister never could get along. That's alright. Your old man will be there to break up the fights. Well, when do I blow this joint? I never did like their peach cobbler. Too much cinnamon. Don't mess with my peach cobbler. I'll cut you over my pie."

I called Diane on the way home and gave her the news. She was ecstatic.

I was happy too but my old, faithful friend fear reared its ugly head and threatened to rob me of my joy. All I could do was pray that God was leading me in the right direction.

Then it hit me, what if this whole thing was being orchestrated by not just God but the ancestors? If that was true, then the question wasn't where they were leading me but what were they leading me to?

CHAPTER
Twenty-Five

The family, all seven of us, made arrangements to relocate back to the windy city, the place where the journey began for Mama, Daddy, Diane and I. Diane, Brandon and the kids arrived a few weeks after Darryl and I. They found a lovely, red brick home two blocks from one of the best schools in the city. Darryl, Daddy and I moved into the condo. Every time Daddy walked into a different room, he would shout, "Hallelujah! Praise the Lord!"

I guess that meant he liked our new home. Darryl said he was blessing the house but I had already done that.

Even though we were living there temporarily, Darryl encouraged me to decorate the condo to my liking. Truth was I did feel a little displaced. I'd just moved in with Darryl and now, only two months later, I was moving again.

It wasn't like the place needed decorating. It was superbly furnished. The living room had big, deep couches covered in an egg white material. The corners of the couch were filled with chocolate-colored suede pillows. Thick, bushy, mocha rugs covered the floor. Chrome tables with bamboo plants in different sized planters filled with seashells and shiny marbles were placed strategically around the couches. Small sand-filled meditation trays were positioned next to blue tea lights around the table.

Every room in the condo had been arranged according to the principles and rules of Feng Shui. It was a simple but stunning home filled with a tranquil energy. None of us could've asked for more.

Daddy's bedroom had a plush leather recliner with a built-in Shiatsu massager and a flat screen TV with over nine hundred cable channels. But what really sold him on Chi-town and our new dwelling was his new nurse, Mrs. Jaspers.

Mrs. Evelyn Jaspers was one of those women who had aged with grace like Cicely Tyson or Nancy Wilson. She was a buxom Black woman with breasts like watermelons. Her waistline was still washboard flat in her golden years. Her hair was a bergamot press and curl turned under in a perfect bob. She wore make-up but it wasn't overdone. Just enough to compliment what she already had.

Before she retired, Mrs. Jaspers had been a nurse for thirty-five years. After only a month of the retired life, she realized she was nowhere near ready to sit at home and rest. She returned to nursing but worked only with private clients. She put Daddy in his place the first time they met. Reminded me of my mama.

Darryl and I zeroed in on a little romantic energy between them.

In the short time she'd been with us, not only had Daddy's health improved, he started shaving every day and wearing dress shirts to breakfast.

Every morning when Mrs. Jaspers arrived, Daddy would be sitting in the living room, clothes starched and pressed, hair slicked back with coconut-scented pomade, looking sharp as a tack. It was good to see my father come alive after everything we'd been through.

Daddy wouldn't go near my spiritual room but he was totally cool when clients came to get readings. He stayed with Diane and her fiancé every other weekend so that Darryl and I could have some alone time. The kids loved having their Grandfather in the same house.

The first three shows we filmed ran like clockwork. On the night that the fourth show was scheduled to air, the seven of us were having dinner together at the condo. Daddy turned the volume up on the TV and shushed us to be quiet. The President was getting ready to make an announcement to the world at an emergency press conference in Washington, D.C.

The news was devastating. America was on the brink of going to war with the Middle East. The leader of that country had issued a warning that if the U.S. tried to attack them, they'd release a biological agent that would exterminate every living thing in North America. According to them, they had undercover ops in every major city ready to begin spreading the secret weapon.

When the President's speech was over, Daddy led us in a moving prayer. Then he told us what he thought about the Middle Eastern president's decision using words I hadn't heard him use in 20 years.

"Bastard! They gon' fool around and kill everybody! I sholl hope that Obinka guy wins the next one. He gon' have a helluva mess to clean up though. What we need is a prayer vigil. Bring all the religious men in the world together. Let them walk to the White House. Somebody gotta stop these idiots before they destroy the whole world. I…."

Suddenly, Daddy grabbed his chest. His lips contorted into a grotesque expression. He leaned over in an awkward position that resembled the leaning tower in Italy. I jumped up, tried to break his fall but it was too late. He fell across the couch and landed on top of the glass coffee table. It crumbled under the weight of his massive body.

"Call 911! He's having a heart attack."

CHAPTER
Twenty-Six

Daddy was in a coma. He'd had a massive stroke and the doctors said his chances of surviving weren't very good. One more time, I called on the Spirits to help me. I was in my spiritual room, praying hard, asking God to intervene on my father's behalf. I heard the front door open. Darryl called out.

"Violet, where are you?"

"I'm back here." I answered. My face was wet with angry tears.

Darryl pulled me to him. I couldn't talk. All I could do was shake my head.

"Violet, listen to me. I need you to pay attention. If we're going to save your father, you need to be present. What are the Spirits saying? Is there something you can do?"

"Why does bad stuff keep happening to me? I can't stop crying. I can't…"

The doorbell rang. I heard Diane's voice from the front door. Darryl left my side to let Diane in. I stayed in my spiritual room where I felt safe and comforted by the ancestral energies that dwelled there. I heard Darryl tell Diane where I was. She'd never come into the room where I did my spiritual work but today she walked right in and sat down on the other side of the table.

"Well, what are they telling you? Is Daddy going to die?"

She started crying too. I gave her a piece of tissue.

"I don't know. I haven't asked them."

"What are you waiting for?"

She always knew how to take charge in desperate situations.

"Are you going to stay in here while I do the divination?"

"I'm not going anywhere until you tell me what's going to happen with my father."

"He's my father too." I said in a spoiled tone.

"Stop being silly and throw the damn shells, Violet."

She would never cease to amaze me.

Six months ago, she thought my spiritual practice was make-believe, now she wanted me to cast the shells. I guess I should be happy. But under the present circumstances, all I could do was follow directions.

I did the libation, lit an incense stick and rang the bell to call the ancestors. Darryl and Diane watched in silence while I positioned three cards face down in front me on the table. When I turned the first one over, I couldn't conceal my anguish. It was the card of death.

"I can't do this! Why do they keep letting stuff happen to people I love?"

Darryl got up and walked over the table. He steadied my hand. Together, we turned over the second card. It was Babaluaye, the Shaman.

I was paralyzed with fear. I couldn't move. Darryl stood frozen next to me.

Diane stepped up and turned over the third card. It was Yemoja, the mother of all humanity. I could hear the desperation in Diane's voice. "What do they mean, Violet? Is Daddy going to pull out of it?"

I looked at the cards and tried to pick up what the Spirits were trying to tell me. I swallowed hard, told myself to pretend I was reading a client.

"The first card is the card of death. Death is trying to claim him. The second card is the High Priest of Shamanism. Babaluaye. That's the kind of strength it's going to take to save Daddy. The third card is Yemoja, the great mother. The spirit that took the slaves into her bosom when they were thrown or they jumped off of the slave ships. Mama's here. She says Daddy stuck somewhere between here and there."

Darryl made a suggestion, "Can you do an offering or something—you know like what you did for me?"

"I don't know, Darryl. For the first time in my life, I don't know what to do."

I put my head down and started crying again. When I looked back up, the room was filled with a bright, white light. My heart started pounding. I looked at Diane and her face transformed into someone else's face. Darryl's face turned into liquid. His features became unrecognizable. First my feet started shaking, then my legs and thighs. Next thing I knew I was standing up. My shoulders were crouched like an older woman. I heard Darryl calling me from some far off place but for the life of me I couldn't get my mouth to form an answer. When I finally spoke, the words that came out weren't my own. Someone or something had entered my body.

"I'm Anna." The Spirit said through me.

Darryl's voice trembled when he answered.

"Hi Anna." He hit Diane on the arm and told her to say hi.

"Hi An-nnn-ie." Diane said, her voice shaking too. "Where's my sister? Wait a minute. Our great grandmother's name was Anna! Are you her? What did you do with Violet?" Diane was talking ridiculously loud.

"Be quiet and listen, Diane." Darryl told her assertively.

"She's here but I'm talking to you 'cause she can't. There's a store on Eggleston Street-right by the train station. You'll see Saint Lazarus in the window. The man that works there, he's the only one that can help your father. Take ninety-five dollars and a bottle of rum when you visit his store. All of you should wear white. Do whatever he tells you to do. Your father's life depends on you following what he tells you. The girls in your sister's dreams—she will need your help to save them. But first you must save your father. And tell Violet, no matter what happens, she mustn't give up the fight."

I felt my body shaking uncontrollably again. When the shaking stopped, I opened my eyes. I was in a daze, like when you wake from a deep sleep. My mouth was dry. So dry I could barely talk.

"What happened? Can I have a drink of water? I'm really thirsty."

Darryl ran to the kitchen and got me a glass of cool water. Diane helped me drink it so I wouldn't spill it down my blouse. I was still very weak and a bit disoriented.

Diane was shaking her head in disbelief. "You'll never believe what happened. I wouldn't either if I hadn't seen it with my very own eyes."

Darryl finished the story. "The spirit of Anna took over your body. She said that she came to talk to us because you couldn't. Look, I'll tell you all about it in the car. You need to change clothes. Put on something white, all white. We need to leave right away. We have to go to this store she told us about. Do you have something that Diane can wear too?"

"I think so, what's going on?"

Do what he says and stop wasting time.

Mamiwata was here.

178

"Something about a girl that's been kidnapped. You're gonna have to save her but first you have to take care of your father. We'll talk in the car. Let's go."

When Darryl told me what my great grandmother had said, I almost couldn't believe it.

It was the same thing Mamiwata had told me in my dreams.

When we got to the place where Anna had told us to go, we looked around for the store. We couldn't see anything so we got out of the car and walked down the street.

"I don't see the store she was talking about."

Darryl answered, it seemed like something or someone seemed to be driving him.

"Let's just keep walking. We have to do exactly what she told us to do."

When we got to the corner, I saw a huge statue of a brown skinned man on crutches with a dog by his side. The statue was in front of a small store. The place had Spanish writing painted on the window in gold and white. The sign read, "Botanica De St. Lazarus."

"We found it! That's St. Lazarus! Now I understand why she sent us here. During the enslavement, the African Gods were synched with the Catholic Saints in an effort to keep them hidden from the slave masters. Babaluaye became Saint Lazarus. Chango became the Saint Santa Barbara and so on. Whoever works here works with the powers of Babaluaye. That's the Orisa that Anna said could heal Daddy. We need to find him or her right now."

We rushed into the store. A small, stocky Latina woman sat behind the counter. Around her neck were long necklaces in various colors like the ones Dr. Bones used to wear. Mamiwata told me how to greet her.

She is a high priestess. Cross your arms over your chest and say Ben-de-ce-on.

I crossed my arms over my chest and repeated what Mamiwata told me. It must've been the right thing because the woman stood up, crossed her hands over her chest and said, "Santo. How can I help you."

"We're looking for St. Lazarus?"

"St. Lazarus? Oh, you want the Baba. He's in the back. Wait here."

We waited nearly thirty minutes before an older man with hair the color of clouds, dressed in impeccable white, wearing twenty or thirty beaded necklaces, emerged from the back of the store. He spoke no English. The lady had to translate.

Mamiwata told me, *he's a Chief Violet. You must drop to the floor, put your forehead to the ground and keep your arms at your side. The proper greeting is Ah-bor-oo, Ah-bor-ay, Ah-bo-see-say. Don't get up until he taps you on the back.* Mamiwata told me.

I led. Diane and Darryl followed my motions. The man said a sentence or two, then tapped us on the shoulder and gently lifted us up off the floor. He said something else to us in Spanish. We looked at each other, totally lost.

"Maria wh-eel es-plain." The man said in bad, broken English.

"His name is Baba Ocha. My name is Maria. He wants to know if you want divination. He wants to know why you are here."

"We...my father's in the hospital. The ancestors sent us here to talk to him about how we can save him." I almost lost it when I said those words.

Maria told us, "The reading is sixty dollars. If there are ebbos it will cost you more."

"What are ebbos?" Diane asked.

I cut her off, "That's fine. Can he do the reading for us right now?"

Maria nodded and locked the front door. We followed her and Baba Ocha to the back of the store. In the back room, large statues of the Saints loomed from perches covered with satin cloth and lace. Ceramic pots of all different colors decorated with the images of the deities stood illuminated by candles that gave the room a mysterious glow.

Decorated candles with foil tops concealing their magic, along with dozens of jars filled with herbs, seeds, perfumed water and other tools of the religion, were lined up perfectly on wooden shelves. Maria lit a charcoal on a hotplate and sprinkled granules of fragrant incense on the glowing red coal. The room became warm and airy as Baba Ocha poured what I knew was libation and recited at least a dozen prayers to the Gods. When he was done, he looked over at me and said something to Maria.

"He needs to know your father's name."

"Herbert Theodore Brown."

Baba Ocha said Daddy's name out loud and sprinkled a little water on the mat in front of his shrine. He took a large group of shells in his hand and dropped them on the mat. Picked them up and dropped them a second time.

I noted that he used the same amount of shells that Dr. Bones used for divination. I counted them. There were sixteen altogether. Two of them were white side up. He stared intently at the shells and then spoke to Maria in Spanish.

"Baba Ocha says this man's life is in danger. The Egun are calling him home."

I fought back the tears. Baba Ocha cast the shells again. Maria interpreted.

"Baba Ocha says your father can be saved but it's going to cost you."

I looked at Maria, "Tell him, whatever it costs we'll pay. Just tell us what to do."

Baba tossed the shells again. This time he shook his head back and forth. His face bore a grim expression. He talked a long time to Maria and it seemed he'd never be finished. My nerves were on edge. She finally told us what the shells had told him.

"Baba says you must give a bottle of rum to Esu before you leave here tonight. You must bathe your father for three days in the herbs of Pau D'arco, Rompazarguey, Rosemary and Sage. Clean the floor where he sleeps with the blood of a rooster mixed with water, ammonia and sea salt. During this time you must continuously burn a white, seven-day candle. Give an offering to the shrine of Saint Lazaro. He wants a brown paper bag with seventeen dollars and a pound of black-eyed-peas inside. Your father will pull out of it. Baba Ocha can't tell you when but he says pay attention to the number three. He has everything here that you need. The offering for Baba's work is a hundred and twenty one dollars. The herbs, candles and other things will cost an additional thirty dollars."

"I have ninety-five dollars on me. Will you take a check for the rest?" I said before the last words were done coming out of her mouth.

It was almost midnight when we got done. The last thing to do was to prepare the floor wash and that meant sacrificing a rooster. Maria went into a side room and came out with a small box. I heard something fluttering around inside of it.

"Diane, are you sure you want to stay here for this part?"

"I think I'll go sit in the car if you don't mind. I'm already gonna have nightmares for a month."

"I'll keep Diane company." Darryl offered.

Darryl and Diane walked outside. Baba Ocha, Maria and I finished up.

Baba Ocha took the bird from the box feet first. It flapped its wings in a last ditch effort to get away from its inescapable fate. My heart was beating so hard I thought it was gonna burst through my chest.

The rooster became silent, almost as if it knew what was about to happen. Baba Ocha prayed for the bird then cleaned its beak and feet with a few drops of water. He pulled feathers from parts of the bird's body and dropped them in front of a shell encrusted pot.

He slid back the lid of the pot. Told me to close my eyes while Maria held the bird upside down and he did the sacrifice. He put some of the bird's essence into a jar, mixed it with a bit of water and handed the receptacle to me in a white towel.

I fought a wave of nausea as I stuck the now warm jar in my purse, took out my checkbook and wrote him a check. I gave him an extra twenty dollars for helping us on the spot. I was turning to leave when the Baba called out to me.

"Senora, the rum."

"I brought it with me. Think I left it up front."

Maria walked out with me. There on the counter was the bottle of rum that the ancestors had told us to bring. I took it out of the bag and handed it to Maria.

"You must take it to Baba. He will offer it to Esu on your behalf."

We went back to the shrine room. I handed Baba Ocha the bottle. He took the cap off with his teeth. I noticed that his energy had become increasingly intense since he did the sacrifice. His eyeballs were almost bulging out of their sockets.

"It's the offering. It heats things up." Maria said, noticing my expression.

He filled his mouth with the fiery liquid and turned to a small red saucer holding a cement head that had eyes, nose and a mouth made of small shells. He spit the rum on the head of the statue with a forceful spray.

He opened a plastic container and retrieved four pieces of fresh coconut rind. He shook them over his head and dropped the pieces in front of the figure. All four pieces fell white side up.

"Alafia. Maferefun Babaluaye." Baba Ocha said in a grateful tone.

Baba Ocha and Maria kneeled to the floor. Maria waved me down too. We kissed our fingers and touched the ground three times in a row. Maria explained the nature of the ritual.

"We do this to express our thanks for the blessings of God over this ritual."

Baba Ocha cast the coconut rinds again. They fell two dark and two light. He went to his ancestor shrine and dropped the rinds a third time. They fell three white and one dark.

"Something is missing. The ancestors want something else." Maria announced.

He spit a little rum over his ancestral shrine, lit a cigar and blew the smoke over the pictures. After a moment, he turned to me with the messages he'd received.

"You mus' make' Ocha."

Maria explained, "You have to become a priestess. The spirits say they've already initiated you in your dreams. Now you must go through the ceremony."

Baba said some other things to her in Spanish. It must've been good news, because Maria's eyes lit up.

"You have much Ase' to do this work. The Orisa are going to use you to make this world a better place. Work with your spirit guides and with Ogun to remove your obstacles. The spirits told Baba that you're a daughter of Yemoja. She is your guardian angel. Do you know who Yemoja is?" Maria told me excitedly.

Yemoja was the name of the deity Mamiwata had told me about in my dream. "Yes, I know Yemoja very well. Tell Baba I said thank you. And tell him I'll never forget this day. *Never.*"

Baba Ocha got up and walked over to me. He crossed his arms, touched his left and then his right shoulder to mine. It was a sign of deep respect and acknowledgement. He hugged me tightly before we went our separate ways.

Go to the hospital, now! Mamiwata spoke to me in an urgent tone. I hugged Baba Ocha one last time and walked quickly to the car.

CHAPTER
Twenty-Seven

Three days had passed and Daddy still hadn't come out of the coma. I called Maria at the Botanica.

"Be patient. The Spirits work in God's time and the Orisa always keep their word. Even when our faith in them dies they fulfill what they promise."

Over the next couple of days, I almost moved into Daddy's hospital room. All of the nurses knew me by first name. The food staff had started delivering two dinners, one for Daddy and one for me.

I took showers in the doctor's lounge. I used the wireless service in the nurse's station to check my email. I sent Amy a message about what had happened to my father. She wrote me back saying that she understood but explained that the show had to go on. The producers were looking for another psychic to replace me. My heart sank. My world was falling apart.

Darryl came by on his lunch break. I told him what Amy had said.

"Maybe there's something else you're supposed to be doing."

"Like what?"

"I don't know. Ask the cards or the shells or somebody. If you're worried about money don't. Your man took care of business. If I quit the firm today, we'd never miss a meal or a mortgage payment."

"I can't expect you to take care of me."

"Why not? Isn't that what people who love each other do during hard times?"

"Darryl, you don't understand. I don't have a job. I have the money from my 401k but that's not going to last forever. What the hell am I going to do if Amy finds another psychic to take my place?"

"Violet, I want you to go home and take a break. I'll stay here with Dad. Go soak for an hour or two in one of those eucalyptus baths you like to take and get your head together."

"You'll call if anything happens?"

"I'll either call or come home. Now get outta here."

I kissed him on the lips and headed for the door.

I was home alone trying hard to relax but the house was too damn quiet. I nuked a veggie chicken patty, layered some lettuce and tomato, spooned a dollop of mayo on top and took a bite. I sat back and turned on the boob tube just in time to hear an announcement being made by the President's military council. I half listened for a few minutes. I was about to put an end to the reporter's banter but Mamiwata told me to keep listening.

"America's troops are on high alert. We've sent up a warning flare asking them to disarm their nuclear weapons. If they don't respond, our troops will ascend on foreign soil with one goal—to put the enemy of American freedom out of business. We know there will be innocent victims but in a war, sometimes you have to sacrifice a few to save the many."

My mind rolled back to the horrific scenes from my dream. I imagined the Okinawa City bombing times ten. Maybe this was the future they were warning me about. Maybe this was what they wanted me to stop from happening. But how? I was only one person.

The voices of my ancestors spoke together in one powerful tone.

If this war happens America will perish. Your soldiers will die in the thousands. Plagues will cover the earth. Your generation and three generations to come will live under the reign of the white cloud. We have been preparing you for this moment your entire life. You must gather the spiritual leaders of the world. The Buddhist, the Hindu, the Catholic, the Jew. Gather the Protestant, the Muslim, the Christian too. Gather the African Priests, the Cherokee Chiefs and the Wiccans together. Bring the Mormons, the Monks, the Seers and Shakers. You must organize a day of worldwide prayer. The people of this world must unify and let go of their petty differences. They must unify to save the world or they will perish together.

I sat there on the couch completely sure that the ancestors had gone off the deep end. How in the hell was I supposed to do something like that? The people that worked in that seamless dome in Washington were virtually untouchable. And why on earth would the gurus around the world lift even a tiny little finger for me? I was nobody, just a lonely psychic who'd found love for the first time in her life. A woman whose father was fighting to stay alive. And then the ancestors added insult to injury.

Call the United Nations. There is a woman there that will help you.

"The United Nations! Do you understand what you're asking me?"

We've tried to stop every World War before it happened.

"Who are you?"

We are the circle of wives. The five who gave birth to your spirit guide, Mamiwata. We are the first mothers of the world. The one they call Lucy was one of us. But that is not her real name.

I'd read about Lucy. Archaeologists had uncovered her bones in Africa. Her bones were supposed to be the oldest ever found. They'd nicknamed her the Mother of Civilization.

"What is her real name?"

Auset. You know her as Yemoja.

Everything the ancestors had spoken in my ear over the last few weeks came flooding back to my mind, including the words that my father spoke seconds before he had the stroke.

We need a prayer vigil. Bring all the ministers in the world together. Let them walk to the White House. Somebody gotta stop them before they destroy the planet.

Daddy had always been a spiritual man, a Seer in his own right. He was trying to tell me what God had put on his soul but his heart gave out on him before he could finish. Even so, there was no way I could pull anything like this off by myself.

Talk to those people at the television station. Ask them to broadcast it on their show. Set up a small office at the house. Ask your friends to help.

What friends? I couldn't ask Darryl to do anything else. He was already carrying us. And Diane was flying back and forth to California for her job.

Go home. Go back to California. In exactly three days, you must begin preparing to return home.

"What about my father? He's too sick to travel. I can't leave him here. I won't leave him here. You're crazy!"

I ran to the room where my altar was and in a single swoop knocked all the pictures off the table. I picked up the tarot deck and threw it across the room. I gathered the tablecloth in my right hand and ripped it from the table.

I looked up at the barren table. My mouth gaped open.

In the center of the table were my shells. All four of them were white side up. *Alafia.* The way was open. God had spoken. This too was part of my destiny.

I dropped to my knees sobbing harder than I ever had in life. My chest heaved up and down as my desperate and confused wails filled the room.

I heard the front door open and shut.

"Violet! Violet, where are you?"

Darryl was home. That could only mean one thing. Daddy had died.

I heard his heavy footsteps behind me. I couldn't bring myself to turn around and face him. I didn't want to know.

"What happened in here? Never mind. Violet! You've gotta get up and come with me to the hospital. Your father is awake. He's asking for you. Come on baby. I need to take you back right now."

It was a sign from God. They'd given my father back to me and now I had to pay up. My offering was the march. That was my sacrifice for them returning my life giver back to the world of the living.

Baba Ocha said it would be three days before Daddy came back. The clock read 11:53pm. Seven more minutes and it would've been day four.

"God, next time could you speed things up a bit?"

"What?"

"Nothing, baby. Help me find something to put on."

CHAPTER
Twenty-Eight

Two days later Daddy was home. The doctors called his recovery nothing short of a miracle. It was the second huge miracle I had experienced in my life. Most stroke patients had to go through months of rehabilitation. Daddy was able to walk around a bit and had begun feeding himself. If the doctors only knew where that miracle had come from: a priest of an African religion and a chicken.

Mrs. Jasper moved in so that she could tend to Daddy around the clock. I think that made my Daddy happier than he would admit. "One of the perks of surviving the big one," that's what he called it.

On the third day of Daddy being home from the hospital, we were all in the dining room having breakfast together. Darryl had flown in his personal chef, Maynard, to help Mrs. Jasper out. Maynard, a big brawny man with a 1970's afro, had the overhead

TV on in the kitchen. Daddy started waving his hand, demanding that everybody be quiet and listen. An emergency broadcast was underway.

"Daddy, I don't want you watching this stuff. That's what got you upset the last time. You're just starting to feel better. This might be too much for...."

"Violet, hush! I can't hear. Turn it up, Maynard."

I was getting up to unplug the TV when, once again, fate stopped me dead in my tracks. The words of the broadcaster would change the course of my life forever.

"The United Nations has taken a stand against the president's decision to go to war. Military heads were seen arriving at the White House for a private meeting. The *U. S. Biological Warfare Team* has been placed on high alert. Hear the full story on the four o'clock news. And remember, you heard it first on News 6, KTRU, the station on America's frontlines."

It was so quiet in the dining room you could've heard an ant crawling across the carpet. Darryl stared at me from across the table.

"Tell your father about the dream, Violet. He'll understand."

Daddy looked over at me. His eyes had that glow, the glow that meant he wouldn't accept no for an answer.

He laughed a little bit. "I know all about your little room back there, so don't worry 'bout me thinking you crazy. Sides, my son-in-law told me a little something 'bout what y'all did to help me get well."

I rolled my eyes at Darryl and answered Daddy's question.

"The night you came out of the coma, I had a vision. When I first started having the dreams, I would see these five women. They were in a cave in the woods helping this lady give birth. The baby they gave birth to—Mamiwata—is the main one that talks to me. The rest of them are you and Mama's relatives. Anyway, the Spirits told me to organize an international day of prayer with all the spiritual leaders in the world and have them convene at Washington, on the Whitehouse steps. They also told me to call some woman at the United Nations. I told Darryl there was no way…"

He didn't wait to hear me confess my lack of faith.

"Violet, if God gave you a vision like that you need to follow through. That's the kind of vision God gave Martin and Malcolm. What would've happened if they let fear stop them from following God's directions?"

"Daddy, I can't believe you're saying that. It's no coincidence that both of them are dead. Did you ever think that some people in the world might not be too happy about me trying to prevent this war from taking place?"

"Violet, God knows I don't want nothing to happen to you but if God wants you to do this then you have to do it. You're God's messenger and we have to help you get the message to God's people. Now, what them spirits of yours tell you to do first?"

"I can't believe you're serious."

I looked around the room and every one of them, Diane, Brandon, Darryl, Mrs. Jasper and even Maynard, were looking at me, waiting for me to tell them what we were going to do.

"Well, first of all, they told me to move back to California."

"Well, what are we waiting for? Let's get packed." Daddy ordered.

"What about me?" Mrs. Jasper looked at Daddy, then at me.

"Pack your things, honey. And bring that wedding gown you keep tucked away in your closet. Diane and Violet ain't gon' be the only ones getting married."

"Are you proposing to me, Mr. Brown?"

"You heard me right, woman. I want you to be my wife.'

"Daddy! You and Mrs. Jasper….that's wonderful. But we pushed the wedding back to September 4th. Remember? Back when Darryl got shot."

"Whatever day y'all get married, me and this here fine lady gon' get married too. Now let's get this show on the road. We gotta keep them crazy folks from destroying God's sweet earth. Then I'm gon' eat some wedding cake and celebrate some real independence."

Darryl hired three extra packers and two moving trucks so we could expedite our move back to California. Brandon was the CEO of a mid-size accounting firm with offices in three states. His corporate offices were in Chicago but he had a small office in L.A. He and Diane decided to move the main office to California and make the office in Chicago a local firm to support his remaining clients.

Brandon was Christian just like Daddy. When he spoke, his southern twang tantalized our ears.

"Vi-let, you know I on't understand how the si-kick thang works. But I believe that the Lord above gives people certain gifts so they can do His work. When I met your sister, I was coming out of a bad marriage and an even worse divorce. On top of all dat, I found out I couldn't have children. And them high paid doctors, they couldn't tell me nuthin. Well, Diane and those beautiful kids changed all of that fir me. Now I have two wonderful kids and a wife to be. Whatever I got to do to keep those warmongers from destroying what I have, I'll do it. God forgive my sefish motives. But like they say, he who is without sin cast the first stone."

"Brandon, thank you for being the only real father my niece and nephew have ever known. I have a gift for you, brother-in-law. You and Diane are going have a baby of your own."

The Spirits told me that a bundle of joy would soon be coming into their life. Brandon looked like a deer looking into headlights.

"Brother-in-law, there's nothing wrong with your equipment that minor surgery won't fix. There's a small blockage there. Get it checked out and you'll see."

Brandon's olive skin flushed with embarrassment. After all, we were talking about his private body parts.

"I-I'll get it checked out when we get to L.A."

Daddy came in ordering everybody around. Destiny was calling us again.

Three days later we were packed up and ready for California.

Daddy limped into the living room leaning on his cane. "Truck's downstairs. Time to blow this joint! Where's Evelyn? Anybody seen Evelyn?" Daddy asked with a huff.

"Who is Evelyn, Daddy?"

"That's Mrs. Jasper's first name."

I'd been calling her Mrs. Jasper for so long I forgot she had a first name. Daddy taught us to address elders by their last name and a surname. His addressing her by her first name confirmed that our father had truly fallen in love. Daddy hadn't loved a woman since mama died. That was over twenty years ago.

"I'm right here, Herbert. Did you take your medicine?" Evelyn answered.

"Stop fussing, woman. Of course I did."

Brought back old memories hearing Daddy talk like that. Love is the best medicine in the world. The twists and turns of life would never cease to amaze me.

"Alright everybody, as Daddy says, let's get this road on the show," I commanded the troops.

CHAPTER
Twenty-Nine

Darryl's house was ceiling deep in boxes. The chill of the pre-dawn beach fog woke me around four a.m. Had my teeth clattering.

Thin shorts and a tank top weren't cutting it. I'd forgotten the temperature in Los Angeles dropped ten degrees at night. I tip-toed down the hall and turned up the heat a notch. Didn't want to wake Darryl or Daddy so I grabbed a throw from the linen closet, flipped the switch to turn on the gas fireplace and curled up on the couch. I intended to read for a while and go back to bed. Minutes later, my reading materials were flat down on my chest. Eyelids grew heavier and heavier. I dropped off into a deep sleep. My spirit left my body and began its travels.

I saw a girl running across a large field. Men were shouting at her, firing their guns in her direction. Deadly bullets hurled toward her frail body. There was something around her neck. A necklace.

I ran as fast as I could to catch up with her and see it clearer. She made a beeline in the direction of a distant car. When she got to it, she slithered through the window, shifted the vehicle into gear and floored the gas pedal. The car skidded off creating a bumpy path in the tall grass.

My spirit sat in the passenger seat beside her. She wrapped her hands around the stones in her necklace and began to pray.

"B'ao ku ishe o tan. Ohun ori wa se. Ko man ni s'alai se eo. Ebo fin, Eru da. Ebo fin, Eru da, Ebo fin, Eru da. Where there is still life, there is still hope. The ebbo is complete. Evil forces depart!"

I knew those words! Those were the words spoken by the circle of wives when they blessed the sacred necklace. When she opened her hand, I saw the stones glistening in a pool of sweat. The same necklace that the wives placed around the neck of one of my grandmothers hundreds of years ago.

I felt the car drop on one side like a balloon being pierced by a sharp object. A bullet had punctured one of the tires. The girl kept driving, pushing the wounded vehicle as fast as it would go. When she got to the edge of the bush, she jumped out of the car and ran toward the river. My spirit followed her to the river bank. When she got to the edge there was no way to get down to the water unless she jumped some fifty feet into the icy, rock-bottom. The men were closing in on her fast. She had to make a choice.

I felt someone tap me on the shoulder. I turned around to see an apparition standing behind me. *"You must save her. You are descendents of the same mother. You must retrieve the necklace. You will need it to complete your mission."*

I heard a loud splash. I turned around and saw the girl's lifeless body floating face down in the river. I started screaming, telling the girl to wake up.

In the real world, Darryl was calling, trying to beckon me back to the present. I could hear him but I couldn't find my way back to him. A sudden splash of cold water yanked me back through time.

I blinked my eyes open, wiped away the water dripping down on my face and neck. I looked around and realized I'd not only been gone from my body, I'd been gone from this existence.

"Violet, you alright?" Darryl asked. There was concern in his voice.

"She fell—I mean jumped. I gotta help her. She needs my help."

"It's a dream, Violet. You were calling out in your sleep. Calling somebody named *Olokun*. I tried to wake you up. When you wouldn't come out of it, I got worried. Had to splash you with some cold water to bring you back."

"There's someone...a girl from Africa. Somehow she's related to me. These men were chasing her. She jumped off a cliff into a river. I gotta help her."

Darryl walked around to my side of the bed and sat down next to me.

"Violet, *we* need your help. Your husband, your father and your sister. I've always had faith in your spiritual guidance but this time...this time I gotta say I'm not feeling it. Us, your *family*, we need to be the priority right now."

I got angry with him for the first time since we got together.

"I know this sounds crazy but I think Olokun's my family too. I really need you to support me on this. Ever since I was a small child my guides have been giving me a message about doing something that would change the world. This is it. I just know it."

"Violet...I'm not doing this. Did you forget I got shot last month? Your father just had a heart attack a few weeks ago. The *Spirits* directed you to organize some kind of peace movement. I don't see how this family can endure any more than that right now. Our plate is full."

I started crying. I didn't understand either. So much had happened over the last six months. From losing my job, to going on national TV, to meeting the man of my dreams and almost losing him and Daddy. Darryl was right. It was too much.

"What do you want me to do!" I screamed up at the sky.

Darryl thought I was talking to him. "I want you to slow down. Map things out. We need a plan, Violet. There's a saying. If you don't have a plan, you plan to fail."

"How am I supposed to plan what I don't understand!"

"Calm down, baby. First, we need to get our house in order. After that, everything else will fall into place. Come here. Come to me."

I went over to him. He pulled me into his warmth. Melted my anger like ice in the sun with a few kisses.

"I've gotta go into the office for a few hours. When I get back, we'll sit down and talk about how we're going to do all of this."

I kissed him on his smooth forehead, worked my way down to his lips, slipped him a bit of tongue. He tasted like cinnamon toothpaste. I leaned into his firm chest again. Let him caress my behind before he let me go.

"I'm sorry I yelled at you. I'm just.....overwhelmed and tired. Sometimes I don't understand this life of mine anymore than you do."

"I love you, woman. More than you'll ever know. We'll figure everything out. *Together.* For now, I need you to make a plan. When I get home, we'll talk about it and figure out our next steps."

CHAPTER
Thirty

I was on the phone telling Amy about my vision for the peace march, about bringing all the religious leaders together to pray for peace. She ate the idea up like it was vanilla ice cream on top of hot apple pie.

"Fabulous! I love it! The J.B. Good Show is in, Violet. We'll need exclusive rights to the footage. And you know I have to get the official go ahead from the execs but you have my vote. J.B. Good loves anything that has to do with peace, green living and all that eco-sustainability stuff. I'll get a contract to you and we'll finalize all the details. You know, now that I think about it you should...."

Amy was on a tangent now. Her business mind was busy creating a road map for the project's success. That's what Darryl was talking about—planning things out. Guess he was right about that. Amy interrupted my revelation.

"When do you want to do this thing? You have any dates in mind?" Amy asked, trying to iron out the main details.

"No date yet. When do you think we should shoot for?"

"I'd say at least five or six months. You're gonna need time to plan an event of this magnitude. You might wanna explore hiring an event planner, unless this kind of thing is your forte. Maybe you could find a sponsoring organization or something. A church, synagogue or some group that already has a following and the contacts you need to pull something like this off."

I opened my journal and wrote what Amy said down. I'd show Darryl. I was going to plan this event like nobody's business.

"Any particular organizations you recommend?"

I felt Mamiwata's presence come into the room.

"There's lots of good ones out there."

Mamiwata gave me a name.

The International League of Women United.

"Amy....you ever heard of an organization called *The International League of Women United?*

"No. Can't say I have. But hold on a second. I'm on-line. I'll google 'em."

I heard her tip-tapping on the computer.

Her tapping made me think about my recurring nightmare, the one where the bombing happened.

"Found them! Their web site address is www league of women dot com. They look interesting. Worked with the United Nations and....let's see...they've done a lot of global work, especially in Africa. I think you should give them a call."

"Maybe I will." I told her writing down the web address.

"Okay, keep us posted on everything. Once you get things in motion we'll set a date for you to come on the show."

"Thanks, Amy. Thanks for giving me another chance. I'll be in touch as soon as I have something concrete."

CHAPTER
Thirty-One

Their receptionist answered on the second ring. "International League of Women United."

"Hi…um…this is Violet Brown. I work with…I work with the J.B. Good Talk Show. It was suggested I contact your organization regarding an event I'm coordinating."

"You need to speak with our project director. Hazel Miller. Just a minute, I'll connect you."

I had no idea getting through would be this easy. I wasn't prepared to make a presentation just yet. I started panicking until Hazel Miller's voicemail chimed in. I left her a message, asked her to call me back as soon as she could. After I left the message I got scared again.

What was I gonna say when I spoke with her? I couldn't exactly tell her I'd had a psychic vision. Maybe I needed to explore other organizations. Surely this wasn't the only one that did this kind of work.

I was on the way to my altar to consult the ancestors when the phone rang. I figured it was Darryl or Diane but it wasn't either of them. It was Hazel Miller.

"This is Hazel Miller. I'm returning your call."

"Uh…Hello. My name is Violet Brown."

"Yes, I know. You work for the J.B. Good Show. How can I help you?"

"I….I'm organizing a march. It was suggested that I get in touch with your organization to see if you would be interested in working with us."

"I'll be frank with you Ms. Brown. We're not fans of the J.B. Good Show. We asked them to cover a story about a woman being stoned in Ziberia. They turned us down cold. Said the story wasn't interesting enough. We don't want our organization exploited in the name of daytime television. Out of curiosity, may I ask what the cause for your march is?"

I realized I'd messed up telling her I was with the J.B. Good Show. I thought it would hold more weight if I said I was with a TV network. If I changed my story now it would make me look bad.

"The cause? Oh—it's a march for world peace."

"Who've you invited to speak?"

"Invited? We…..we're reaching out to leaders of religious movements. People like the Dalai Lama, Minister Louis Farrakan, Rev. Jesse Jackson and…."

"So you're organizing a celebrity march."

"No, they'll be regular people there too."

"Miss Brown, we're all regular people. At this time I'm not sure what my organization can do to help you. We work mostly on human rights issues with a focus on victims of human trafficking and the rights of women living in third world countries. Right now we're knee deep in a case involving a Ziberian woman."

"My ancestors were Ziberian." It came out of my mouth before I could stop it.

"I see. Well….you may've heard about her case then. Woman named Ayoola Omikunle. An activist. Our group had partnered with hers to support legislation that would've put an end to a very controversial practice that kills hundreds of women in Africa every year."

"Did you say her name was Ayoola?"

"Yes, did you know of her?"

"I—I….no. I just know that name."

"You might've heard about her work with the Mefa-Eru."

"The what?"

"The Mefa-Eru. Girls who've been enslaved by traffickers"

I had to open my big mouth and tell her about my ancestors.

"I read something in the newspaper about it."

"We're pretty tied up with trying to find her daughter. She was kidnapped a few months after her mother was killed. She may have information about her mother's killers that could help us with our case. There's a big article about it on our website."

"I'll check it out."

She paused for a minute like she was thinking something over. "I tell you what. Get me a proposal about your march and I'll give it some thought."

"Thank you! I…I'll get it to you right away."

"I have to run it by the board before I make my decision but we'll check it out. Sorry to rush off the phone but I'm late for a meeting."

"Thanks for taking the time to speak with me. I'll get that proposal out to you asap."

"Good day, Miss Brown."

I entered the address for the League of Women's website. Surfed around the site a bit and learned a little more about their organization. I clicked on the link to their on-line newsletter, skimmed through it looking for the article on Ayoola Omikunle.

My mouth dropped open when I clicked on the URL for the picture. Ayoola Omikunle looked just like my grandmother on my mother's side.

Ayoola had a sharp nose and heart-shaped lips, cinnamon-colored skin and reddish-brown hair. I zoomed in closer and noticed something else familiar. Around her neck were the same kind of beads that Dr. Bones wore.

I read the report that The League published about her case. According to the military police, Iya Ayoola was killed because she resisted arrest.

Three sentences at the bottom of the page almost made me faint. I read them a second time to be sure of what I was reading.

Iya Ayoola Omikunle Fayemi is survived by her daughter, Olokun Ayoola Fayemi. At the time this article went to press, Olokun's whereabouts were unknown. Unnamed sources say she may've been taken to America as part of a human trafficking ring currently under investigation.

Olokun was the name of the little girl in my dream!

Was it possible?

No way. It had to be some kind of eery coincidence.

As I sat there pondering, a spirit spoke to me.

Didn't I always tell you there are no coincidences, Violet? That was Mama.

"Mama, what are you trying to tell me?"

Mama didn't answer

I ran to the altar room, picked up my cowry shells, sprinkled a couple of drops of water and cast the shells.

"Is the Olokun girl on the League website my biological ancestor?"

The mouths of the shells shouted their answer. *Alafia.*

In a daze, I bent down to the floor, kissed my fingertips and touched the only earth I could reach at the moment.

Crying tears of joy, I ran back to the office and called Darryl on his cell phone.

"Baby, you have to come home right now! You're not going to believe what just happened. I think I found my ancestors."

"Violet, didn't we just talk about this?"

"This is different. I'll tell you all about it when you get home."

"I'm parking the car. I'll be right up."

When he walked in, I took him by the hand and dragged him to the computer.

"Can a brother get a glass of water? Maybe a little something to eat? I just got home. I'm exhausted. I can look at whatever it is in just a minute. How's your father doing?"

"He's fine. He's over at Diane's house. You have to come right now. You have to see this. Dinner'll be ready in a few minutes."

He followed me to the room where our computers were. I pulled up the website, clicked on the newsletter and scrolled down to the bottom of the article.

"Read those three lines."

When he finished reading he leaned back in the chair.

"It's pretty damn coincidental that the daughter's name is the same one from your dream. But I don't want you to get your hopes up. A lot of people in Africa have the same name. Just like there's thousands of people in America named Kimberly."

I sat back in the chair. "It's her, Darryl. I just know it. She's in trouble. I have to help her. What they do to those girls is….it's horrible."

"I understand what you're saying but I need you to get some information. Will you at least research this a bit further before you move forward?"

"I'll call the lady at the League back and see what else I can find out."

"What lady?"

"Oh, I didn't tell you that part yet. I talked to Amy today. The J.B. Good Show is gonna support the march. When I told Amy my vision, she suggested I get an organization to sponsor us. When she said that, Mamiwata whispered the name of…. Oh. My. God. Mamiwata told me the name of the organization that would connect me to Ayoola's daughter!"

"Violet, you're getting all worked up again. I want you to calm down. Slow down and tell me everything."

Before I could finish, the smell of burning food tickled my nostrils.

"Oh shit!"

I dashed down the hall to cut the stove off.

"Her name is Hazel Miller." I said, loud enough for people next door to hear.

"Stop yelling. I'm right behind you. Did you say her name is *Hazel Miller*?"

"Yep."

"I know that name." Darryl said, sitting down in the kitchen. "Is the website for that org still up on the computer?"

We went back down the hall to the office.

Darryl opened the browser, clicked on the link for the staff of *The League*.

"I'll be got-damn. That's my bosses' wife. That's Hazel Miller, the wife of millionaire attorney, Robert E. Miller. You hit the jackpot by calling her."

"Baby, what are you talking about?"

"Our firm handles the financials for their organization. That's how I know her name. Damn, this is some *Twilight Zone* kind of stuff. I get it. I finally get it. I guess you aren't crazy after all."

CHAPTER
Thirty-Two

I n a large warehouse in the most crime-ridden part of Downtown Los Angeles, Fagunwa Ogunlano, a Ziberian soldier from the National African Alliance, reminded himself of the promise he'd made to Ayoola Omikunle two years ago.

His thirteen-year old daughter Adina had gotten sick after she was kidnapped and raped by an NAA solider. Fearing she'd contracted the AIDS virus, Fagunwa brought her to Ayoola for evaluation. Ayoola and her team of nurses concluded that Adina hadn't contracted the AIDS virus but was infected with a rare and sometimes fatal fever. Using a powerful concoction of healing herbs and a series of ancient rituals, Ayoola healed his daughter. Fagunwa made a vow to Ayoola that whatever he could do to end the NAA's brutal regime, he would do it.

Risking his own life and the lives of his wife and children, Fagunwa had traveled from Africa to America where the notorious

General Mbele Mubosa had launched a human trafficking ring under the NAA umbrella.

Fagunwa understood fully what he was up against in taking down the General's operation. Either he would destroy the General's regime or it would destroy him. There was no middle ground.

A tall muscular man with a neatly trimmed mustache and short cropped afro, Fagunwa sat down at a small desk and plugged in the flashdrive that contained the files he'd copied from the General's computer. He entered the NAA's executive level password and clicked on the document hoping and praying it had the information he needed to convict the General.

Three documents popped up on the screen. He clicked on the one titled, *NAA Financial Records*. As the content of the document came into view his mouth dropped open like a trap door.

In front of Fagunwa's eyes was three years worth of financial records for the NAA. Some of the expenditures were in code but because of his rank, he knew what the codes stood for.

The information he had was extremely incriminating. Multiple government agencies, both American and African, would be hit hard if the General went down. Passport agencies, an airline company, a shipping agency, two police departments, a dozen American military officials were all listed on the spread sheet under the debit category. The NAA's partnerships ran wide and deep.

Fagunwa skipped to the page shaded in green which listed the company's assets and cash currently on hand. An unbelievable number leaped off the page.

$46,560,224.22

The General had made millions auctioning girls to his corporate clientele. It sickened Fagunwa to think about the horrors those girls had suffered not to mention the anguish endured by their families. Fagunwa's daughter had almost become a victim of General Mubosa's regime. If it weren't for a spy from Ayoola's organization she wouldn't have made it out alive.

Fagunwa skimmed the other files. Most of it was contacts and resource data, all of the people who made the General's machine run like clockwork.

It was painfully clear that his boss had spent a great deal of Ziberia's money doing what the Americans called, "greasing palms." But the bulk of the profits had remained in General's pockets.

Fagunwa signed into his e-mail box. Without a moment's hesitation he electronically sent the files to the contact Iya Ayoola had told him to work with in America. Hazel Miller, the project director for the *International League of Women.*

When he was done transferring the files, Fagunwa carefully deleted all records of his sending the document and went about the process of shutting his computer down.

A year ago Mrs. Miller had approached him about going undercover to help take down General Mubosa. Fagunwa had to think long and hard about her proposal. Going undercover required him and his family to relocate outside of their beautiful country. It was a huge price to pay but it would be worth it to see the terrible crimes stop and the Mefa-Eru set free.

As he powered his computer down, his colleague Sergeant Abayomi trotted into the office. Fagunwa's heart went into overdrive as Abayomi made his way around the desk to where he could see the screen.

The computer screen went blank just as Abayomi reached him. Fagunwa didn't think he'd seen anything but he couldn't be sure.

Abayomi had a message for him. "The General would like to meet with you right away."

"Did he say what this meeting is about?"

Abayomi ignored his question and stepped away to answer the phone. Fagunwa pulled the flash drive from the computer and slipped it into his jacket pocket without being seen. He went to the men's room and lifted a loose floorboard in back of one of the toilets. He wrapped the drive in a small piece of cellophane from a pack of cigarettes and tucked it neatly underneath the tile. When he came out of the bathroom he heard Abayomi tell someone on the phone that they were on their way.

"You know the General doesn't like to wait." Abayomi warned.

When had he become the authority on what the General liked and disliked?

Fagunwa went into the other office where there was a private line and called his wife.

"I may be late tonight. Don't wait up for me."

It was their code. She knew he was telling her to get out of there and take their children to a safe house.

"I love you, Fagunwa. Thank you for saving us."

"It's not over yet." Fagunwa told her.

Abayomi knocked on the door. "We better go now."

CHAPTER
Thirty-Three

I dialed the number to the League's offices. This time an answering service responded.

"I'm trying to reach Mrs. Hazel Miller. It....it's an emergency."

"I'm sorry. Mrs. Miller has gone home for the day. Is there a message?"

"No....I'll....I'll call her back tomorrow."

Darryl walked in the room with two plates of slightly burned soy chicken wings, green salad and crispy scalloped potatoes.

"I couldn't save the broccoli." He handed me a plate. "Who was that you were trying to reach?"

"Mrs. Miller. I wanted to ask her a few questions. She's gone for the day."

"Would her home phone number work?"

"That's right! Your bosses' wife. Could you make the introduction? She might freak out if I call her at home."

A few minutes and a couple of hellos later, Darryl handed me the phone.

"Why didn't you tell me you were the wife of one of my husband's senior partners?" Mrs. Miller rattled off.

"I didn't know I was at the time."

"The League will be glad to assist you. I'll be out of the office for a few days but I'll follow up as soon as I get back. Have you emailed me your proposal?"

"Haven't had a chance to send it yet."

"Why don't you wait until I return. There's something wrong with our office email. One of those darn internet viruses."

"I'll do just that. Mrs. Miller...before you hang up, I have a couple of questions about the case you told me about."

"For security reasons I can't say too much. There's a lot of information online about the case. In the meantime, I have a question for you too, Mrs. Brown. Or is it Mrs. Collins?"

"Soon. It'll be Mrs. Collins very soon. What's your question?"

I smiled at the thought of being Darryl's wife.

"Were you on a TV show several months ago?"

Another J.B. Good fan. "Guilty as charged."

"I thought so! You were incredible."

Sometimes it felt uncomfortable when people found out about my gift. Things were never the same after they knew who and what I was.

"Thank you, Mrs. Miller."

"Please call me, Hazel."

Hazel was high society all the way. I could see her sipping club soda, nibbling on gourmet crackers and caviar at her women's meetings. Seemed like her political and community work kept her grounded.

"Did you have a question for me, Violet?"

"My question has to do with the daughter of Ayoola."

She hesitated before answering.

"I have to remind you that some of the information about this case is classified. Only because Darryl's like a son to my husband am I even talking to you about this. Hold on---I have the updated report in my briefcase."

I heard her shuffling through papers.

"Ayoola's daughter's name is Olokun. I'm sorry to tell you this but the report says she was found dead last week. The military ruled her death a suicide. The League isn't buying one ounce of their story. We'll do a full investigation before issuing a conclusive report on this case."

I choked back the tears. "Does the report say how she died?"

"May I ask what your interest in this case is?"

I chose my words very carefully. "I've been doing some research on my genealogy. There's a remote chance we're related."

"That....that would be incredible."

"Keep in mind the individuals who provided this report are suspects in an alleged murder case. And again, I need to emphasize the confidential nature of what I'm about to tell you."

"Mrs. Mil...uh, Hazel, you have my word that I won't speak of this to anybody."

"The soldiers claim they found Olokun dead in a river. They couldn't retrieve the body because of its location. Cause of death is listed as suicide. According to the arresting soldier, Olokun escaped from the warehouse where they were holding her and jumped into the river to avoid being caught and arrested."

"Does the report say where she was last seen alive?"

"Downtown Los Angeles."

"Thanks, Hazel. You'll never know how much this means to me."

"You're quite welcome. You'll give my best to Darryl won't you?"

"I most certainly will."

I ran upstairs and relayed the entire conversation to Darryl. He sat up in the bed, turned toward me with love in his eyes.

"Wow. You dreamed all of it—the Mother, the daughter—you saw it before it went down didn't you?"

"And you know what else? She's not dead. Olokun didn't die when she hit that water. I have to find her, Darryl. She needs me."

"The men that killed that girl's mother are not to be played with. You gotta let the professionals handle this one. I'll do everything I can to help you but I'm not losing you over a stranger, even if you *are* related."

I climbed on top of his warm body and kissed him.

"Don't try to change the subject, Violet. I'm serious. Let the police handle this."

"Fine. I'm just gonna do a little research."

"I'm a lucky man." He said, sliding his warm tongue in my mouth.

"Why don't you show me instead of telling me how lucky I am?"

"You ain't gotta ask this brother to taste the caramel twice."

CHAPTER
Thirty-Four

The atmosphere in the warehouse was thick with anger. General Mubosa ordered soldiers around like they were servants on a plantation.

General Mubosa was built like a totem pole. His chin bled into his neck in layers of fat. His eyes protruded like bubbles giving him a perpertual look of surprise. When he was angry, he looked like a human toad.

"I am sick of your incompetence! You say the girl is dead? I want her body back at this warehouse by nightfall! Now go!"

The soldiers raced out of his office.

Fagunwa and Abayomi walked in. Both fell to their knees in the traditional Ziberian salute. General Mubosa didn't bother rewarding them with the gesture to rise, just started belting orders out.

"Sergeant Fagunwa, I want to know how a girl who was under your and six other soldier's supervision, was able to escape from this warehouse?"

"I wasn't there when the incident happened, Sir. If you just take a look at my report, it..."

"I don't give a damn about your report! Tell me what happened!"

Before Fagunwa could respond, the General turned his rage on Abayomi.

"Sergeant Abayomi, were you there when the girl escaped?"

"Yes, sir. I was...." The General didn't let him finish his rant.

"So I have two incompetent soldiers."

"Sir, let me explain." Abayomi began.

"I don't want an explanation. I want you to find and kill that girl! If she talks to the wrong people it could jeopardize everything we worked hard to build. And I will not have that. I won't go down alone! Do you hear me?"

The General stared down his nose over his glasses at the two soldiers, both of whom were still kneeling down on one knee.

"Stand up and answer me!"

The two men leapt up.

"Fagunwa, I want you to know that we're watching you. I understand you had a private conversation with the girl a few days before she disappeared. What did you find necessary to say to her without anyone around?"

"She was going for a walk by herself. I merely told her to get back to the compound—that the wives weren't allowed to go walking by themselves."

"I'm relieving you of your duties at the compound. You will work here in this office as my assistant. Sergeant Abayomi will clean out your desk. Is that understood?"

The General's henchmen unbuttoned their jackets and let Fagunwa see their guns.

"Yes, sir! I am honored to work at your side and I hope that I will...."

"Silence! I'm not finished. And I didn't tell you to speak."

The General was so angry the veins in his neck were popping out.

"I also had special software put on all the computers. I see you've been emailing someone here in America. Who is she?"

Mrs. Miller had prepped him on how to respond in the event that someone found out about their correspondence.

"My oldest daughter is applying for admission to a school here in the United States. They give scholarships to girls to do medical research."

The General looked at him like he wasn't sure if he believed him.

"Ha! Do you know that American women become whores by the time they're sixteen? Is that what you want for your daughter?"

Fagunwa was tempted to tell him that American girls were no more promiscuous than African girls. But seeing how angry the General was, he decided to keep his opinions to himself.

"No, sir!"

"Take these files and get them organized. When you're done with that, I need a fresh pot of coffee and something to eat. Abayomi, have one of my wives sent over."

"Yes, sir! Right away." Abayomi and Fagunwa said in unison.

Fagunwa knew he'd have to expedite his plan. The general was closing in on him. Fagunwa noticed a slight grin on Abayomi's face as he walked out of the office.

That's alright. He won't be smiling for long.

CHAPTER
Thirty-Five

With *The League of Women* pretty much on board, the vision for the peace event started to come together. After hours of brainstorming, Darryl and I came up with *World Peace and Unity March* as the theme for my inaugural event.

After I emailed Hazel the proposal, I turned my attention to finding Olokun. To find her I had to understand who she was. To understand who she was I had to understand where she'd been. I reached out to Hazel to learn more about Ziberia, the country where Olokun was born. Hazel had an encyclopedia of knowledge about that corner of the African continent.

"Ziberia is a beautiful country rich with African culture and history. Its tribal nations number in the hundreds. Among the most popular are the Zulani, Uligbo and the Fausa but the largest tribe is the Zoruba whose ancestors were among the largest population of Africans brought to the U.S. during the slave trade. Most

Americans have no idea that Ziberia is the tenth largest producer of oil in the world. It was there that the famous *Shell Corporation* discovered billions of dollars worth of crude oil bubbling under the soil."

"I don't understand—if there's oil in Ziberia why is there so much poverty? Why are the people there still struggling?"

"Because their forefathers sold the land for pennies to American and British owned oil companies. And the expansion of those companies had a devastating effect on the environment. Between 1976 and 1991 oil spills destroyed massive amounts of Ziberia's farmland and wildlife. One tribe in particular, the Ogoni, led peaceful protests against the oil giants. But the military leaders---who were banking on the millions they would make from the oil, responded by waging war on the Ogoni people. Thousands were killed and injured before the war ended. In the end the Ogoni relocated."

"That's horrible. What a sad story."

"No need to feel sorry for them. They're a resilient people. Despite their challenges they continue to achieve great things. Hold on, Violet. Call coming in."

When she came back I said, "Did you receive the email with my proposal?"

"Yes. And I'm delighted to confirm that we're going to greenlight your project. This march is going to be a huge success."

"That's...amazing news! Thanks, Hazel. Thanks for everything."

"Thank you for caring enough to do this work."

I went to the altar room and set everything up to do a reading on finding Olokun. Before I could cast the shells Mamiwata spoke. *Dr. Bones. Call Dr. Bones.*

I searched through the box with my stuff from the desk at my old apartment. In the bottom of the box, underneath my CD's and mp3 was the brochure and business card Dr. Bones had given me with the number to his clinic in New York. He answered on the first ring.

"Violet Brown. Knew you'd be calling. You've been on my mind all day. Saw your TV show. You've come a long way my sister."

"That was an experience." I said laughing.

"I bet it was. How've you been? Get initiated yet?" He chuckled a bit.

"In my dreams but not in the physical."

"The two are basically the same. The dream state is actually more powerful. That's another conversation. What can I do for you?"

"It's a big request. Not sure how to ask you."

"Just ask."

"Let me start from the beginning."

After an almost two-hour long conversation I caught him up on the particulars of my soap opera life. Told him about moving to Chicago, moving back to L.A., Darryl being robbed, Daddy having a stroke, organizing the march. I saved the part about my search for Olokun for last.

"That's what I need your help with. Olokun might just be the last living descendent of my clan. And Darryl won't let me do this alone."

"I don't blame him. You're about to play a dangerous game with some very high stakes. Your timing on calling me is pretty interesting. I'm preparing to leave New York and move back to Los Angeles. Moving in three days. Working on a few projects there and spending so much time in the city it makes more sense for me to move than spend a mint flying back and forth."

"You gotta be kidding."

"Hold on a minute, Violet."

I knew what he was doing. *Divining.* Asking his ancestors for guidance.

In what was actually a few minutes but seemed like hours, he came back to the phone.

"We're gonna find her. Your sister. But I'm not gonna kid you, it won't be easy. We'll need to do a few things beforehand to ensure our safety."

"Can you do them there in New York? I'll send you the money and..."

"We'll get it done when I get there. Right now I've gotta go. A client is coming in. I'll email you the particulars. Get some rest. You're gonna need it."

I called and updated Darryl on the progress, told him I contacted Dr. Bones.

"That the guy you met in the park when you were sixteen?"

"That's him."

"You barely know that man."

"I know his spirit. Who's more qualified than him to help me find Olokun?"

"Here we go with that *spirit* stuff again. Let's talk about it when I get home. I'm late for a meeting."

"There's nothing to talk....."

"I *said* we'll talk about it when I get home. You gotta let me be the man in this relationship, Violet. You know I respect your gift but asking me to sit back while you run around with some guy you barely know is ludicrous. Taking chances on your life to save some girl you never met--even more crazy. It's a lot to tolerate. Imah need you to work with me on this one."

"Fine. We'll talk later. You still love me?"

"What kind of question is that? Of course I love you."

I failed to tell Darryl that Dr. Bones was on his way to California or that he'd already agreed to help me find Olokun. My plan was to soften that blow by cooking him a six-course, vegetarian soul food dinner. I hooked it up like my life depended on it. Barbeque tempeh, ginger-garlic collard greens, baked yams, cornbread and brown rice seasoned with sweet corn and butter. He ate every single drop. I brought him his cherry pie dessert wearing a black lace thong, matching garter with thigh-high panty hose and a see-through, black chiffon robe.

I let him take me right there on the dining room table. He worked me like a night job, had me calling his name in three different languages.

When we finished, we curled up on the couch, stomachs full and bodies sweaty from our sensual meal. I chose that moment to drop the news about Dr. Bones being on his way to Cali.

"Woman, you've completely lost your mind. Call that man back and tell him you changed your mind. If you don't, I will."

"I've known him since I was sixteen. If he wanted to hurt me he had plenty opportunity."

"You've only been in his physical company a few times. Surely you aren't basing your trust on that?"

"The ancestors told me..."

"Don't start with that *ancestors* stuff."

It was our second real argument. I had no idea how stubborn my man could be but I was about to find out.

I tried wearing him down some more. When we got in bed I mounted him, teased him until his manhood gave me its full attention. I inched down on it, eased him inside of me and rode him like a wild stallion. I was sure he'd softened up but after he'd taken all I had to offer he let me know he hadn't budged an inch.

"That was good, baby. Real good. But don't think I've changed my mind about you and that Bones guy going to find your sister. I meant what I said. Leave it to the professionals."

"The police are understaffed and overwhelmed. I have to do this. Plus there's no time to find someone else. You gotta trust me, Darryl. How can you marry me if you don't trust me?"

"Maybe we need to rethink the whole marriage thing."

I chose not to dignify his vindictive statement with a response. I surrender to the hope that a good night's sleep will bring him to his senses.

"Good night, Darryl. I'll talk to you in the morning."

He was still sulking when we woke up. Barely talked to me all day. I let him be where he needed to be but inside I worried Darryl was getting tired.

Dr. Bones arrived in Los Angeles a few days later. I made up a story about meeting Diane for lunch so we could work on our plan to find and rescue Olokun.

Turned out Dr. Bones knew somebody who ran a security company that catered to the buildings in Downtown Los Angeles. He had his guy ask around to see if any of the guards had seen anything that looked out of place. If a group of girls was living in a warehouse in the heart of downtown somebody had to have seen something.

While Darryl was at work, I broke down and told Daddy a little about what was going on.

He slid his travel bible down in my purse. "Don't you worry 'bout nothing. I got you on the prayer list at church. Darryl's name right under yours. Only thing I got to say is this, I know you're a strong woman but in a marriage you gotta pick your battles. You gotta know when to let up. You get what I'm saying, Slim?"

"Yeah, you're telling me don't let this cause a problem in my marriage."

After dinner, Darryl and I sat down to talk. I gave him the details on the plan Dr. Bones and I had come up with. Asked him for his input. Kept my mouth closed and listened to what he had to say with an open heart.

"You went ahead with this without talking to me. That doesn't make me feel real good."

"I didn't know what else to do. His inside guy says he thinks Olokun and the other girls are in one of two warehouses. He's leaning toward the second one."

"These are cold-blooded killers you're talking about going up against."

"We're not taking any chances. We've consulted the oracle, given offerings to the deities for our protection and we have the inside track on what to expect when we get there."

"I'm getting a bad feeling about this. Only way for me to be okay is....I wanna go with you. Least I can protect you if I'm there."

"That's not gonna work. We want them to believe we're there to make a delivery. What shipping company sends three employees to drop off a few boxes? Maybe...maybe it would work if you waited in the van."

"Fine. I'll wait in the van. But tell your boyfriend your husband's tagging along."

"Boyfriend? Are you jealous? Is that what this is about?"

"When is this going down?" He ignored my last question.

"Forty-eight hours."

"Not a lot of time."

"We're gonna find her. I know we are."

Before we went to bed I sent Amy an email. Gave her the good news that I'd found a sponsoring organization. When I hit the send button it dawned on me how one thing had led to another, how each door had opened another.

Doing the J. B. Good Show led me to quit my job. Quitting my job led me to the job in Chicago. If there hadn't been the threat of war, Daddy wouldn't have had a stroke. If daddy hadn't had the stroke, I wouldn't be doing the march. If I hadn't done the march, I wouldn't have found out about Olokun.

In some ways life was like a tree with a million branches. Some of the branches have roots in places we can't see. If we water our roots, the trees produce the fruit that feeds our soul. When our souls are full, the world is a better place to live.

I prayed my roots would always be fed and that my family would be protected while I was out saving one of our fallen trees....

CHAPTER
Thirty-Six

"What are you doing behind the General's desk?" Abayomi snapped, sneaking up behind Fagunwa.

"Checking to see if his trash was full. There a law against that?"

"The General has cleaning women to do that but if you'd like to apply for the position, I'll see what I can do."

Fagunwa refused to let Abayomi get to him. Abayomi would pay for what he'd done just like General Mubosa would. For now, he had to stay calm and follow the plan.

General Mubosa walked in shortly after Abayomi. He was flanked by two armed soldiers. He glared at Fagunwa with a fiery rage in his eyes.

"Sergeant Fagunwa, join us in the conference room. We have some questions to ask you."

The group filed into the conference room. Fagunwa took a seat close to the door in case he had to make a run for it. General Mubosa tossed a folder across the conference table to Fagunwa. Inside the folder were pages of emails Fagunwa had over the last few days.

"We pulled those messages from your in-box. Why don't you tell us again about this Hazel Miller from the International League of Women?"

Fagunwa glanced at the e-mails. "I explained this already. It's nothing. They're supposed to announce the winners of the scholarship this week. My daughter is a competitor, may even be the winner of their contest."

General Mubosa gave Fagunwa a look that said he knew he was lying but he also knew they couldn't prove anything. Not yet.

"Speaking of your daughter and her mother, where have they disappeared to?"

They'd been to his home.

"My wife went home to visit her mother."

"We'll have to send one of our men to pay them a little visit."

Fagunwa fought to contain the fury bubbling in his soul. If they put one hand on his family...

"This is nonsense, General. Sergeant Abayomi is trying to frame me. Make it look like I'm doing something against our military to promote his own agenda. Why don't you admit it, Abayomi? You want to be the new Commander. That's what this is about."

Fagunwa's words did exactly what he hoped they would. Deflected the General's attention away from him onto Abayomi.

Abayomi jumped up, sent his chair flying backwards. It almost hit General Mubosa in the head.

"You're a liar, Fagunwa! You were seen talking to the girl. One of the soldiers saw you. Now she's missing." Abayomi shouted.

Fagunwa turned to the general. "What did that man see? Nothing! I was giving her an order. Did you forget that I was the one who helped capture her? Why would I want to free her after tracking her for months?"

The General smashed his fist on the table.

"Stop this madness! Both of you will control yourselves!"

General Mubosa stacked his papers neatly in front of him, took a few seconds to compose himself. He looked back and forth at Fagunwa and Abayomi.

"Sergeant Fagunwa, perhaps I put too much into these ungrounded reports. You have been a loyal follower of the Alliance. I am aware that some of my men are vying for the commander position. But it is my judgment and my judgment alone that will determine who'll be named the next commander."

Abayomi sucked his teeth and shook his head in disbelief.

"With all due respect, Sir, Fagunwa is lying to cover up his little plan. I know all about it!" Abayomi said, making one last failed attempt to convince the General of his colleague's guilt.

"Did I ask you to speak, Abayomi?"

"No sir."

"May I continue?"

Abayomi nodded without speaking.

"As I was saying, there is a way for you to prove your innocence Sergeant Fagunwa."

He slid the phone over to where Fagunwa was sitting. "You're going to call this...Mrs. Miller. You will say exactly what I tell you to say. If you don't, your head and my bullets will become great friends today."

Fagunwa swallowed hard.

"No problem, sir. What do you want me to say?"

Thankfully, when Fagunwa asked to speak with Mrs. Miller and told them who he was, they told him Mrs. Miller was out of town on business.

The General looked at him like he had dirt on his collar.

"When she returns, we'll get to the bottom of this. Everyone out! I need to think." The General said clearly enraged that his top man might've betrayed him.

"Yes, Sir." They said in unison.

General Mubosa's voice trembled with anger when he spoke. "Fagunwa, don't go too far my friend. I might need you to do some work for me."

"I'll stay close, Sir."

CHAPTER
Thirty-Seven

Alfred. After all these years I finally knew his real name. We were booking a hotel suite in downtown L.A. so we could set up shop near the warehouse.

"We're all set. I'm gonna head home and try to miss that five o'clock traffic. I'll be back in the morning." I handed him the room key.

He smiled like he knew something but couldn't say it. "I have something for you, Violet. Come up to the room for a minute so I can give it to you."

Upstairs in the room, I sat on a brown leather couch and waited for him to come out of the bathroom.

He came back with a small blue gift bag. He sat down on the couch next to me and handed it over. I slid the bag between my legs.

"Dr. Bones.....Alfred, can I ask you something? How do you deal with it? Knowing things before they happen. It's so hard for me sometimes."

"I don't mind you calling me Dr. Bones. I use tai-chi and herbs to keep my body temple strong and focused. I keep my shrine in order so my ancestors can protect me. I look to the Orisa to look after my house and my family."

It was the second time since we met that I noticed his eyes. They were beautiful—a light hazel color with thick lashes. They were so close to his skin color you had to be close to him to see them.

"So...are you married? Do you have children?"

"No children except for the spiritual ones. And I'm married to Ifa. Many beautiful sistahs have crossed the threshold of my heart but none of them made it their home. Ifa has said it is coming time for me to marry. So I'll be ready when she comes. I may have more than one wife—it depends."

"She or they will be very lucky to have you."

"Modupe. That's kind of you to say."

"What does Mo-du-pway mean?"

"Thank you—it means thank you." He looked at her with knowing eyes. "Violet, I don't want you to worry. We're gonna find your sister. It won't be easy. But don't give up when things get a little tough."

"I won't stop until I find her."

My body felt heavy. "I guess I better get home. It's getting late. I'm tired. Darryl will be worried. I'll be here first thing in the morning to rent the van."

"I have some herbs for that. I'll give them to you in the morning. Goodnight beloved. Ayanmo."

"Ayanmo. I've heard that word before."

He cupped my face with his warm strong hands. I felt a stirring in my loins.

"It's a saying in the Ifa tradition. It has to do with reaching one's destiny. When I say it to you, it means that I wish I was supposed to be more than your teacher."

He walked off toward the bedroom. "Did you open your gift?"

I pretended he didn't drop that bomb on me. "I'll open it when I get home."

"If you wouldn't mind, I like to be present when you open it."

I opened the bag and found a tiny, purple leather pouch inside. I emptied the pouch into my hand. A group of white glossy shells slid into my palm. I spread the shells out on the table. Counted sixteen shells all together.

Sixteen. The number given to priests and priestesses in the tradition.

"I have the four you gave me but what am I supposed to do with these?"

Dr. Bones didn't answer. He went into the bedroom and closed the door.

I headed for the parking lot. Drove home in complete silence. That night I didn't get a wink of sleep.

CHAPTER
Thirty-Eight

Hazel Miller pulled into the parking structure, parked in her reserved space and headed toward the elevators. When she pressed the up button, she noticed a man sitting behind the wheel of a long black limousine at the top of the lot. The driver seemed to be talking to somebody but she couldn't see anyone else in the car. Hazel thought he might be talking on one of those speakerphones. She brushed it off figuring he was probably a chauffeur for one of the executives in the building.

Hazel walked through the reception area, said her hellos, accepted a few welcome backs, collected her messages and headed to the massive space she claimed as her office. She was eager to get to her email. She knew it was full after that nasty virus had infected her computer.

She stopped in the kitchen to get a cup of tea. When she set her purse down, the messages she had collected on the way in went tumbling to the ground. As she bent down to pick them up, a name caught her attention. Sergeant Fagunwa, an ally from Ziberia who was working undercover on the kidnapping case involving Olokun, the daughter of a murdered activist, Ayoola Omikunle.

Hazel forgot about making her tea and hurried down the hall to her office to call Fagunwa. She froze in her tracks when she saw a strange man coming from behind her desk. He had a walkie talkie in one hand and some other electronic contraption in the other. When the man saw her expression he started explaining.

"We got it fixed." He pointed at her computer. "It's working just fine now. You have a wonderful day, Mrs. Miller." The man said before darting out of the door.

She wondered how he had known who she was?

"Um, excuse me. I didn't get your name or the company you work for."

"Arnold. I work for Tower Technology"

She took note of his piercings and tattoos. "Thank you, Arnold. You have a good day too."

Hazel was sure Arnold wasn't their regular computer guy. For a moment she thought she might be overreacting. Maybe the regular guy was out sick. She made a mental note to check Arnold out with the computer maintenance firm that took care of their office.

Hazel dialed the first few digits of Sergeant Fagunwa's phone number and hung up. She thought it might be wise to first check her email and see if he'd sent her a message. Sure enough, there was an email from him with a file attached to it.

To:Hazel Miller, Project Director
Hmiller@leagueofwomen.com
cc:HumanRightsWoman@aol.com
Sent: July 10, Time: 0800
From: Sergeant Fagunwa, NAA
Sfagunwa@naa.com
Re: Scholarship Information

Dear Mrs. Miller:
Attached please find my daughter's scholarship application.
I believe you will find everything in order. We look forward
to your response.

Sincerely,
Sergeant Fagunwa Adewale

The mention of the scholarship was a cue to let her know
that their operation was in danger of being exposed. It was also
a warning that he was in danger and that his family was being
moved to the safehouse they'd set up on the outskirts of town.

Fagunwa's email had a file attached to it. When she saw the
file's name her jaw dropped. *NAA Financial Reports.* If this was what
she thought it was...

When the file was done downloading she moved the arrow
over it and clicked the button to open it up. A few cyber seconds
passed before the document loaded onto the screen. Her hopes
were shattered when she scrolled down to read the data.

The data was completely scrambled. Nothing but letters and
numbers in random grids.

She tried reopening the email and downloading the document
again. Nothing. It just wouldn't work. She wondered if the virus
had infected her e-mail or if maybe the files were encrypted?

Her eyes pivoted to the to/from section of the message. She
noticed that Fagunwa had sent a copy to her personal email address

too. Holding her breath, she went to her AOL account and signed in. When the file was done downloading she clicked on the open button and crossed her fingers. The document popped up on her screen. As she scrolled down to where the first paragraph should be, a wide smile stretched across her face.

Fagunwa had sent her the financial records of the headman of the National African Alliance!

Downstairs in the lobby, the bald, pierced, tattooed computer guy from Hazel's office called his superiors with an update on her computer system.

"It's done. The file is dead. We uploaded a killer virus onto their server. I just confirmed that it wiped everything off her computer's hard drive and corrupted the messages in her e-mail box. We re-installed the server this morning and made sure all the incoming messages are routed through our network. Looks like the message the General was concerned about also went to her AOL account. I couldn't hack that one—a lot of firewalls to break through. But our virus should've corrupted the file. Situation is handled. Please advise on next steps."

His superior office was quiet for a few seconds. "Leave her alive for now."

"Ten-four. You want me to trash her office after closing time to send her a message?"

"No. We can't give them a clue that we're on to them. She might have to be our ransom if things don't go as planned.

"Ten-four. Take me off the clock. I'm going to lunch."

On the other side of town, Violet's Father, Mrs. Jasper, Darryl, Diane, Brandon and the children were having brunch at a local diner.

"Darryl, I admire you. Trusting my sister with a man she hardly knows. Letting her traipse all over town to find some girl she hasn't ever met. Damn—you're a saint." Diane quipped, chewing on a piece of bacon.

Darryl wasn't sure if what Diane just said was a compliment or an insult. Violet had warned him about how sarcastic her sister could be.

"Without trust, what kind of relationship do you really have? Violet's a grown woman and this is really important to her."

"My sister is as stubborn as a mule once she makes up her mind about something. You know anything about this Dr. Bones person?"

"Only that she met him in the park when she was sixteen and they've kept in touch ever since."

"I remember that story. Me and Daddy thought she was making the whole thing up. I hope he's not some nutcase."

"Diane, that's enough." Her father told her, giving her a look that said, STFU. "Go get me some more of those potatoes from the buffet."

"How's your golf game these days, man?" Brandon tried to distract Darryl.

Darryl ignored his question.

"Diane, are you trying to tell me something? Is Violet in danger? You know something about this man that I don't? Violet told me he was okay. Truth be told, I was never okay with this."

Darryl looked away, like he was reflecting on something that happened in the past.

"Maybe I should've gone with her. She said they were just picking up the van and renting a hotel room." Darryl said out loud but to himself.

"A hotel room? What do they need a hotel room for? I..."

Brandon shot Diane a look that made her close her mouth mid stream. He made another concerted effort to intervene on his woman's messiness.

Darryl slid his chair back, pulled out his wallet and put three twenty dollar bills on the table.

"Diane, can you drop your dad and Mrs. Jasper off? I gonna drive over to that hotel and make sure Violet's okay."

"Hold on a minute. They're making a broadcast about the war." Brandon yelled.

Everybody turned their attention to a TV that was mounted on the wall of the small café. At the bottom of the screen the words "breaking news" flashed.

Someone in the diner yelled for the waitress to turn up the volume. The newscaster's voice chimed in.

"If no treaty is established over the next few days, U.S. military forces will begin preliminary air raids in the Middle East. The threat of biological warfare looms over the country. Will the United States be able to establish a peaceful agreement with foreign ministers? Get the full story on tonight's eight o-clock news right here on Channel 6."

Darryl thought about Violet's dreams. She had seen a vision of America being victimized by foreign terrorists a second time. Bottom line, he had to help Violet find her sister before her dreams became a tragic reality....

CHAPTER
Thirty-Nine

After we picked up the van, Dr. Bones and I went back to the hotel room to review our plan. As we walked through the lobby to the elevators people nodded at us like we were a happy couple on vacation together. Nothing was farther from the truth.

I was dressed casually. Blue jeans, purple blouse and a matching camisole that highlighted the crown of my twin peaks. Dr. Bones looked majestic in all white—shirt, pants and shoes. I had to admit, we would've been a stunning couple.

We sat on the plush couch in our hotel suite's living room. As we talked, our knees brushed. And every time our flesh connected, my skin sizzled. As we went to pick up a document we needed to review, he took my hand, pressed it gently to his lips and kissed each of my fingers. When he was done, I let my arm drift down to my side.

Dr. Bones' power was pure, his strength enveloping. My heart pounded wildly as I leaned over and put my lips on top of his. I kissed him softly on and around his mouth. I was thinking about taking it further but he stopped me.

"No, Violet. It would be different if....your love is already with someone. This...what we feel is natural. You're scared and worried about your sister. I'm lonely for a woman like you in my life. We can't let things get out of hand. There's an African scripture, an Odu from the sacred Ifa oracle that reads: *bit by bit is how we eat the head of a rat.* Do you know what that means, Violet?"

"No. But I'm sure you're gonna tell me."

"It means that little by little, we can accomplish the things in life that are most difficult. Bit by bit, we can heal our people and make this world we live in a better place. Bit by bit, we can all become better people."

I started crying. I thought about all I had faced to get to this point. Remembered all of the lonely days and nights before I met Darryl. The agony of losing my mother when I was so young. Daddy's heart attack. The weight of the gift the ancestors had given me in being able to see the future.

"I love Darryl. But it's so hard sometimes. Making him understand who I am, what I deal with everyday of my life. Some days I wanna go somewhere and live on an island. I wish....I wish he understood what it's like to be me."

"That's the burden of those God chose for this path. We must tell the truth even when it is unpopular. Even when it alienates us. But in the end, like the wisdom Otura Meji, which says, "The truth will rise, pressed up to the earth.""

I looked away from him and confessed. "I've always been attracted to you. Even though what we have seems to be no more than a spiritual connection I always wondered if...I thought maybe we were meant to be more."

"The feeling is mutual. Ever since the day I met you in the park I felt the connection. But I knew we weren't meant to be together in that way this time. I had to honor that."

I melted into his arms. Felt the magnitude of our spiritual kindred.

"When you say you knew we had a connection—what do you mean? And how do you know we weren't meant to explore this.... us?" I asked him seriously.

"The man you love—the man you and the Orisa have chosen for you—that man is waiting at home. I'm here as your teacher this lifetime."

"How can you be sure? You said you might have more than one wife. Maybe I'm meant to have more than one husband."

"There will be times when you feel Darryl is not giving you enough but remember, you are seeing his sacrifice through your eyes. Often we're blind to all our mates endure on our behalf. He has what your soul needs. You need each other to fulfill your mutual destiny."

"Darryl's a good man. One of the best I've ever known. I love him with all my heart. I wanna be his wife, spend every night in his arms. But there's something I feel for you too. Not sure what it is."

"Lust. Curiosity. The mystique of me being your teacher. But you don't know me as a man. I'm human. I have faults just like the man you're with. One of us has to be strong enough to keep this right where it is."

"Thank you for—for coming through the park that day. You helped me make sense of this life. For that I'll always be grateful."

"Our journey is not over, Violet. Actually, it's just beginning. Do you have the shells I gave you?"

"I haven't taken the pouch from around my neck since you gave it to me."

"It's time."

"Time for what?"

"You're going on a ride with me. It's time for you to initiate yourself."

CHAPTER
Forty

Fagunwa saw a tall, neatly shaved man wearing an NAA uniform standing guard outside of the office. On his lapel was some kind of executive badge of honor.

He went to the window and spoke to him. "What's going on? I thought the General called off the supervision."

"Sergeant Fagunwa, I need to talk to you. I'm not here on behalf of the General."

"There's nothing to talk about."

"She wrote you back."

"Who wrote me back? Who are you?"

"Mrs. Miller. She got the file."

Fagunwa wasn't taking any chances.

He knew there was another soldier that was a plant but he had no way of knowing if this was him.

Fagunwa stepped out into the reception area.

"I don't have any idea what you are talking about."

"We don't have much time. You have to leave here right away."

Fagunwa stood watching him for a sign he was lying.

"They have her. Olokun. They're saying she's dead but she isn't. They're holding her captive in the back of the warehouse.

"You are mistaken. Olokun ran away."

"The girl's mother is still alive too."

It was clear that someone had been talking to the man from inside of the Resistance movement but Fagunwa still couldn't reveal his position. It was way too dangerous to chance.

"Are you saying Iya Ayoola Omikunle is alive?" Fagunwa asked, trying to see how much the soldier really knew.

"There are two Americans, a woman and a man. They are planning to make a fake delivery to the warehouse tomorrow. The woman is coming to rescue Olokun."

To have this kind of information, the soldier had to have contacts that ran wide and deep.

"What is your name, soldier?"

"I am Ade Olatunji Mubosa. I knew Iya Ayoola. We....we were going to be married after her husband was killed." Olatunji said, choking up.

"Iya Ayoola would never marry a man who worked for the General. Wait. Mubosa? Are you related to the General?"

"I'm his son."

"You're his son?"

"Let me help you understand, Sergeant. My father is the leader of the NAA. He had my mother killed because she objected to what he was doing with the Mefa-Eru. After she died, he gave me a choice. I could join his military or join my mother. I chose to work for his army. That way I would have a better chance of taking him down. I met Iya Ayoola right after her husband died. I was going to marry her. Then my father....he had her killed. He thought he did anyway. He knew I loved her. That was the day I vowed to destroy him."

"I'd heard that you were estranged from your father."

"I rarely come into the compounds unless...."

Fagunwa watched him closely for any sign that he was lying. "Unless what?"

"Unless they're going to kill one of the girls. I am the executioner. That is my job in my father's military. What my father doesn't know is that I've been letting them go. I take them far away from here under the guise of executing them and put them in the hands of someone who will protect them. Listen, we have no more time for small talk. We must get you out of here. They're coming to kill you."

No one except the most trusted supporters of the movement was privy to the information Olatunji had. Fagunwa had no choice but to trust the man.

"Why should I trust you?" Fagunwa asked him.

"Because I want what you want. To return our country to its greatness. Ziberia was the most beautiful land in the world before the military took over."

"What you said about Ayoola still being alive. Is that true?"

"I've told you enough to make you trust me. Now let's go before it is too late."

Fagunwa grabbed his backpack from the warehouse, strapped it on his back and stuck his gun in the small of his back.

"Sergeant Abayomi moves the checkpoints every night at ten. There's nobody on the roof for about fifteen minutes. That's when we can get them out of there." Fagunwa told him.

Fagunwa took out the map of the warehouses. "I also have this—it's a map of the warehouses where they are keeping the girls."

Both of them understood the odds against him. If the General's men found out that there was a plot to free the Mefa-Eru, the girls would be killed to prevent them from talking.

If Fagunwa was to survive, it meant leaving his wife and children behind. He wasn't sure he could do that.

There was one thing he was sure of—he had to stay alive tonight.

CHAPTER
Forty-One

Tammy, a rail thin Asian woman with bleached blonde hair sauntered into Hazel's office.

"Yes, Mrs. Miller."

"Did you find out about the computer repair guy?"

"I talked to the repair service this morning. Tower Technology isn't scheduled to come out until tomorrow. They don't know who the man was that came to our office the other day."

"I had a feeling he was phony. Until further notice, I want you to check all repair and maintenance personnel out with their superiors unless they're our regular guys."

"No problem, Mrs. Miller."

Hazel knew too that the man who'd been in her office was the one who sabotaged their computer servers. The authorities were getting close to toppling the General's regime. He and his henchmen were trying to cover their tracks. They'd go to any length to protect their operation.

Hazel remembered that the hallways and elevators at the League headquarters had hidden cameras in them. That meant the building's security might have gotten a picture of the man. She called Tammy into her office again.

"Tammy, when the Tower's guy comes tomorrow, have him reevaluate our computer system and give me a report on this supposed virus that took us down. I also want a full work up on any spyware installed on my computer and my laptop. I want to know the times and dates when my email was accessed between the dates I was in New York. And call the building security and have them give us a copy of the tapes from this floor and from the parking lot for the last week."

"Mrs. Miller, are you thinking that the virus that took out our system was done intentionally?"

"It's a possibility. There's more but I'm not at liberty to discuss the details just yet."

"It's strange you would say that. Just this morning, as I walked from the parking lot into the office I saw a man standing near your parking space."

"What was he doing?"

"He was talking on a cell phone. I heard him say something about a team in Africa. I didn't think much of it at the time since we're not the only international agency in this building. But there was something weird about him. He was wearing a business suit but his vibe just didn't fit with his look."

"Thanks for the information, Tammy. After hearing what you've just said, I think we need a little more security. Call *Anderson Armed Guard Services*—you know, the ones we used when Desmond Tutu came to visit—and arrange for two officers to man our entrance and the parking lot. I think I should inform my husband's law firm of this matter as well. And call Mike Peterson at the

United Nations and tell him I need a meeting with one of his people. Don't talk to anyone but Mike."

"Got it. I'll get on this right away. When do you want the meeting scheduled?"

"His first available time, even if it's midnight tonight. Tell him this is code red. He'll know what I'm talking about."

Hazel wanted to send Mike Peterson an email but she didn't trust the privacy of her internet transmissions from work. She decided to work from home for the rest of the day where the computers hadn't been tampered with. Plus, the security system at home was connected to the police department.

She called her husband's office from her cell. She knew he wouldn't be too happy that she was just telling him about the ordeal. She got his receptionist.

"Harriet, let me speak to Robert. It's urgent. Pull him out of a meeting if you have to."

She was right. Robert was pissed he was just finding out.

"I can't believe you're just telling me about this. I want you to promise me that you'll let the authorities handle things from here on out. These guys are bad news and their connections are global. They'll squash you like an ant and think nothing of it. I'm calling Ron Dantz over at the CIA. You remember Ron? I went to school with him."

He opened up his contact list on the computer.

"Of course, I remember Ron. But I have a feather in my cap that the CIA doesn't. Darryl's fiancé thinks she might be related to Ayoola's daughter. She's also a big-time psychic. They featured her on the J.B. Good Show."

"Hazel, I want you to listen like your life depends on hearing what I have to say. If this organization is what I think it is, it's worth millions.'

"Some very important and powerful people are going to go down if this operation is exposed. Darryl's wife-to-be is bonkers if she thinks she can tiptoe in there and walk out with their property. Psychic or not, unless she has a learjet or one of those bewitched noses, they'll take her out. I'm calling Ron when we hang up. Did you call Mike Peterson?"

"We're trying to set up a meeting with him and his people asap."

The phone buzzed letting Hazel know another caller was on hold.

"I gotta run hun, another call is coming in. By the way, I'm gonna work from home for the rest of the day and tomorrow."

"I want you to be careful. You hear me, Hazel? Don't take any chances. I'll be in Hawaii overnight on business. I'll call you as soon as my plane touches down."

She pressed down the buzzer to the reception area.

"Yes, Tammy. Who is it?"

"Mike Peterson is on line two."

"Have him call me on my cell." Hazel said heading to the balcony to talk in case her office had been bugged.

After she told him the entire story, Mike put her on hold.

"Hold on a minute, I have a report from the Ziberian embassy. It came in yesterday. There's something familiar about this story."

After he glazed over the story he told her, "Our intel thinks the United Nations in Africa might have some corrupt agents working for them. Your best bet is to rely on the feds. The good news is this, since this Violet woman is American, I might be able to get some agents in there to intervene if things get crazy. But she's gonna have to get out of there fast. All hell is going to break out when they find out we're on to them. Let's hope no one tips them off that somebody's on their trail. Where's your plant now?"

"She's not our plant. Our guy is a Ziberian soldier who worked his way up to be the head guy's right hand man. I don't know, Mike. I..." Hazel's intercom buzzed again with an incoming call.

"Tammy, I'll call whoever it is back later. I'm on a very important call."

254

"Mrs. Miller, I'm sorry to bother you, but the man on the phone said he's the son of the General of the New African Alliance in Zibokute, Ziberia."

"What? Keep him on hold for a second. Let me get my tape recorder. Put him through when I tell you I'm ready."

She clicked back over to Mike Peterson.

"You'll never believe who is on the other line."

"Who?"

She started to tell him then decided against it.

"Some guy who works for the New African Alliance."

"Be careful, Hazel. It might be a set up. Call me back when you get done and be sure to tape the conversation. I'll get on the horn and see what resources I can drum up for you."

"I will. And thanks so much Mike. We'll talk later."

She clicked the tape recorder and called Tammy on the intercom.

"Tammy, go ahead and put him through."

"Is this Mrs. Hazel Miller?"

"Yes, it is."

"I have some information for you. I hear you are working on the kidnapping case of Ayoola Omikunle's daughter?"

"Yes, the case information is on our web site. What can I do for you?"

"This is Ade Olatunji Obakoso the son of General Obakoso. I have spoken with Fagunwa. We are working together to bring my father's military down."

The mention of Fagunwa made Hazel's palms start sweating.

"Is this a secure line you're calling me from?"

"Yes. I have it checked for bugs everyday. I know that you have the reports. But I have something else that might interest you."

"Reports—what reports? What might interest me?"

"I believe I have the location where the girls are being kept."

"And why would you give me this information?"

"I have my reasons and I don't have time to explain them right now. But I will tell you this. There is an American woman. She is looking for Ayoola's daughter. She could be placing herself in great danger."

"I don't know her but if I did, why would she listen to me?" Hazel was purposely vague.

"You're right about that."

"What exactly do you want from me?"

"Do everything you can to get those girls out of there by tomorrow morning or you'll find nothing but dead bodies in that warehouse. My father and his men rely on my radio station for their internal transmissions. I will tell them that the network has gone down. They'll get on a remote network which only works for an hour. One hour. That's all you have. I take the network down when your people are in place. You get those girls and your team out of there."

"I don't even know if you are who you say you are."

He ignored her and kept talking.

"We don't have much time."

Hazel thought about the situation in its entirety. If Olatunji were a fake, he wouldn't have known about Fagunwa or about Violet. Fagunwa would die before he exposed their plans. She didn't have a choice. She had to trust him.

"Here's what we'll do...."

Darryl called the hotel where Violet had told him she and Dr. Bones were meeting. The operator connected him to the room but no one answered the phone.

When he was about ten minutes away from the hotel, he tried to reach Violet on her cell.

No answer.

Darryl's mind was spinning with scenarios and none of them were good. He spun the wheel again. It landed on Mrs. Miller.

Hazel's assistant picked up. "This is Darryl Rollins, one of the attorneys from Hazel's husband's law firm. Is she available?"

Tammy was being extra cautious after the computer guy incident. When Hazel left the office she'd instructed her not to give out any information to anyone unless she personally authorized it.

"She's gone for the day."

"Is she at home? It's urgent."

Tammy didn't want to be rude but she couldn't take any chances.

"I'm sorry Mr. Rollins but I can't give out any information."

"Can you just tell her that I called and to call me as soon as she can. It's really important. She has the number."

"I'll give her the message."

He tried his bosses' home number but nobody answered. He thought about calling Bob at the office but remembered he'd gone to Hawaii on business. Darryl turned off the freeway and jumped back on the 405 heading north. It was time to pay a visit to the Miller estates.

CHAPTER
Forty-Two

"**S**ergeant Fagunwa's gone, sir. I checked the entire warehouse." The officer told Abayomi.

"I knew we should've kept him under surveillance. I'll put an order out to my men to be on the lookout for him at local bars and nightclubs. Call into the base and see if anyone has seen him. While you're at it, issue a bulletin for his immediate capture and detainment." Abayomi commanded.

"Yes, sir! And what if he resists?"

"We need to bring him in alive."

"Understood, sir!"

Ten miles away, Sergeant Fagunwa sat quietly in a booth in the back of a seedy bar in the run-down part of Chinatown. A couple of hours had gone by since he fled the warehouse. Hidden by a small crowd on a tiny dance floor, he watched as three of the General's men entered the bar. Two soldiers stood guard at the front door while the other one went to the bar and asked the bartender a question. The bartender shook his head no. Frustrated, the third man scanned the patrons for his target.

It didn't take Fagunwa long to figure out that they were looking for him. Fortunately, the club was busy and a group of gyrating bodies blocked the guard's view of him. He had only one chance to get out of there.

He stood slowly, shielding himself with a Eurasian girl with big hair and eased out of the back door. He made a break for the trees, then, when he was sure the coast was clear, he traveled along a stretch of dry terrain where the river once flowed. He trotted through that eery darkness for a good two miles. Worried he might be lost, he powered up his phone and downloaded a map to the safehouse. As soon as he copied down the route, he disabled his GPS and turned off the phone so the soldiers couldn't zero in on his location.

He sat down on a pile of bricks and tried to catch his breath while he reviewed the map. The plan was that he would meet his wife there in twenty-four hours. The League would pick them up and take them to another safehouse that was three miles from his current position.

He'd have to travel through the night to get to the safehouse before sunrise. He would've tried to drive it but too many people in the NAA knew his face. Plus, Abayomi had men posted at every point of entry.

He saw a car coming down the road. The car's lights flashed in his direction.

Fagunwa dove into a ditch and prayed he hadn't been spotted. He heard the car pull over and a car door open and shut. Footsteps moved across the earth toward where he was hiding.

He heard a voice whispering in the night.

"Fagunwa. Fagunwa, are you there? It's Olatunji. Come. We must get you out of here."

He lifted his head, dusted the dirt from his face and shirt, and stood up.

"I couldn't wait for you at the bar. The General sent his men and I had to make a run for it." Fagunwa told him.

"I know. I heard them talking on the radio. We have to get you out of here fast. My father's men are stopping at nothing to find you."

Fagunwa climbed up the hill and got in his car.

"You have to get into the trunk. There's a blockade just up the road. They might check my car. Hurry."

"They'd check the vehicle of the General's son?"

"My father cares about one thing—keeping the money flowing and the girl's held hostage. He has enough money and resources to buy almost anyone. We can't risk them finding you or finding out I helped you. Once we get out of downtown, I'll let you out. Now get in before it's too late."

Fagunwa got out of the car and curled up in the trunk. Before Olatunji laid the drop cloth over him he asked, "Where we headed?"

"We're going to the radio station. We'll be safe there. From there I'll put my plan into motion."

When the trunk closed and the darkness enveloped him, Fagunwa realized for the first time in his life he was scared. Not only was he scared of what they'd do if they found him. He was afraid of what would happen to his wife and child if he and Olatunji's plan to take down the General didn't work.

He knew what would happen. Three funerals. Him, his wife and his daughter. No mourners. Like thousands of other soldiers who tried to fight the regime, the military would blame their deaths on some unfortunate accident.

He promised himself he wouldn't let that horror happen to them. Not now. Not ever.

CHAPTER
Forty-Three

D r. Bones and Violet were on the elevator having a heated discussion.

"If you wanna survive this, this is what you have to do. You need all the power and magic of your ancestors to overcome the evil that is following you."

"Are you talking about me getting initiated?" Violet asked him in a huff.

"That's exactly what I'm talking about. I've already set everything up. All you have to do is say yes."

"I-I…need to talk to Darryl. This is a big step. I don't know if I'm ready."

"You can call him from the car. I had to keep your initiation secret because of what's going on. Your sister's life depends on us getting through tomorrow."

They drove the Harbor freeway, switched to the 91 and headed toward San Fernando Valley. The mountains grew bigger and the distance between houses increased.

"So you've been planning this all along but didn't tell me?"

"Like I said, I had to keep it a secret because if anyone knew, they might try to sabotage us."

"I keep trying to call Darryl but the signal won't hold. Are we almost there? Seems like we've been driving for hours."

"We're minutes away. Just relax and surrender."

As we exited the freeway, I saw a woman standing near a huge tree. The woman raised her hand and gave them a short wave. I snapped back around and tried to point the woman out to Dr. Bones. But when I turned around the woman was gone.

"Did you see her? That woman? She was standing there by the tree."

"I didn't see anyone, Violet." Dr. Bones said, smiling knowingly. "But sometimes the spirits show themselves to let us know we're on the right path. Did you know her?"

"I don't know. She looked like….she reminded me of the spirit woman in my dreams. Mamiwata. But it couldn't be her could it?"

"Of course it could."

We pulled into the driveway of a large complex. There was a large house with several small cottages behind it. A rod iron gate swung open as we entered the premises. As we drove toward the main entrance I saw tall, looming statues of African figurines lining the driveway. It felt like we'd entered a palace.

"What is this place? What or who are those statues?"

Dr. Bones pointed to a statue to my right. "That one there is Shango, the God of justice. Remember I told you about Shango?"

"Whose place is this?"

"My teacher. He will supervise your initiation."

A bark-colored woman wearing a colorful scarf and matching dress opened a second gate. When she saw who was in the car, she dropped down on one knee, bowed her head and said some kind of greeting to Dr. Bones.

"Aboru, Aboye, Abosise Awo. We are honored to receive you and your guest. Your rooms are prepared and we are ready to begin the ceremonies."

He tapped her on the shoulders and said some kind of blessing over her. "Ogbo Oto. Please rise, Iya." Dr. Bones said, heading down the hall.

"What does that mean? Aboru, aboye…."

"It roughly translates to, "May a calm messenger receive my prayers.""

"And your answer?"

"The jest of it is, "May you live long and well.""

More statues lined both sides of the hall in the foyer of the building. Dozens of small wooden sculptures with protruding features. Bowls of fruit, candles and water were strategically placed on a large altar.

I hooked my arm around Dr. Bone's arm. "Who is that?" I pointed to one of the statues on the altar beside us on the floor.

"He represents the deity Eshu. Eshu protects the house and the people who live here. There are twenty-one of them because it is said Eshu has twenty-one roads."

The woman who had let us in returned with two other women. One of them looked fairly young. All three of them had a regal beauty and an unmeasured grace about them.

What looked like the eldest among them spoke, "I am Apetabi. We will show you to your sleeping quarters. If you are hungry, we have food cooked and waiting for you down the hall. The Araba says to get some rest. He will see you shortly. It will be a very busy evening."

Dr. Bones nodded his head and followed the women to a room down the hall. I stayed close behind him but the women stopped me at the door.

"Your room is down here. The women's quarters."

I looked at Dr. Bones. "I need to call, Darryl. He's probably worried sick."

"Give me his number and I'll call. You'll be fine. I'm right down the hall."

After I wrote down Darryl's number, I followed the women to a modest sleeping area. My bed had been sectioned off.

"Are you in need of food at this time?" The Apetabi asked me.

I shook my head no, then remembered what Dr. Bones had told me about turning down food in African culture.

"I'm famished." I told her.

"After you wash up, come to the kitchen."

"Where is the bathroom?"

"Follow me, Iya." She said, handing me a towel and some black soap.

"I'm not an Iya. I mean, I haven't been initiated."

"You will be soon. Make sure you wash with the soap."

I always knew it would happen—my initiation. I'd dreamed about it many times. Still I was frightened. Didn't know what to expect. Didn't know the people here. I wished Darryl was by my side.

I used the potty then refreshed my body a bit. The soap smelled nice, a mixture of amber and musk. I washed my face, brushed my teeth, tied my locks up in the large purple scarf I had around my neck. When I exited the bathroom, one of the Awo's wives was waiting for me in the hall. I was instantly sorry for taking so long.

"I'm so sorry. I didn't know you were waiting."

"Follow me please." The woman answered dutifully.

She led me to a humongous kitchen and handed me a piping hot cup of tea, a bowl of rice and beans and a warm buttery roll.

"You must keep up your energy sister. The night will be long and you must remain alert for all of it."

I started to ask her what they had planned but decided against it. Sometimes it was better not to know. After my meal, I followed Oshara--who I found out was the Awo's fourth wife--down the hall back to the sleeping quarters.

"Do you require anything else?"

They were so disciplined. I felt guilty for accepting their hospitality.

"No, please, get some rest."

I stretched out in the bed listening to the night sounds, thinking about the journey ahead. All of a sudden the reality hit me hard. I thought about Daddy, Darryl and Diane and was filled with worry for a minute.

I closed my eyes and remembered Darryl's gentle touch and the wonderful smell of his body. What the hell was I doing out here in the middle of nowhere, searching for some strange girl I never even met? I should be home with my man in our big, beautiful home snuggled up watching a good movie.

I sat up in bed, slipped on my house shoes and tiptoed down the hall to Dr. Bone's room. I'd had enough of this. I wanted him to take me home. I tapped lightly on the door and whispered his name.

"Baba Alfred, are you asleep?"

He spoke to me through the door.

"Not anymore. What can I do for you, Violet? Are you still hungry?"

"No. Can I talk to you for a minute?"

There was a pause before he answered. "Yes, Violet. Come in."

I sat down on the edge of the bed. He turned over on his shirtless back, folded his hands behind his head. Moonlight shined through the golden corneas of his eyes. His energy was gentle and comforting. It calmed me immediately.

"Did you get in touch with Darryl? I know he's worried crazy. Cell phone died so I can't call."

"It is part of the purification process to feel lonely. You're being prepared for what is to come. The ancestors. They're working with you."

He handed me his cell phone, turned over on his side, pulled the cover up and across his muscular chest.

"I called your husband but there was no answer. Try him again if you like."

As I dialed Darryl's cell number I noticed that his phone was about to die too. Darryl's phone rang once, twice and went straight to voicemail.

I tried to sound calm when I left him a message. "Darryl, this is Violet. I'm at Dr. Bones' teacher's....Shit!" I handed the phone to Dr. Bones.

"Your phone just died."

"If he's the man you say he is, he'll understand. Eventually."

"If it was me, I'd cut my losses and kick him to the curb."

"Thank God you're not him."

"I feel like I'm in a crazy dream. One of those dreams where the same scene keeps playing over again and again."

"That's because you're living your dreams. This is where the dreams were leading you. Remember when your Spirit Guide showed herself to you on the road? She wanted to let you know you're exactly where you're supposed to be, that there are no mistakes on the road of destiny."

I lifted his blanket. Slid into the bed beside him. I turned over on my right side facing away from him. He draped his left arm around me, pulled me close.

"I'm scared, Alfred. On the other hand, I feel protected. Like nothing can touch me. It seems like my other life is so far away. I get the feeling that the old me is dying and another me is being reborn. I don't understand it."

After a few minutes, Dr. Bones turned me around to face him. He put his finger to my lips.

"Violet. Sweet Violet. Yes, you *are* being reborn. This is your Sankofa. You're returning to the greatness you once were in another life."

He kissed my neck until I was moaning. I slid my hand down to his manhood. My fingers touched the tip of it. He throbbed in my hand. Once again he stopped me.

"No….this is…wrong. Acting on lust won't take away the fear."

"You're right. I'm so confused….I shouldn't've….I shouldn't have done that. What's right never comes from doing wrong."

"I shouldn't have put my lips to your flesh. We're lonely. Craving things that gives the human soul comfort. As priests, we must learn to overcome our base emotions. It's just as difficult for me. I'll always care for you, Violet. But we're not meant to be together in this life. Trust me, I checked."

"What if the oracle is wrong?"

"Your path has already been decided. Tell me you don't love that man and I'll marry you today. In fact, I'll have my teacher marry us tomorrow if you can honestly tell me you can live without him."

"Darryl is everything I want, everything I prayed for. Took me forty years to find him. I want to spend the rest of my life with him, whatever life I have left, if I make it out of there tomorrow."

Alfred looked out at some invisible entity, "We knew each other long ago. In another life. People often confuse the feeling of remembrance for love. We remember what we had in that life but it doesn't mean we're supposed to have it in this life. As much as I wish things were different, you belong to him."

He turned his face from me. There were tears in his eyes. "I'm not so manly I don't feel."

"Thank you, Alfred. Thank you for having the strength not to ruin the sacredness of our kinship. I'm going to bed now."

There was a fire raging between my legs.

"Violet, in a few hours, after we've rested our bodies, I must prepare you for what the oracle has shown us is coming. Great turmoil lies ahead. Together we will help bring down some very powerful people. Understand this: they will kill us before they allow us to destroy their operation. This is why you must be initiated. You're going to join the spiritual lineage of some of the most powerful Ifa priests in the world."

I remembered the priestess at the Botanica told me I would be initiated in Africa. Was this what she was seeing?

The moment felt right but I still didn't feel ready. I didn't really understand what the Ifa religion was all about. What did being *initiated* mean? Were they going to cut me? Make me drink blood? I needed to know more.

"I need to study. How can I move forward when I don't know what this is all about?"

"What you need to learn will come a little at a time."

"What about my father—you know he's had to bend a lot to accept what I do with the ancestors. And what about Darryl? I think the man I'm going to marry should be here with..."

Dr. Bones sat up in the bed and looked me directly in the eyes.

"We don't choose when we come into the priesthood. The divine time chooses us. Not because we're special or wonderful but because we need it. But nobody's going to force you to do anything. It has to be your choice."

"This….this is a lot."

"You've known me long enough to know that I would never let anything happen to you. You trust me don't you?"

I shifted my weight to the other foot. "Of course I do but this is….this is a big step."

"Your Ori has to be in alignment with this."

"I have one last question. What am I gonna wear?"

He laughed a bit and told me, "The wives will give you something appropriate to wear."

I stood over his bed. "You know, ever since the day I met you it seems like we can't talk without you telling me some life-shattering news."

He glanced at his watch. "You have about two hours before we have to be up. If you can't sleep, I suggest you at least lay down and rest your body. Tomorrow is the day of reckoning. Tonight is the night you will be reborn."

"There you go again."

"Good night, sweet Violet."

CHAPTER
Forty-Four

Darryl drove up to the gate at the Miller's estate and pressed the call button to notify the security office of his arrival.

"Darryl Rollins. I'm one of the attorneys at Mr. Miller's law firm. I need to speak with Mrs. Miller. It…it's an emergency." He told the guard on duty.

"I'm sorry that won't be possible. Mrs. Miller doesn't have any appointments booked today."

"Like I said, this is an emergency. My wife's in danger. Mrs. Miller may have information that could save her."

"Hold on a minute."

The intercom buzzed a minute later.

The security officer told him, "Please proceed to the second Security gate."

Darryl drove a few feet to another gate where a second security guard stood waiting.

"We need to see your identification."

Darryl took out his driver's license and gave it to the man. The guard checked to make sure the picture matched the person, wrote down the pertinent information and handed Darryl's license back to him.

"You can go on up."

Darryl sped up the hill and parked behind one of the three Rolls Royces in the circular driveway. A liveried butler let him in and led him to the sitting area.

"Stanley Ruthers at your service, sir. May I bring you something to drink?"

"I'm kind of in a hurry."

The butler gave him a look that said his impatience wouldn't be tolerated.

"Some water would be fantastic."

"Sparkling or still."

"Sparkling would be awesome."

"With lemon or plain?"

Darryl felt like yelling, *just bring me a damn glass of water!*

"Lemon is great. Fine."

As Stanley the Butler left to fetch the water, Hazel Miller walked in. Darryl stood to receive her. She wore a floor length, white silk caftan and had a lovely gold scarf wrapped elegantly around her neck. Gold earrings that looked like they cost a mint framed her pleasant but troubled face. The youthful glow in her facial features said she'd had a few Botox treatments here and there but not to the point of looking unnatural.

Hazel extended a manicured hand for him to shake, "Darryl Miller. It's good to see you. I never had a chance to thank you for all the work you and your team at the firm did for the League. Sorry about the security but we've had a few incidents at work and had to step up our system. Please, sit down."

"I hope you'll accept my apology for coming by unannounced. Your office told me you were out for the day. Figured you were working from home. Tried your cell but the call rolled straight to voicemail. I'll get right to the point. I'm here to see if you have any information about my wife. She's gotten herself in the middle of something....something that might be dangerous."

"Darryl, being that you work for my husband's law firm I know you understand my having to say that what I'm about to tell you is classified information."

"I understand completely. Do continue."

"I don't want to alarm you but you have good reason to be concerned. It seems as if your wife may've walked into the middle of a sting operation involving a crime unit from Africa. They're being funded by corporations and government agencies right here in the United States. We don't know how wide and deep this goes. One of Ziberia's top ranking military officials has been implicated."

Darryl was speechless. He sat back in a fluffy, white linen armchair grazing his beard. Stanley the butler walked in with his sparkling water and sat it on a tray with a frosty glass of ice and lemon wedges with a cocktail napkin on the side.

"Uh, Stanley, I think I'm going to need something a little stronger."

"I'm at your service, sir."

Hazel told him, "Stanley, bring out the mobile bar and all the mixes. Bring some snacks too. I've suddenly got a little appetite."

"Right away, Madam."

Darryl, would you like to join me for lunch? Stanley makes one of the best Ruebens this side of the West Coast. He has the mustard flown in from Germany."

Darryl's stomach growled at the thought of food. He hadn't eaten all day.

"I'd love to. I better call home and let Violet's father know I'll be a little late coming in."

"I agree. We've got to come up with a plan before you leave here and that might take some time."

While they ate, Hazel filled Darryl in on everything. The computer virus. The plant the League had working for the General. A woman named Ayoola whose daughter had been kidnapped by the General's men. She also told him Violet's last known whereabouts.

"How do you know where she is when I don't?" Darryl asked Hazel, worried as hell and getting more worried by the second.

"Well, because of the possible UN involvement in the scandal, the government has gotten involved. A group called the GSF-- *Government Special Forces*—has been tracking Violet and her friend. *The League* works closely with the GSF. Anyway, they've followed Violet to the compound of a highly respected African leader."

"Guess I should thank technology. Nothing we can't do without being seen anymore. Where are they going next?"

"Rumor has it that Violet and her friend from New York, are going to try to rescue the daughter of Ayoola Omikunle. GSF intelligence officers have been trying to locate a group of kidnapped girls who were brought to America by traffickers. Yesterday, our agency received intel on their possible location. We think the girl your wife is trying to help is one of the girls being held at the same compound."

"Violet told me they're in a warehouse somewhere downtown Los Angeles."

"There are hundreds of warehouses down there. We need the exact one. If we get the location wrong and the General finds out we're onto them, those girls are dead."

"Violet's in real trouble."

"All we can hope for is that our people get to Olokun before Violet does."

Darryl wiped the mustard and mayo from the corner of his lips and took a few sips of the sparkling mineral water Stanley brought him. Both were delicious.

"I've been trying to get Violet on her cell since this morning. It's rolling to voicemail which means her battery probably died."

Hazel poured herself a drink from a pitcher of gin and pineapple juice with slices of fresh pineapple in it. She offered Darryl a round. He declined.

"Think I better stick with the mineral water. I'm driving."

"The GSF is able to track her moves through her cell phone's GPS system but if her phone is turned off, it'll be hard for them to get an accurate signal."

Darryl stuffed the last bite of the tasty sandwich into his mouth, added a few barbecue potato chips to the mix and washed it all down with the water.

An idea popped into his mind but in order for it to work, the timing had to be exact.

Hazel continued, "Our sources say your wife and her friend are planning to make a fake delivery to a warehouse where the girls are being held tomorrow morning around nine a.m. If we can get a message to them that the police are handling it, we might just have a chance to save them."

"I'll keep calling her. If I hear anything, I'll let you know. I need to ask you one last favor. Would you mind getting the word to Bob that I'll be off work for a few days?"

"No problem. I'll tell him I authorized it." She chuckled at that one. Then she got serious.

"Be very, very careful with these men. I'd never forgive myself if something happened to you or your wife. They killed Olokun's mother for speaking out against them."

He took her hand. "You're a kind and thoughtful woman, Mrs. Miller. I appreciate your concern but where I grew up, I dealt with bad men on a daily basis."

"Please, call me Hazel." She motioned to the butler. Stanley, please see Mr. Rollins to the door."

"Stanley, you think I could get one of those Rueben's to go?"

"My pleasure. Right away, sir."

Darryl weaved and bobbed through rush hour traffic. While he drove, he brainstormed ways to keep Violet safe in the middle of a war for power and money.

An idea popped in his head. It could work with a little help from someone who worked in the field of public relations. He'd put in a call to Ron, an old college buddy and executive for a major PR firm. If he got Ron on board, he could pull this thing off and save Violet at the same time.

He also had to tell Violet's sister and father something. He didn't want to upset them but they had to know the truth. Violet was in trouble, big trouble.

He decided on a half truth. He'd tell them that at the moment, Violet was safe and that they were very close to finding her.

After putting in a call, he sent an email to Ron. He didn't dare say anything to him about the case over the phone but he let him know the call was urgent.

Violet's father was taking a mid-afternoon siesta so Darryl chilled in the library and watched the evening news. Half listening, he poured himself a glass of iced tea, added a generous helping of Cruzan rum and nibbled on a second helping of Stanley's famous Rueben sandwich. While he ate and drank he checked his work email. He'd just reclined in the massage chair when a news headline caught his attention.

Military leaders in the Middle East threaten to use biological agents if U.S. invades airspace.

The phone rang. Darryl rushed to pick up the receiver thinking it was Ron returning his call. It wasn't Ron—it was Violet's mystery man, Dr. Bones.

"Darryl, this is Dr. Bones. Your wife wants you to know she's safe and will meet you at the hotel in the morn…."

"Let me speak to Violet! Hello? Anybody there?"

The phone line went dead.

CHAPTER
Forty-Five

Around three a.m. the wives awakened Violet and led her to the courtyard. After a long prayer, they blindfolded her and gently began to cut away the clothes she wore. A large piece of fabric was wrapped around her body and tucked in like a bath towel.

Nosy and a bit scared, I peeked through the bottom of the blindfold to see that I was now dressed in all white. I looked like a snow bunny in mid-summer.

Dr. Bones explained that we were going to hike to a nearby river. We walked in silence while the birds and other forest animals sang a song of rebirth and evolution. When we got to the river, the priests washed my head with the amber and musk smelling soap. While they washed, they sang a litany of hymns and spirituals sung by slaves on plantations and railroads while they picked cotton and swung hammers twice their weight.

Those songs were followed by drumming for the deities. The louder they played, the more intense the energy became. By the time they were finished, I felt like my feet were on fire. Hundreds of Spirits were rushing in. Some were crying while others were dancing and clapping. My mother stood to the side nodding her approval.

After the cleansing, the priestesses led me back to the courtyard and removed the blindfold. I was instructed to sit on a low stool before a giant shrine to Yemoja, the deity who ruled the ocean. Yemoja said she had claimed me as her child.

Oshara clicked on an electric razor. When I realized she was getting ready to cut my hair off, I jumped up and out of the chair.

"Hold it! I didn't…I didn't sign up for this."

"The cutting of one's hair is symbolic of returning to the state we were in at birth."

"You can do anything else but my hair stays."

After I sat back down, Oshara caressed my head gently. "Initiation teaches us that our truest beauty is inside. We were whole before the body took on form."

"That sounds real spiritual but I'm not walking around baldheaded."

"Today you will become a Bride of the Orisa. You and Yemoja will become one. Your life will no longer be your own."

I knew I was being vain, maybe even a tad bit stubborn but this was a lot to swallow. I was in the middle of nowhere. I was about to be scalped in preparation for induction into an indigenous religion. And what if Darryl didn't like her without hair?

Oshara opened my hand, placed four shells on my palm and closed my fingers around them.

"Do you trust your ancestors?"

I thought it might be some kind of trick question but I answered anyway.

"Yes, I trust my ancestors."

"Then ask your ancestors what you should do. Cast the shells, daughter."

The ancestors would understand my dilemma. I said a short prayer, shook the shells over my head and asked the spirits for guidance.

"Is it necessary for me to sacrifice my hair to be initiated?"

I let the shells drop on the mat. All of them fell white side up.

"You have their answer, Violet. The rest is up to you."

I shook my head in disbelief. "Me and my ancestors are gonna have to have a talk when I get home. Fine. Go ahead and cut it."

Oshara prayed as she cut my hair.

"Bless her life, old great ones. Guide her on the path of righteousness. May she release the old to embrace the new path ahead of her. May she live to see her grandchildren grow old. May she realize her destiny in this life."

Then she called down the deities in a rhythmic chant.

"Esu. Obatala. Osun. Yemoja. Sango. Oya. Ogun. Esu. Bless the head of your daughter. Give her peace, clarity and focus. Cleanse away her negative thoughts. Help her fulfill her destiny in this life!"

My beautiful locks tumbled down over my shoulders and down my back like leaves returning to the earth. When Oshara finished, I looked down and saw my hair scattered on the ground in what looked like a spiritual mosaic.

I knew intuitively that each lock represented something about myself that I didn't love.

Suddenly I was glad my hair was gone. A powerful peace crept over me unlike anything I had ever felt before.

Dr. Bones began playing a soft melody on the congas. He kept playing while Oshara finished shaving my head. When she was done, I felt light-headed, like my spirit was floating up in the ethers somewhere. I ran my hand across my bare scalp. To my surprise, my head felt good without hair. Felt like I'd shed the weight of forty years and then some.

I felt a soft pressure at the crown of my head but I was too far gone to care what was going on. When Oshara was done shaving, she poured a warm herbal mixture over my freshly shaven scalp. The water made me feel good—like I was in my mother's womb again. Oshara poured and prayed over my head for what seemed like hours.

When she was done Oshara asked, "How do you feel, Iyawo?"

"Iyawo? What's that?"

"It means, bride of the Orisa."

"I feel light. Like I'm floating. Bet I look pretty funny don't I?"

"You look lovely. The light of the Spirits surround you."

A short, stout man with a pleasant face walked through the courtyard flanked by two male priests. Dr. Bones whispered in my ear. "That's the *Araba*. Kind of like the Pope of the Ifa religion. When you meet him, keep your eyes to the ground. Salute him as soon as you enter the shrine and never sit anywhere that you're higher than him."

"Got it."

The Araba went into a small building in the center of the courtyard. Dr. Bones took Violet's hand and led her in that direction.

"I'm nervous. What if he doesn't like me?"

Dr. Bones smiled lovingly. "Don't worry, he'll like you. Just follow the protocol and everything will be fine. He did a special blessing over your sacred implements. Your *Olokun* has the ashe of the ancestors inside."

"Olokun. That's the name of the little girl we're looking for. In my dream the spirits told me her name was Olokun."

"That's correct but we gotta go. Can't keep the Araba waiting."

They entered a dimly lit room. The entire space was a huge shrine.

There were at least fifty pots in the room of all sizes and shapes. These pots looked different from the ones I'd seen at Baba Ocha's shop. The Araba's pots were mostly terra cotta and wood. Some of them were painted with images of the Orisa. There were more statues too. All African and very elaborate. Some were almost human size. There was a large flag with an African motif that stretched across the wall's width and height.

I kept my eyes downcast as we entered. I nearly tripped over my feet trying not to look up. From the corner of my eye I saw a small terra cotta pot on the steps by his large, brown ashy feet. It was painted blue and decorated with cowry shells. Afraid I'd make a mistake and look at him, I kept my eyes on the Araba's toes. When we got closer, Dr. Bones dropped to the ground and saluted him.

"Aboru, Aboye, Abosise Araba. I am honored to greet you."

Violet followed suit and repeated the greeting exactly as she heard it.

The Araba nodded his head knowingly. "Ogbo Ato. Raise your eyes child and look at me."

I darted my eyes toward Dr. Bones. He had told me it was disrespectful to look the Araba in the eyes. I didn't want to disobey the Araba but I didn't want to break protocol either.

"It's okay, Violet. He wants to *see* you."

I slowly raised my eyes to meet the Araba's intense glare. When their eyes met, his eyes bulged with a sign of recognition. He was quiet for a minute then he picked up a staff that was decorated with strips of fabric and painted with a white chalky substance.

He twirled the staff contemplatively. "So you are one of Mamiwata's descendents. Are you aware of the powers you've inherited?"

"No—yes….a little."

He rose from the chair. Dr. Bones rushed to assist him in standing up.

"Come here, child."

I inched closer to him. My heart pounded madly. I was sure he could hear and maybe even see it.

"Please remove your gelee."

I unwrapped the white scarf Oshara had tied around my head.

The Araba put the pot to my head and began a series of prayers. First the pot felt heavy, like it weighed a ton. Then I didn't feel it at all.

My spirit left my body again. I was hovering on the ceiling watching him pray over me.

When he was finished he placed the pot in my hands.

"Today is the first day of the rest of your life. Today you are reborn. I hereby grant you the priestly name, Adeomi. Crown of the Sacred Waters."

He placed several strands of beads around my neck that looked similar to the ones I'd seen Dr. Bones wearing.

"Now that we have saved you, you must save the rest. You odu in Ifa is Eji Ogbe. Only Orunmila knows who will have salvation. Remember, bit by bit is how we eat the head of a rat. You must always observe good character no matter what others do. Many will envy you and try to cause your downfall. Do not worry. Orunmila will use their betrayal as seeds to grow your good. You will be a great diviner as was Osun who walks very close to you. You must become Iyan'ifa when the time is right. You will return to Africa one day with your husband and child. It will be a daughter. Go forward Adeomi. You came all this way to save our daughters. Your good deeds have set you free."

"I-I-I....thank you, sir."

Dr. Bones quietly led me from the room. When they got back to the compound Dr. Bones instructed me to pack up my things and prepare to leave.

As I gathered her things I felt a strange surge in my soul. It snaked its way up my third eye and played a vision of my life to come. My body was there at the compound but my heart was roaming the Spirit world. I felt tall—tall like the Jolly Green Giant from the green bean commercials. The ancestors were whispering in my ear. Whispering that I would do great things in this lifetime. That nothing and no one could keep me from fulfilling her destiny.

It all sounded so amazing. But I had no idea how tall and dangerous the mountain was that I had to climb to get to my destiny.

It wouldn't be long before I found out...

CHAPTER
Forty-Six

D arryl heard the front door open and close. Thinking it might be Violet he jogged toward the front of the house and saw the night nurse leaving.

He turned to the sound of footsteps behind him, saw Pop Brown coming down the hall.

"Morning, son-in-law. Had me a good sleep. Feeling like a million bucks. You heard from Violet yet?"

"Morning, Sir. I heard from her teacher. She's doing fine. You hungry?" Darryl said, trying to change the subject before he asked more questions.

Darryl knew Mr. Brown knew he was lying but for some reason, his Pop-in-law let it go.

Mrs. Jasper was out of town visiting her sister who'd come down with the flu. Darryl could tell the old man was lonely for his lady friend and that he was worried as hell about his daughter. There was nothing either of them could do but wait.

Darryl prepared a light breakfast for them. While they ate they watched the morning news. When the news went off, Mr. Brown went back to his room to take a shower and get dressed. Darryl sat at his desk going over some briefs for an upcoming case.

He couldn't concentrate. His shoulders were tight. He decided to take a hot shower to relieve some of the stress. He was just about to step under the water when a call summoned him back to the bedroom. He prayed it was Violet but it wasn't. The caller ID read Stanton Public Relations. Ron was calling back.

"Hey man." Darryl said, wrapping a towel around his waist.

"Sorry for calling so early but my plane just landed a few minutes ago. I got your message. You said it was urgent. What's going on? You finally getting married or something?"

"You got jokes, huh? Actually, I *am* trying to get married but I have a little problem."

"Shoot from the hip man. You know I have your back."

When Darryl got through telling him what he needed and the parts of the story he could tell him without putting his wife in danger, his friend got quiet. When Ron finally spoke, he kept it real. Ron always told it like it was, even in high school.

"Damn man, you're asking for a whole lot."

"I'll owe you big if you help me out."

"We go way back and you know I'll do what I can do. Where's that you said she is now?"

"With some dude in a hotel downtown L.A. or at some compound in SFV. One of the two."

"You let your wife-to-be hang out with some broh you barely know? You really trust this sista."

"You'd have to know her to understand."

"Gonna cost you but we can do what you asked. I hope she's worth it."

"She's worth every cent, man."

"Auight, you send me the information I need. I'll get back to you first thing in the morning with details."

"Thanks, I owe you one."

"Naw man, you owe me three for this one. Hey, before we hang up, I wanted to tell you that I saw your ex the other day. Angelia was with her. Your baby girl's getting tall. Y'all ever work that thing out?"

"I let it go. Could've taken her to court but I didn't wanna put my daughter through the custody drama. Her mother will come to her senses. Hopefully before Angelia graduates high school."

"Don't let it be too late, man. Brothers got rights too. You-on't want her to grow up and be asking you how come you didn't try to see her. Better the mother mad than your children. Trust me man, I know what I'm talking about."

How Ron had gotten a law degree and spoke such poor English baffled him.

"Yeah, thanks man. Hey, she tell you where she's living now?"

"She's back at her parent's house over there off of Wilshire and Rossmore."

"Thanks man. Stay Black."

Part one of Darryl's plan was in full effect.

Darryl sat back in the chair and thought about his daughter's almond-shaped eyes and copper colored hair.

He decided right then and there that when this mess with Violet was done, he was gonna put in a call to one of his lawyer buddies that handled custody battles. Angelia *was* his child too. Ron was right about that.

He needed to update Hazel but it was way too early to call. He'd ring her in a couple of hours and tell her what was going down. He wondered if her contact had been able to get word to Violet to back off?

Outside of Hazel's estate, three men in a van were putting on ski masks and loading up their guns. One of them called into a base camp for instructions. The other turned up a flask of brandy and passed it around to his friends.

The man on the radio asked somebody on the other end, "Do we have the word? Do you want us to take her?"

He listened for the transmission. When he received it, he updated his compadres.

"Base camp says to wait. They're holding out for some additional information. Relax your weapons fellas. It might be a while."

For some reason, Hazel couldn't sleep. She had the feeling she was missing something, something important. She got up, went to the kitchen and put on a kettle of hot water for some herbal tea. Mimi, one of the night staff, came staggering sleepily into the kitchen.

"Does Madam require something?"

"No, Mimi. Sorry to wake you. I'm fine, really. Just a bit of insomnia. Please go back to sleep."

"Are you sure I can't get you anything, Madam?"

"I'm sure."

Tea in one hand, file folder in the other, Hazel headed to the study. She sipped and glazed over the financial reports of the NAA. She'd read them over a dozen times but she had the nagging feeling there was something she wasn't seeing.

The report listed the sources where revenue had come from and had the bank names and locations of the accounts where money had been deposited. The bulk of the accounts were offshore but one of the banks was in America. Hazel thought the number to the American bank account looked familiar.

She studied the account number again.

"Where have I seen these numbers?"

Suddenly she remembered where she'd seen them.

The bank account of the League of Women! This was the account that their payroll checks came from. That meant that someone from the NAA had access to the League's payroll records. The only way to get access to the League's payroll account was through the company that processed their payroll checks and that was…

"Dear Jesus, Lord Almighty. Bob's firm!"

Hazel got so excited she knocked her tea over on the desk.

"Someone from Bob's law firm is involved with this scandal. That's how they knew I was going out of town. That's how they knew what was going on with the case. Who could it be?" She said talking out loud to herself.

She had to get in touch with Darryl. She signed on to her computer and sent Darryl an email telling him that there was a strange discrepancy in her accounting statement and that she needed to talk to him about it pronto. Just as she was signing off, Hazel heard keys jingling at the front door.

For a minute, her heart raced. She thought a stranger might be trying to come through the front door. Then she heard him call out her name.

"Hazel? Hazel, where are you? It's me, honey. I'm back."

Hazel scurried downstairs to greet her husband. She had so much to tell him—so much had taken place while he was away.

"I'm so glad you're home. You're never going to believe what I found out."

"What's wrong, Hazel? And don't try to hide it. It's all over your face."

She told him what she found on the report.

"Have you told anyone else about this?" He asked her, walking upstairs to their bedroom.

Darryl. She didn't want her husband to think she'd told someone else before she talked to him.

"No, not yet. But I thought Darryl should know about this. His wife is involved."

"Let's keep this under our hat for just a minute. You never know how outsiders might react."

When had his right hand attorney become an outsider?

"Can we talk about this in the morning? I'm exhausted. This merger is killing me. Let's get some rest and we'll hash everything out in the a.m."

How could he go to sleep after being told that someone from his company was using her agency's bank account to launder money from a child kidnapper?

Hazel knew something was wrong.

She didn't want to believe what was going through her mind but something was definitely wrong here.

Her husband undressed, slid into his pajamas and robe.

"Bob, I can't sleep. I'm going to the study and read for a while."

"Can I at least get a kiss goodnight?"

Hazel gave him a quick kiss on the cheek.

"Now what kind of kiss is that for a man who's been gone for two days?"

"Sorry, honey. I didn't brush my teeth."

She hurried down the hall to the bathroom, closed and locked the door and sat on the edge of the tub thinking. When she heard his light snores echoing down the hallway, she tiptoed downstairs to the study. She sat down at her husband's desk and sipped the remainder of her cold tea.

For the first time in the two decades they'd been married, Hazel didn't know if she could trust the man she married.

She spun around slowly in his chair. Her eyes drifted downward to her husband's briefcase. She never went through his things but tonight she couldn't stop herself from peeking inside his attaché.

At first glance, there seemed to be nothing out of the ordinary. A dozen or so legal files, his work phone and a second state of the art cell phone. Hazel unsnapped the pocket just above the base of the case. She moved two fingers around inside the fold until they settled on something she could grasp. She slid out an airline ticket stub. She figured it was just his boarding pass from his travel today and was about to put it back when something on the ticket stub caught her eye.

The destination city—it was all wrong. What in the world would Bob be doing in Ghana? He was supposed to be in Hawaii.

Hazel marched upstairs to their bedroom with the ticket stub in hand. She flicked on the light and snatched back the covers.

"Robert Dean Miller, I need you to wake up and talk to me this instant!"

Startled, he stared up at her with a look of disbelief.

"Have you gone mad? What is it that can't wait until the morning?"

"What is this? I found it in your briefcase." She held the ticket up for him to see it.

"Why are you going through my things? Let me see it."

She held it up to his face for him to get a closer look.

"Why it looks like an airline ticket stub."

"That's exactly what it is. And I want to know what you were doing in Africa when you were supposed to be in Hawaii?"

"I wasn't in Africa, Hazel."

"It says right here, Accra, Ghana. Isn't that in Africa?"

"Let me see the stub, Hazel."

He took the stub from her and held it under the light.

"I can't read this."

He put on his glasses.

"Did you look at the name on the ticket? This was stapled to an expense report. It must've come off. This stub belongs to Martin Lund. His expense budget was a bit off so I'm reviewing his reports for errors. Now can I get some sleep?"

"Bob, did you hear what I told you about the report from the NAA and the discrepancy on my accounting reports?"

"Sort of. Okay, I was half-listening. Something about an account being screwed up and the firm's payroll department being the cause of the mistake."

He sat up in bed, "I'll talk to Martin in the morning and get to the bottom of it. Told you I'm jet-lagged. I just need a few hours of sleep."

He took off his glasses, placed them on the nightstand and took a sip of water.

"Robert, someone at your law firm is using my agency to launder money. This is serious. We could get in big trouble."

"What are you talking about? You didn't say anything about laundering money. Let me see that report! Why didn't you say that?"

"I did but you weren't listening!!"

He took the report and slammed his glasses back on his face.

Hazel felt embarrassed for suspecting her husband. She was so upset by this whole mess she didn't know what to think or who to trust.

He glanced at the column on the report that listed the receivables. "Jesus. You're right. Somebody's been funneling revenue from an unidentified source into your payroll account. Marty—he's the one who manages the firm's payroll. Maybe that's why his numbers were off. And you think this has something to do with that human trafficking case?"

"I think it has a whole lot to do with it."

"I think we should notify the police. This is over our heads."

"How do we know the police aren't involved?"

"Don't get paranoid on me, Hazel. We have to trust somebody."

"*Who* to trust is the question." Hazel said, feeling nervous about the whole thing.

Hazel sat down on a chair next to the bed and told her husband the entire story. He was just about to pick up the phone and call the authorities when the doorbell rang. Both of them snapped their heads around toward each other.

"You're not expecting anyone are you?"

"Absolutely not."

"No one ever comes to this house without our security calling."

Hazel slipped on a pair of jeans, sweatshirt and sneakers. Her husband grabbed a pair of sweatpants and slipped on his tennis shoes.

Hazel pressed the intercom that went to the security booth. It rang and rang but no one answered.

"Bob, something's really wrong. They're not answering. Why didn't security call up and alert us that a guest was coming?"

"I don't know but I'm going to find out. In the meantime, call the police."

Hazel grabbed her cell phone and dialed 911. When she put the phone up to her ear, all she heard was a busy signal.

"Oh my God. I think they've blocked our outgoing calls."

"Stay calm, Hazel. Did you try the landline?"

The doorbell rang a second time. Hazel snatched the phone off the nightstand.

"It's dead, Bob. We have to get out of here. You don't know how dangerous these people are. They'll do anything to..."

The doorbell rang a third time. They heard someone fiddling with the door.

Bob paced back and forth across the plush carpet.

"Listen, you remember how we used to joke about the laundry chute being an escape route?"

"Yes."

He went to the nightstand and took out a small revolver. He tucked the gun into his pants at the small of his back. "I want you to slide down that chute, exit through the housekeeper's door and get some help. I'll stall them until you get back."

"Bob, I can't leave you here."

"Get outta here now!"

"Okay! You don't have to yell!"

Hazel hurried down the hall with Bob on her heels. "Kiss me, Bob."

"Hazel!"

"Kiss me right now!"

He leaned over and kissed her on the lips.

She looked into his eyes. "I love you, Bob."

"I love you too. Now go!"

He helped her up and into the chute, gave her a shove and sent her sliding down into a dark hole. Just as he closed the hatch the front door crashed in.

CHAPTER
Forty-Seven

"**D**addy and Darryl are probably worried out of their mind by not being able to get me on my cell."

The van's air conditioning was on the blink. Hot, dry San Fernando Valley air poured in through the open window. Violet felt like she was about to suffocate.

Dr. Bones turned into a shopping plaza. "I need to stop for gas. I think there's a cell phone store next door to the station. You can buy a car charger."

"It's seven-thirty. They're probably not open yet. You think we'll make it to the warehouse on time?"

"There's nothing to think about. We make it on time or everybody dies."

CHAPTER
Forty-Eight

Olatunji and Fagunwa drove along the side streets of downtown Los Angeles. Block after block of urine-smelling pavement, shopping carts filled with old newspapers, aluminum cans and empty water bottles.

Olatunji knew exactly where the checkpoints staffed with his father's henchmen were located. Still, it was no easy feat avoiding them. Somehow he managed to weave a path toward the outskirts of downtown.

There was one more blockade to pass through. Olatunji hoped to use his clout as the General's son to get through without incident. With his fugitive once again tucked neatly in the trunk of his car, Olatunji pulled up to the gate.

He rolled down the windows and flashed his badge. When the soldier realized who he was, he greeted him properly by lowering his head and crossing his right arm over his chest.

"Honorable Ade. We greet you with respect sir. We apologize, but we are having a problem today. Your father has told us that every car must be searched."

"Surely he didn't mean for you to search the car of his own son."

"He told us that there were no exceptions."

Olatunji bluffed him. He pulled out his cell phone and began pressing in numbers. "I will call him right now. I hate to bother him with this but I don't want you to…."

The soldier looked nervous.

"No—ah…sir, please, go on through. I wouldn't want to bother the General. I'll let him know you came by."

Olatunji winked at him and snapped his phone closed. "You're a smart soldier."

Once they were past the blockade, Olatunji pulled over in an alley and let a sweaty Fagunwa out of the trunk. The trunk added ten degrees to an already sweltering morning. Olatunji began to worry about the man's health.

"You don't look too good. Are you alright?"

"I'm a little weak. But I'll be okay. Let's keep going."

"We got to get you inside. The city is closed up tight with my father's men."

Fagunwa's mouth was as dry as a desert. "You have any water?"

Olatunji reached behind him and grabbed a few bottles of water from the cooler in the backseat. He also retrieved a bag with some food in it and gave it to Fagunwa. Fagunwa downed the entire bottle of water in a few seconds and munched the sandwich down in four bites.

"I was very thirsty."

"We have to keep moving. Put this hat on and slide down in the seat."

"I need to use a phone and a computer."

Olatunji thought for a minute. "I have my phone turned off in case they're tracking me. I have a small office at the Radio Station. You can get on-line there."

"I have to get in touch with Hazel Miller. She's working on the case and may have valuable information."

"You can call her from the landline."

"What's at the radio station?"

"I'll tell you about it when we get there. Right now I need to focus on keeping us alive."

Olatunji turned the car around and started heading toward the freeway.

"You're a smart man. Your father underestimates you."

"Only because I want him too. Fasten your seat belt Fagunwa. It's time for us to take a drive."

CHAPTER
Forty-Nine

Darryl was in the kitchen brewing a pot of coffee. Pop Brown and Mrs. Jasper, who'd just gotten back from Tampa, were seated at the table. Darryl joined them with an overflowing plate of some of Mrs. Jasper's soulful cooking.

Pop Brown was absorbed in the morning paper. "Herbert Theodore Brown, if you don't lower that newspaper and talk to me I'm going to stick a hole right through it with this fork. I just got back from Florida and I'd like to be able to at least see you." Mrs. Jaspers threatened, her fork held high in the air.

"Okay woman, don't get violent on me. You know I like to stay caught up on world news. America's about to go to war. Plus, I'm trying to find us some oxygen masks on sale in case they drop the A-bomb on us."

She rolled her eyes and turned toward Darryl. "Darryl, how are you doing sweetie? You like those eggs? That's my mama's recipe. You put cheese in before and after you cook 'em, little diced Onion and bell pepper and just a pinch of brown sugar. By the way, son, how's Violet doing?"

"Mrs. Jasper, these are the best eggs I ever had. Thank you for taking such good care of us." He tried to avoid the question about Violet.

"You welcome, baby. My pleasure. Now what about Violet? When she coming home?"

"Violet? She---she's doing some studies with her teacher. I expect her shortly. I might have to go and pick her up." Darryl answered carefully. Not careful enough to fool Pop Brown.

"What's going on with my baby? Don't lie to me, son. Violet done went up there trying to tell those people what to do, didn't she? I don' told that girl to keep her mouth shut. But her mouth is just like running water—always flowing from somewhere."

"I don't have any details right now. But I know she's okay. As soon as I hear something else you'll be the first to know."

Pop Brown walked off shaking his head.

The phone rang. Darryl figured it was Hazel. She'd promised to call with an update on how things were going.

He glanced at the caller ID before putting the phone to his ear. Violet's cell phone number glowed on the small screen. He snatched up the phone.

"Violet! Where are you? You okay? Why haven't you called us?"

Mrs. Jasper picked up the remote and shut the TV off. Pop Brown walked over to where Darryl was standing and tried to listen in.

"Let me speak to her, Darryl. I'll talk some sense into that girl."

Darryl tried to stall him without being disrespectful.

"Yes, sir. Just a minute, I need to give her some important information."

Violet, where are you?"

She answered, but he couldn't hear her very well with all of the static in the background. There were breaks between her words.

"I'm planning...coming home...later. We're on our way to....."

Darryl had to tell her she was in danger. He didn't want to upset her dad, but he knew there was no way Violet's father was going to let him take the phone into another room to talk privately. He couldn't let the connection be lost before he told Violet what was going on. It was now or never.

"Violet, I want you to listen to me. You're going to have to abandon your search for Olokun. Hazel thinks they're onto you. Get out of there right away, Violet. Get out of there as soon as you can."

There was so much static on the line. He wasn't sure if she heard him. But this time he could hear her much clearer.

"Darryl, I couldn't hear all of what you said. You're breaking up. Are you trying to say someone is following me?"

"Yes, that's exactly what I'm saying." Darryl yelled into the receiver.

Nothing but static came back.

"Violet....look, some people are coming to help you. Reporters. They..."

Violet's father snatched the phone from him. "Now you listen here you hard-headed little girl. Your fiance' here, he trying to keep me from knowing how serious this thang is, but I ain't dumb. You in trouble, Violet. You in over your head. Get your tail outta there. Everythang you supposed to do, you done."

He stood there holding the phone. "Violet, are you still there?"

Darryl took the phone back from him and looked at the screen.

The call had ended five seconds ago. Violet must've lost her signal. He hoped she'd heard enough to make her get out of there.

The phone rang again. Darryl hurriedly pressed the talk button. But this time it wasn't Violet it was Hazel.

"Hazel? Is that you? I was just getting ready to call you."

Hazel interrupted him. She was frantic.

"Darryl! You have to help me. These men—they broke into our house. I had to escape through the laundry chute. I would've called the cops but they somehow locked our phones from making outgoing calls. I ran down to a little donut shop—

Sally's—about two blocks from the house. I found out the firm is involved in the scandal. A guy named Martin Lund. He's been laundering money through my agency for those madmen. Come now! Bob's still in the house!"

If the firm was involved, there was no telling who else might be.

"Hazel, I want you to stay right where you are. Don't call anyone. I'm on my way!" Darryl said, grabbing his keys and heading toward the door.

"Pop Brown, I don't want you to worry. I have everything under control. I'll be back just as soon as I can. Hit me on my cell phone if anything comes up or if Violet calls back."

Violet's father got up slowly and walked Darryl to the door. "Son, you be careful out there."

"I will, I promise." Darryl said, hugging him tightly around the shoulders.

Darryl jetted to the garage, jumped in his car and sped off toward the Miller estate. He tried Mr. Miller's cell phone. There was no answer. He feared the worst. Everybody knew that Mr. Miller never, ever turned off his cell phone. In fact, there was a running joke about it at the office.

The boys at the firm said, "If Mr. Miller didn't answer his cell phone, he's either having sex or dead."

Since he just hung up with Mr. Miller's wife, there was only one option left. Darryl prayed for a miracle.

CHAPTER
Fifty

Fagunwa and Olatunji were almost to the Radio Station when Olatunji got a call from one of his insiders. After he hung up, he gave Fagunwa a chilling update.

"My contact just informed me that a new blockade went up this morning. Gonna need you to get back into the trunk. We may have to go straight to the warehouse."

Couple of blocks later, Olatunji pulled over, opened the trunk and waited for Fagunwa to curl up inside. He put a drop cloth over him and closed the trunk.

Armpits sweating and heart pounding, Olatunji drove up to the checkpoint. He'd planned to use the same *family member* pass on the soldiers as he had the others but there was surprise waiting on him. He saw a car with tinted windows parked on the side of the road. Ziberia's official flag hung on its antenna. The rear end of the car bore government license plates. His father was here.

Olatunji's stomach tightened into a thick knot of nerves. His throat felt like it was closing. He spotted his greatest enemy standing near the control booth next to two of his bodyguards. He hated the sight of him. This was the man who had murdered his own wife in cold blood—Olatunji's beautiful mother.

Olatunji parked behind his father's car. He honked the horn twice, a signal to Fagunwa that there was trouble. His father turned to the sound of the horn, saw it was his son and walked over to greet him.

Two of his henchmen followed closely on his heels. Olatunji recognized Sergeant Abayomi who'd been protecting his father since he was old enough to carry a gun.

A man who has done so much wrong needs constant protection, Olatunji thought to himself.

Olatunji greeted him pleasantly, tried to hide the hate in his eyes. They touched shoulders, first the left, then the right, as was their custom.

"Baba. It is good to see you. I'm sure you've been very busy?"

Olatunji stood to his father's left so he could watch the car.

His father gave orders to a few of the soldiers then turned to his son, "Yes, we are very busy with global enterprises that can bring great resources to our country. So how are things for you my son?"

Fanning himself with his hat, Olatunji answered, "Tense, but calm. The parents they....they want answers but they're afraid to ask the questions."

"They know better than to question my laws. I am creating an economy that will get rid of our country's financial burdens. I'm giving their husbands jobs so they can feed their families. I don't see what they're complaining about. They can always have more children. They're only girls. We hardly ever take the boys."

Olatunji fought the impulse to smash him in the face. He wondered what kind of God had created his father.

"Just silly women. Easy to replace." He answered, his teeth clenched tight in his mouth.

"It would be nice to have my son join me for dinner. I have many young girls you could enjoy free of charge. One of them might make you a good wife."

Olatunji wanted to tell him that the woman he married would have the freedom to choose a husband, but instead he said, "That's a tempting offer. I'll have to take you up on that some other time. I'm meeting a repair man at the radio station."

The General scratched his chin, "Oh, is there a problem?"

"Nothing serious, just a few connectors that need to be replaced."

His father's eyes were cast toward the ground for a minute. Olatunji had never seen his father look down. It was a sign that something was seriously out of place. His father looked up but not at him.

"There's a soldier who betrayed us that's on the run. If you see him, kill him on sight and bring me his head. Fagunwa is his name. He has information that could hurt us. We have to stop him before he causes problems for our operation."

Olatunji couldn't believe his father was using terms like *us* and *we* that alluded to them being unified on any level. He couldn't remember when his father had done anything that was about anyone other than himself.

General Mubosa touched his son's arm lightly.

"Olatunji, I need you to stay close. We might have to kill them. All of them. The girls we haven't sold yet. Perhaps we could use some gas or something? Think about it and let me know. But we can't let them leave. They know too much about our operation."

His father's touch sent a shiver up his spine. "I'll be in touch, Father. Do not worry. Everything will work itself out. I better hurry before I'm late. I had to bring in some specialists and I don't want to miss them."

"Be very careful son. There are two Americans working with Fagunwa. One of them says she is a relative of Olokun. I have my men following them. Just in case."

"I will, Baba. I'll be careful. And I'll watch out for those people you are searching for. I'll call you later. Maybe I'll come by for a late meal."

Olatunji headed for his car. As he drove toward the gate, he purposely waved at his father who gave the cue to the soldiers to lift the gate. He felt dirty from his touch, the touch of a murderer. He couldn't wait to wash it off of him.

As Olatunji drove through the barricade he let out a sigh of relief. But he could only relax for a brief moment.

When Olatunji was out of sight, the General walked over to Sergeant Abayomi and whispered in his ear.

"I want you to put two men on my son. Two of your best men. Just in case."

Abayomi looked at him in disbelief and answered. "Yes sir!"

CHAPTER
Fifty-One

Darryl pulled into the parking lot of Sally's Donut Shop, jumped out of the car and hurried inside. There were two customers at the counter ordering their sugar fixes. He looked around the shop and locked eyes with a man who was stacking bundled newspapers on the table. Across from the newspaper man sat a business woman dressed in a smart black suit getting her dose of morning caffeine.

Darryl went over to the plump cashier. "Have you seen a woman with….."

Before he could finish the sentence the woman pointed around the corner.

"She's in the back. Stands out like a sore thumb in here."

"Thanks." Darryl spun around and made a dash for the back of the shop.

Sitting at a round, sticky table in the corner was Hazel Miller. Her head was down, cradled by a set of perfectly manicured hands and fingers. When she lifted her head, Darryl could see she'd been crying.

"Hazel. Are you okay?"

"I keep calling his cell but no one answers. I was just about to go back to the house and take my chances," Hazel said, sobbing loudly.

Darryl slid onto a chair beside her, wrapped his left arm around her shoulders. "Hazel, stop assuming the worst. I called the police on my way over here. They should be there by now, especially in this neighborhood. I told them we'd meet them over there. They're probably waiting for us."

As they rounded the corner, they saw a row of squad cars lined up in front of the Miller property. Two men were face down on the ground, spread eagle and handcuffed. Yellow tape was strewn across the front entrance of the estate.

One of the officers walked up to the car on the passenger side. "Are you Mrs. Miller?"

Tears and black mascara streamed down her face. "Yes I am. Where's my husband? Is he okay?"

"I have some unfortunate news for you."

"Oh my God! Please don't tell me he's dead."

"Your husband was shot. He's been taken by ambulance to a local hospital. He…"

"Is he alright? I need to know right this instant! Is my husband dead or alive?"

"Hazel, calm down. Listen to the man." Darryl said putting his large hand over her fragile fingers.

"He's listed in stable condition. One of our officers will escort you to the hospital. But first we'll need to take a statement."

The officer spoke directly to Darryl, "His room is heavily guarded. Are you a family friend or a….?"

"He's my attorney." Hazel said, wiping the mascara from below her eyes with a soggy tissue.

"Come on, Hazel. Let's get you to the hospital."

"We have to get a statement from the victim's wife while the details are fresh."

"My husband's in the hospital shot and I have to give some damn report!"

"Can she give the report at the hospital?"

"I guess so. Go on. Go see about your husband."

A motorcycle cop drove a few feet ahead of them all the way to the hospital.

When they arrived, another officer came over and guarded Darryl's car. Taking a cue from the conversation at the house, Hazel told the officer on duty at the hospital that Darryl was their attorney. He waved them right on through.

Mr. Miller was awake but highly sedated. A nurse was recording his vitals. He had an IV attached to his wrist and an oxygen mask on his face. The nurse explained that he looked a lot worse than he actually was.

"Can he talk?" Hazel asked her, holding back tears.

"Oh he's talking. He requested we order him dinner from a certain deli."

Hazel couldn't help laughing at that one. "His wanting food is good."

"Only one of you can be in the hospital room at a time. Police rules. There's a waiting room just down the hall." The nurse told them.

"Hazel, I'll be right down the hall. If you need me just holler."

"Thanks, Darryl."

Darryl was relieved Mr. Miller was going to be okay but he knew that they were far from being through the thick of this crisis. He looked at his watch. It was 8:30a.m. Darryl's big plan was set to launch around nine.

Darryl had arranged for Ron's PR agency to break the story about the kidnapped girls to over a thousand news agencies in Los Angeles and abroad. There would be a side bar to the story about an American woman named Violet Brown who was trying to find and save the children. The sidebar would tell how Olokun, whose mother had been allegedly murdered by the Alliance, was being held by the traffickers. The *League of Women United* would be mentioned as the human rights agency investigating the case. He figured he might as well create a little publicity for Hazel's firm since he was paying for it.

All hell was going to break loose when the government was indicated as possible suspects in the scandal. But if things went right, the press would be all over Violet. And that would prevent her from being killed.

Violet's paparazzi would become her protection. The Alliance wasn't dumb enough to murder an American citizen in front of the cameras.

At least that's what he hoped.

Twenty minutes later Hazel came walking into the waiting room. She looked a mess from crying but there was a smile on her face.

"He'll be alright. The killers thought he was dead. They left him in the foyer and went searching for evidence that could implicate their boss. Bob crawled out the back door and down the driveway to the street. By then the police had come."

Darryl handed her a cup of hot cocoa. "Bob's one lucky man."

"A few inches to the left and that bullet could've pierced his heart. I always told Bob he had an angel watching over him. He always said that angel was me."

"Did they say how long they're gonna keep him?"

"A few days or so. They have to keep an eye on that shoulder wound. Darryl, I don't know what I would've done if you hadn't answered the phone this morning. I'm forever in your debt. By the way, in the midst of my hysteria I forgot to ask about Violet. How are things going with finding her sister?"

"She's close. Very close. Our plan is in motion."

"Plan? What plan?"

"I'll tell you on the ride back. Let's get you some clothes. You're staying at my house tonight. I'll have my driver take you back to the hospital after we get some food in you. My father's fiance makes the best soul food dinner on this side of the West Coast."

"Soul food. I've heard of it but never had the pleasure of sampling it. It's like African-American gourmet cuisine right?"

"Something like that...."

CHAPTER
Fifty-Two

One of the League's plants had gotten nervous and spilled the beans about Violet and her friend's visit to the warehouse. The General sent a green memo to his men instructing them to let Violet and her friend pass through whatever blockade they arrived at without incident. The General was banking on executing them when they walked into the warehouse. Since she bent on reuniting with her African sister, he'd let them die together. A befitting ending to their so-called long lost lineage….

"We must be getting close to the warehouse. I can feel her. Olokun."

"We're just a few blocks away."

"I think I have enough of a charge to make an outgoing call."

She punched his number into her cell and prayed Darryl was still talking to her. He answered on the first ring.

"Violet! You have us all worried as hell. Where are you? Are you okay?"

"We're a few blocks away from the warehouse. I'm okay. We're about to go in there."

"Violet, it's a trap. Don't do it. They're on to you."

"I have no other choice. It's the only way we'll get her out of there."

"I'm on my way. I want you to stay put until I get there."

"There's no time, Darryl. I love you. I love you with everything in me."

"Violet, I organized a media blitz. They're gonna swoop on that place in the next hour. If you can just hold off until then."

"Call the police and tell them to meet us over there at 9:15am."

"Members of the police department might be part of their team."

"It's a chance we have to take."

"I'm almost to you."

"Darryl, if the head guy finds out about the media, he's gonna kill the girls."

Dr. Bones pulled into a 7-11 parking lot.

"What's going on? Why are we stopping?"

"Who are you talking to?"

My hands were damp with nervous perspiration.

"Dr. Bones."

"I think there's someone following us." Dr. Bones told her.

I could tell by the expression on his face that he was getting a message from Spirit. And it wasn't good.

"Darryl, let me call you right back."

"Violet, don't hang up this…"

"I'll call you back as soon as I can."

Dr. Bones reached over and touched her hand, "Violet, I need you to do what I tell you. We're going to beat them at their own game."

They got out of the van and walked into 7-11.

"Did you see that blue car that drove into the parking lot behind us?"

"Yes."

"That's them. The General's men. They're tailing us."

I listened as Dr. Bones put in an urgent phone call to some friends who lived in the area.

About fifteen minutes later, a middle-aged Black man and a voluptuous Black woman came sauntering into the store. When they left, the man was wearing Dr. Bones' jacket and Kufi hat and the woman had on white clothes similar to what I wore. They got in our van and drove away.

We hid behind a magazine rack and watched the car that had been tailing us pull out into traffic behind the van. When they were out of sight, we eased out of the store, slid into a black Chevy Impala and jetted toward the warehouse.

"By the time they figure out we switched cars and passengers, we'll be at the warehouse."

"What about the uniforms? What about the pot with my Orisa in it?"

"Your Orisa is not in that pot. You and your Orisa are one. Its spirit now lives inside you. You'll come to feel it more deeply as you grow in the wisdom and knowledge of our tradition. The pot is sacred, but it's not your source."

I was confused. "If we don't need the pot, why do they give it to us?"

"Until your human vessel is ready for the vast power of the Orisa, you need a physical place to focus your energy, prayers and offerings."

"I still don't get it but okay."

"Violet, I need you to trust me. I promised I'd protect you."

Just as he said the words, the car sputtered, jerked a time or two and shut off. Smoke oozed from under the hood and started seeping into the car.

"Shit. This car isn't going anywhere anytime soon." Dr. Bones said calmly.

I couldn't believe how calm he was in light of the circumstances fate had just placed before us.

Dr. Bones looked down the road. "Ogun will not fail us. Help is coming."

He went into his backpack, took out a jar with an herbal solution in it. He retrieved a long, thick railroad spike from a pouch around his waist.

Dr. Bones looked out at the road and began an invocation. "Ogun! I hereby invoke your power. Remove these obstacles and get us safely to our destination. We need your help, Baba. I give this offering in exchange for my answered prayers and respectfully ask you to make a way."

He shook the shells in his hand.

"Will you make a way for us to continue our journey?"

The shells fell three white and one dark.

"Ogun says yes, but something is missing."

I lost it. Emotions got the best of me. "This is crazy! I'm calling Darryl. He said he was almost here. He must be close now. I'll have him pick us up."

"That might be a mistake, a mistake that could cost us."

I punched Darryl's number into my cell. Once again, Darryl answered on the first ring.

"Darryl, where are you?"

"Woman, if you hang this phone up on me again...."

"I don't have time to explain. I need you to come and get us."

I told him where we were.

"Stay on the phone with me until I get there."

"Fine."

Two minutes later, Darryl's Escalade pulled up. I jumped out of the car and ran to him.

"Violet! Get back in the car! Somebody might see you!" Dr. Bones yelled.

A white van screeched up beside Dr. Bones. Darryl jumped out of the car and went into warrior mode.

It was the team who doubled for us at the 7-11.

"It's okay, honey. They're with us."

"You had me and your Dad worried out of our mind. That's it. No more going at this by yourself. From here on out, I go or you *don't* go."

I looked up and saw the couple who switched cars with us switching places with Dr. Bones. After they drove off, Dr. Bones came running over to Darryl and I.

"We have to change into these uniforms and get to the warehouse now or the girls are dead."

"I'm going." Darryl said in a firm tone.

"Adding another person to the plan at this stage could put us in danger."

"Look broh, I don't know you and you don't know me. But this is my wife and I'm going or she's not going."

"I don't mean to offend you."

"No offense taken. But this isn't up for discussion."

"Only two of us can walk up to the door. They'll know something is suspicious if three delivery people show up at the same time."

"Fine. I'll wait in the van."

"We need to put on our delivery uniforms."

The three of us squeezed into the van and pulled on the navy pants and white shirts that bore the *Jenkins Delivery Service* logo.

"What's next?" Darryl asked in a curt tone.

"Violet and I are going to walk up to the warehouse pretending we're making a delivery. I'll send Violet back to the van to unload while I take the first load of boxes in. While I'm in there, I'll get the girl and go out the back way. My inside guy told me there's a door that leads to the alley on the far right side of the building. You two are gonna wait for me back there."

"And what if your plan doesn't go as scheduled?"

"God help us all."

"I think I have a plan B."

"Yeah, let's hear it." Dr. Bones said, climbing into the driver's seat and starting it up.

While you're inside, the media is gonna start to arrive. They'll be the distraction you need to get that girl out of there. By then the calvary will have arrived to save the rest of them."

"It might just work."

"It has to." I said pulling my seat belt around me. "I'm ready. Let's do this."

CHAPTER
Fifty-Three

Diane, Brandon, Hazel, Mrs. Jasper, Pop Brown and the children were sitting in the living room watching the news and worrying. As usual, the house was filled with the soulful perfume of Mrs. Jasper's southern cooking.

"Diane, turn up the volume on the TV. The midday news is coming on and I gotta feelin' it's something we need to know." Pop Brown said, bending down to hug each of his grandchildren.

Hazel hung up from her call and made an announcement. "I just got off the phone with the police. They have Martin Lund in custody. They're interrogating him about his connection to the case in Ziberia and the laundering of funds from the League of Women United."

"I hope they lock those scoundrels up for the rest of their lives." Brandon said.

"All we have to do is get Violet home safe and everything will be fine." Diane said.

"Hush! The news is starting."

They say through two local news stories. Right before they went to commercial break, someone stuck a piece of paper in front of the anchorwoman that seemed to jolt her.

After she composed herself, the network announced it had "breaking news." The group listened intently as the newcaster made her announcement.

When she was done, Mrs. Miller said, "Oh my God. The media has gotten wind of the case. All hell is getting ready to break loose. Violet and her friend are about to be in the middle of a Mexican stand off!"

The TV showed footage of the police arriving to the scene and the SWAT agents getting in place.

Pop Brown stood up. "I'm going down there! Nobody's gonna hurt my baby."

"Daddy, we have to let the police hand this."

"I need you to get in that car and drive me down there right now!"

"Daddy, I'm not doing it. Your heart can't take the stress."

"Okay, fine."

Two minutes later, Pop Brown came out wearing a *Member's Only* jacket and a *Chicago Bears* baseball cap.

"Daddy, we already talked about this. Darryl called and he's with Violet. He said for us not to worry, they're gonna be fine."

He ignored his oldest daughter and went straight for the door.

"Daddy, where are you going?"

The rest of the group rushed outside on his heels just in time to see a long black limo slide up to the curb.

"He called Darryl's driver. Guess we better go with him. Brandon, lock the door. I have a key." Diane said, getting into the limo and sitting next to her father.

"You don't run me little girl. You might be grown but I'm still your father."

After everybody was in the car, Violet's father said, "Driver, take me 5th and San Julian."

And off they went....

CHAPTER
Fifty-Four

Darryl, Dr. Bones and I pulled up in front of a dilapidated warehouse on 5th and San Julian. I wasn't sure if it was just me being paranoid but the street seemed a little quiet for downtown Los Angeles.

"Either one of you think it's quiet for a weekday in downtown Los Angeles?"

"Yeah, like somebody's waiting for us to get here." Darryl agreed.

"Let's go over the plan one last time." Dr. Bones said, trying to keep us focused.

INSIDE THE WAREHOUSE, GENERAL MUBOSA SLAMMED A PRESS release down on his desk. His left arm swept across the surface of his massive workstation sending the pencil holder, tape dispenser and stapler flying across the room.

Sergeant Abayomi and two other soldiers ducked then backed up a few feet to avoid becoming the target of his rage.

"I want you to pay close attention to what I'm about to say. I want them dead! Not tomorrow, not the next day, today! This Violet person, her male friend and her companion. If I don't see their dead bodies on this floor by the time the sun goes down one of you will die. Every day that Fagunwa and those Americans remain alive, I will kill another soldier. And arrest my son. He might be a part of this, this media attention. Am I understood?"

"Yes sir! General, you should know that we have two of our men watching them. The first chance they have to take them, they will...."

The General threw a glass pitcher of water across the room at Sergeant Abayomi. It crashed against the wall behind him just missing his head.

"Make it happen without our being implicated any further. And prepare to move the girls. We may have to kill them. Now go!"

Sergeant Abayomi and the soldiers exited quickly. One of the men was sweating profusely. Fear seemed to pour from his pores.

"Sergeant Abayomi, I'm turning in my badge. I resign effective today." He tossed Abayomi his badge and headed for the door before he could object.

Jodowa, another NAA soldier, was on the verge of turning in his badge too. His large hands were still trembling from the meeting with the General.

He and Abayomi walked toward the parking lot strategizing on how to handle the crisis they found themselves facing.

"Abayomi, this detail is becoming more dangerous every day."

"Soon this job will be over and you will have a lot of money for your family. We must bring Fagunwa in alive, kill him and get rid of the body. His demise will make our problems go away. Let me make a few calls. I'll get back to you."

"Sergeant, I can kill men all day and all night. But I'm not a killer of innocent children." The soldier confessed.

"It's either you or the girls."

"Maybe I'll quit too." The burly man said with a huff.

"The General is angry because somebody involved the press. The media will try to crucify him over these accusations. He's afraid he might be arrested. As soon as things die down I think he'll change his mind about killing the girls."

"That man is a killer. It's in his blood. Some of the soldiers say he had his own wife murdered. That's why his son barely speaks to him. When a man's own son hates him...."

"Just stay close and be ready. This isn't over yet. I think we can all come out of this on top." The soldier looked at him like he'd gone nuts.

Abayomi talked a good talk but on the inside he knew the truth. The soldier was right. Things were bad and getting worse by the hour.

The General's whole operation was on the verge of being exposed. He himself could be under investigation. His career would be over before it ever got started. He had to rethink his strategy. Perhaps his place wasn't beside the General anymore.

"Maybe you're right, Jodowa. Perhaps it is a bad move to arrest Fagunwa. We'll hold off for now. We'll map out his capture but I don't want the plans executed unless I give the word. Is that clear?"

"Yes sir!"

Abayomi issued a memo to have the girls moved to a secure location. Large tents were set up just a few miles away where the girls would be stored until things cooled down. Metal tanks filled with poisonous gas were brought in and put in place in case of an emergency. The soldiers were instructed on what to do if there was threat of the operation being exposed.

In a small apartment near the warehouse, a tall, stately woman wrapped a large piece of fabric around her head. She took the last sips of a cup of tea and slid a collection of multi-colored beads over her head.

Another Amazon-size woman wrapped her head with a colorful piece of cloth and donned a similar array of necklaces. Iya Ayoola, Olokun's mother, and her best friend Oshunike, were on their way to get Olokun out of the warehouse. They would get her out alive or they would die trying. Iya Ayoola called Olatunji on his cell. He told her where and when to meet him. He explained that one of his American friends was working with one of his students to get Olokun out of the warehouse before the General moved the girls.

"The General will kill them before he lets them take Olokun."

"We know how dangerous this is. I'm calling to ask you to summon them. The Sacred Five. Dr. Bones and his friends will need their protection to survive this. Can you do the rituals?"

"Of course I can. I don't have the necklace but I can invoke them through the Oriki."

"Do it as soon as we hang up. If everything goes well, you and your daughter will be reunited, sitting down having dinner before the sun goes down."

"What a dinner that will be."

"Wait for me behind the warehouse. This will all be over soon."

"I'll leave right after I do the invocation."

"Olodumare will prevail."

"Yes, God will prevail, Olatunji. Ase. May it be so."

Ayoola kneeled, poured a few drops of water on the floor and spoke the invocation that had been used for thousands of years in times of trouble.

"B'ao ku ishe o tan. Ohun ori wa se. Ko man ni s'alai se eo. Ebo fin, Eru da. Where there is life, there is still hope. What Ori comes to fulfill, it cannot help but fulfill it. The offerings are accepted, evil forces depart."

CHAPTER
Fifty-Five

Three uniformed FBI officers had a terrified Martin Lund penned up in a small office interrogating him about his recent trip to Ghana. He still had on his work clothes, a gray and black Brooks Brothers suit. His blonde hair was wild and unruly. He had dark circles under his eyes because he hadn't slept in days.

Martin didn't know how the police had found out about the traffickers but he would die before he told them anything. Those horrible monsters had kidnapped his little girl. He had one more bank deposit to make for them and then they promised to let his daughter go. The last time he talked to her she had sounded so afraid. His wife thought she was at a basketball camp. He couldn't bring himself to tell her the truth.

The officers picked up his wife Susan and brought her to the station. When Martin saw her being led into the interrogation room he broke down.

She ran to him, threw her arms around his neck. "Martin, what's going on? They say you laundered money."

Susan was a petite woman who'd been sheltered all her life. She'd attended boarding school as a child and went to an exclusive all girl university in England. She wore a white velour sweatsuit, Prada sunglasses and Nike running shoes. Her eyes looked just as tired as his.

He had to tell her the truth. His back was up against the wall. He couldn't lie to his wife anymore.

"Susan, I have some really bad news. Something happened to our daughter. I thought I could get her back and make everything okay again."

"Martin, you're scaring me. I called the camp to check on Tracey and they said it's not due to start for another two weeks. Where's our baby?"

He sunk his head into his hands. "They took her, Susan. They took our little girl. When I refused to do their dirty work they took her for insurance."

"Who…who took her Martin?" His wife asked. He could tell she was bordering on hysteria.

"Those animals. They're part of some foreign operation that sells little girls. But not our daughter—they promised me they wouldn't sell Tracey. They promised to bring her back if I did one more deposit."

Susan fainted. One of the female agents rushed over and put some smelling salts beneath her nose. She came to a couple of minutes later.

The agent took Martin to another room.

"We need to know everything if we're going to save your daughter."

Martin told them exactly what happened. "They showed up at the firm's offices one night when I was working late trying to clear out the books for quarter. They threatened to kill my wife and take my daughter if I didn't do exactly what they told me. I was scared. Terrified is more like it. I did the first deposit and thought they'd leave me alone. But they came back and asked me to do a second one. Then I found out that the money was coming from the sale of human beings. I tried to end our arrangement. That's when they started playing hard ball with me. The next thing I knew, they'd taken Tracey."

"Have you given them the last deposit?" Agent Johnson asked him.

"No. I was supposed to make the final transfer today."

"Do you have a contact number for them?"

"No, they always call me. I contact them through an e-mail address. I make the transfer electronically and then I drop off the confirming documents at a P.O. Box. I'm scheduled to make the final deposit this morning."

"When they call you, you're going to tell them that something came up but you are going through with everything as planned. Where are they supposed to bring your daughter?"

"She's supposed to be at the office where the P.O. Box is. When I bring the documents they're going to release her."

"What time do they usually call you?"

"Around this time."

"We want you to accept the call. Once your daughter is safe, we're taking them down. Don't worry, you'll have immunity for assisting us in solving the case."

He breathed a sigh of relief.

Based on the description Martin gave them, the agents created and ran pictures of the men through a special computer database with millions of profiles. They were able to match their faces to known members of a militia that had been on the international hot list for months.

It was almost over but with a case like this, almost didn't count. Almost could mean more dead bodies....

CHAPTER
Fifty-Six

A few minutes after nine, Dr. Bones, Darryl and I pulled up in front of the warehouse. The men got out and started unloading boxes onto a dolly. I picked up a clipboard and pretended I was checking things off just in case they were watching. When Dr. Bones had a full load, we headed for the door of the warehouse.

My heart pounded like congas in a Cuban nightclub. My right eye started twitching in tempo with the beating in my heart. The door flew open before we could ring the buzzer. Two of the General's henchmen armed with what looked like shotguns answered the door with a rude greeting.

"What is this?" A tall man with a deep African accent asked Dr. Bones.

"We're here to deliver your uniforms."

"If you just sign here we'll bring the rest of them in for you." I told the man handing him my clipboard and a pen to sign with.

"We're not expecting any deliveries. You have the wrong address. Now get out of here. You're on private property."

"Is this 1615 South 5th Street?"

"Yeah. But I told you we're not expecting any deliveries. Now get the hell away from here."

It dawned on me that they hadn't made us yet. Dr. Bones was thinking the same thing. This could still go in our favor. But one of us had to get inside.

"We got the wrong building, Samantha. That means we're gonna be late to our next drop off. Listen sir, could I use your facilities? I've been holding it for hours." Dr. Bones said, holding his groin.

Before the man could answer, a large explosion barreled through the warehouse. It came from the back but the vibrations made the front windows rattle.

"What the fuck was that?" The tall guard asked his colleague before they took off in the direction of the explosion.

Dr. Bones turned to me and said, "Get back to the van. Meet me in the alley in ten minutes. Don't be late."

"What are you gonna…"

Dr. Bones took off running, right into the heart of danger.

I ran back to the van and told Darryl what happened.

"He's gonna try to get your sister out of there."

"That place is guarded like Alcatraz. I don't see how he can get her out without being caught."

"God's in the business of miracles, Violet. And that's what we need right now. Let's pray."

"Mama's prayer…That's what she wants. Say it with me."

We bowed our heads. "And though I walk through the valley of the shadow of death, I will fear no evil. Thy rod and thy staff will comfort me…."

Before we could finish praying, another car pulled up the warehouse. Two men and two women got out of a blue Ford Taurus and headed toward the side of the warehouse. The woman looked familiar. She reminded me of my grandmother on my mother's side. They didn't see Darryl and I because we were sitting in the back of the van. But we could hear them talking.

The woman who looked like my grandmother said, "The explosion worked. There are no guards out front. They're probably all in the back trying to see what happened. I think we can sneak inside and get the girls." They headed toward the side of the warehouse just as our attention was drawn to a loud commotion coming from inside the warehouse.

We heard somebody yelling in an African language. At least fifteen men ran out of the warehouse toward the back of the building carrying large buckets of water. Apparently there was a fire.

"He's been in there exactly eight minutes. I think we should drive around to the back."

"Not yet. There's too much activity. Let's wait a few more minutes."

"We can't let Dr. Bones and Olokun get out of there and we're not there to get them."

"Just wait a few more minutes, Violet. Something's not right."

Five minutes later, the front door of the warehouse flew open. Dr. Bones came running out with a young girl in tow. I knew it was her before I saw her face. She was wearing the necklace from my dreams.

"Open the door! Hurry! They're coming!" Dr. Bones yelled.

I slid the door open and moved to the side. When Olokun saw me, her mouth froze in a wide O.

"Modupe Egun. Ibae T'orun. You look like my grandmother." She said.

"We don't have time for reunions right now. Get in the car and we'll talk about who looks like who later!" Dr. Bones said, lifting Olokun up and into the van.

Darryl started the van as Dr. Bones slammed the door shut. Darryl backed up and tried to turn around to get out of there. Before he could put the car in drive, the doors to the warehouse burst open and gunfire rang out.

"Stay down!" Darryl shouted as he hung a sharp left that threw us backwards and into the sidewall of the van. Gunfire followed us. The deafening sound of bullets hitting glass nearly gave me a coronary.

When the gunfire slowed, I stood up, peaked out of the back window and saw soldiers barreling down the alley in our direction.

"Darryl, get us out of here! They're coming down the alley!" I told him.

"There's a bus blocking the exit and I don't think I can get around it."

"Back up and go the other way. Hurry, you have to act fast."

"You want me to head in the direction of the soldiers?"

"Yes. The element of surprise will throw them off. I want you to floor that gas pedal and mow anybody down who gets in your way."

Olokun slid onto her knees, took the necklace off her neck and began to pray.

"The invocation. Yes! Say it. Hurry!" I told her.

"B'ao ku ishe o tan. Ohun ori wa se. Ko man ni s'alai se eo. Ebo fin, Eru da. Where there is life, there is still hope. What Ori comes to fulfill, it cannot help but fulfill it. The offerings are accepted, evil forces depart."

Darry backed up, turned the van around and headed for the alley. He counted off before his foot mashed down on the pedal.

"One, two, three!"

He burned rubber back down the alley. The soldiers scattered like mice as he burned rubber toward the intersection, right into the line of fire.

As soon as he reached the entrance, the shooting started again. He swung left, throwing us against the other side of the van. Just when I thought we were clear, Darryl slammed on his brakes. Dr. Bones, Olokun and I ended up piled on top of each other behind the driver's seat.

"Darryl, we can't take being tossed around."

"I…I can't help it. You won't believe what I'm seeing."

"It better be Jesus and his apostles if you're still in this alley."

"Well, it's not Jesus. But what I'm seeing right now—is one level below seeing Christ himself."

Dr. Bones, Olokun and I lifted our heads just above the dashboard.

"Oh my God. It's….the media. The cameras. They're here in full force."

"Hell yeah! And if they're here, the calvary not far away." Darryl said.

A few seconds later, what seemed like L.A.'s entire police force surrounded the warehouse. Twenty minutes after that, General Mubosa and his men surrendered. The police had them spread eagle on the ground.

We were instructed by the police to stay in the van. It was hot as hell but we didn't care. We were alive. I prayed the girls were too.

"Violet, I think your husband's press release may be the thing that saved our lives." Dr. Bones said smiling.

"That's my man." I said proudly. "I just hope the girls are okay."

"They're free. I can feel it." Olokun said, sounding like a seer.

Just as Olokun spoke the words, a large yellow bus drove around the corner and parked in the front of the warehouse.

"What's going on? That's the bus that was in the back of the warehouse." I asked no one in particular.

"Looks like they're getting it ready to load people on it." Darryl answered.

A few minutes later, the front gate to the warehouse opened and the girls came running out.

"Oh my God. They're free! Yes! Thank you, God!" They're finally free!"

"Yes, they are free, Violet. And it is because of you and your ancestors." Dr. Bones said.

I was crying so hard I could hardly contain myself. Dr. Bones had a few tears in his eyes too. Darryl tried to console me.

"These are tears of joy. Not sadness. Joy."

I looked over at Olokun. She was crying too.

There was a knock on the van's side door. Dr. Bones slid the door open.

"If one of you is Violet Brown, there are some people here to see you."

"That would be my father." I said laughing.

CHAPTER
Fifty-Seven

I heard him before I saw him. "Violet! Violet, you alright?"

"Yes, Daddy. I'm okay. I found my sister."

"Violet, I don't know how you did it, but you saved them girls."

"God saved those girls, Daddy. Trust me on that."

Diane had to drop one of her stale jokes to decorate the moment.

"Violet Brown, you are one cup of crazy and a teaspoon of coo-coo cachoo. But you're still my sister and I'm glad you're alright."

"Me too, Vi-let. I kept praying and praying. I knew the good Lord was gonna protect you and those children." Brandon echoed with his southern accent.

"She's a hero. That's what she is. My wife is a hero." Darryl said.

"And you're my hero, Darryl Collins." I said kissing him.

I turned to Dr. Bones. "I never could've done this without you. I'm forever in your debt, Dr. Bones."

"Alfred. You can call me, Alfred. And you owe me nothing. I did it for the Orisa. For Yemoja. For the great Mothers."

"Diane, where're the kids?"

"They're with Mrs. Jaspers and Hazel. They're fine. Who's this young lady?"

"This....this is Olokun."

"Very nice to meet you." Olokun said.

"You dat' girl from Africa my Violet always dreaming about?" Daddy asked.

"I think so. Yes, sir. I am."

"She say you her sister. Y'all related?"

"I...I think we are."

"How so?"

"Daddy, enough questions for right now. Olokun has been through a whole lot. Let her get some rest and calm down. Then we can talk about everything."

In the front of the warehouse, the General, Abayomi and two of the General's henchmen were being led out in handcuffs.

The two men and two women we'd seen walking down the side of the building right after the explosion walked toward our van with a police officer.

"Ma'am. Do you have one of the children from the warehouse with you?"

Before I could answer, Olokun screamed a shriek so piercing that it made time stop. She jumped out of the van and fell to her knees.

"Yaaaaaa!!! Is....is it really you? Please tell me it is you!"

"Yes, my daughter. It is me. I am alive."

"Oh God, Modupe! Adupe Ancestors. Yetunde! Yetunde! My mother has returned! I thought they had taken you from me."

They embraced, kissed each other a thousand times. Both of them had tears streaming down their faces. Iya Ayoola caressed her daughter's face.

"Mama, I thought I would never see you again."

"I am here, daughter. We had to make them think they'd won to beat them."

The two men introduced themselves.

"I am Olatunji, the son of General Mubosa. I am also Ayoola's husband."

"I am Fagunwa. I am a friend of Dr. Bones. Together Olatunji and I helped take the General down. I was the inside man for The League.

"So you're Hazel's inside man."

"And I am Oshunike, a family friend." Olokun's Mother's friend said.

"Auntie Oshunike, it is so good to see you." Olokun said, hugging her tightly.

"And you, my daughter."

The police van carrying General Mubosa and his henchmen rolled by them. Fagunwa waved goodbye to the General and winked at Abayomi.

The General shouted at his son through the window as they carted him off.

"This is not over! I will destroy you the same way I destroyed your mother! You are my son. My flesh and blood. How could you betray your own father!"

Olatunji walked over to them. "Hold on just a minute officers. Please, if you would, allow me to say goodbye to my father."

The officer rolled down the window just enough. When he was close to his father, Olatunji spat in his face and said, "I might be your son but I am nothing like you. You will pay for what you have done to those children and to our great nation. Long live Ziberia! May God have mercy on your soul."

CHAPTER
Fifty-Eight

Olokun and her entourage stayed in Darryl's guest house. We spent the first two days sleeping, getting massages and eating fabulous soul food meals cooked by Mrs. Jasper. After the dust settled, I called Hazel Miller. She filled me in on the drama that went down at her camp while I was saving Olokun. Darryl had told me most of it but Hazel colored in the blank spots. After she finished her story, I told her what I thought she could handle of my journey.

"The important thing is that they caught those criminals. And that horrible General—thank God he's been stopped. And thank God Martin and Susan's child was returned unharmed. And you were able to save Olokun and find your sister. What more could we ask?" Hazel said, grateful everything had turned out okay.

"Hazel, you make our life sounds like one of those blockbuster movies. But you're right, this was one helluva journey. Next weekend, Diane, Daddy and I are getting married. We're having a triple wedding. Three weddings in one. Then I'm going on a long vacation! You'll be there right?"

"Bob and I wouldn't miss your wedding for the world. When you come back from that honeymoon we've got a lot to talk about. I informed the board of my intention to retire. I want you to take over my post as executive director of the League."

"I'm deeply honored, Hazel. I'll accept your offer on one condition. That the World Peace March is my first official project."

"It's a deal, Violet. We don't have to wait for a war to happen before we bring the world together in the name of peace. If the U.S. hadn't signed that peace treaty with the Middle East a few days ago we'd be in the midst of another crisis."

"Hazel, what I'm about to tell you is gonna sound a little strange. But I think Olokun stopped America from going to war with the Middle East. When we were in the van and the soldiers were shooting at us, she did this invocation to call down the Spirits to help us. I've had dreams about a massive bomb being sent to our country. The dreams were vivid which makes me think it was more than a dream it was a premonition. I saw and heard people screaming, the ashes falling from the sky—it was terrible, just terrible. So when she said the prayer to save us—while that spiritual portal was open—I asked the Sacred Five to save America."

"I've always believed we have angels watching over us."

"I think our country could really benefit from a mass gathering focused on religious unity."

"If anyone can get these religious fanatics to unify it's you."

"I'll give it my best shot."

"You do that. You do have an amazing story, Violet. I really think you

should write a book about your gift. I know a few publishers that might be interested."

"I'm no writer."

"That's what Sidney Sheldon said twenty million copies ago. Speaking of the march, I was going to surprise you with the news that we have a big corporate sponsor signed on. Since I already opened my big mouth I'll go ahead and tell you that they agreed to sponsor two mega speakers. The Dalai Lama and Marianne Williamson."

"Oh my God, you're kidding. The Dalai Lama? Marianne Williamson?"

"Yep. Dalai Lama's representatives called this morning and said they'd penciled the *Peace & Unity March* into his calendar. With those two signed on, we can get any one else we want."

"You are an amazing woman, Hazel Miller. You truly are. Can I hug you?" I asked her before making my way down the hall to the living room.

Daddy, Mrs. Jasper, Diane, Brandon and the kids had just arrived to visit my African sister, great Aunt and her family. Diane had lots of stories to tell them about me when I was a child. Hazel said her good-byes. She had to leave to pick up her husband Bob from his physical therapy.

When Darryl got home, he and Olatunji hung out in the media room watching b-ball and soccer. Olatunji gave Darryl a book on Yoruba culture. Darryl introduced him to the world of American sports via our plasma television.

While the men hooped and hollered over the NBA dunking and slamming, the women hung out by the pool eating tacos, laughing and swimming. Iya Ayoola and I caught up on nearly four decades of our lives.

I told her about my mother dying when I was young and my challenges growing up psychic. She told me about almost being killed and losing her husband while fighting for the rights of Ziberian women. We were more alike than we realized. Olokun listened quietly as we talked.

Iya Ayoola slipped and told me about Dr. Bones and her friend Oshunike. Apparently they'd made a love connection and had been talking on the phone everyday. Destiny at work again....

Daddy, Mrs. Jasper, Diane, Brandon and the children had to leave because the kids were tired and Daddy needed some rest.

After the game went off and the kitchen was tidied, our African family joined us at the kitchen table where we talked, ate and laughed until the sun came up.

It was an evening filled with love and family. The painting was almost complete. And the Gods were right, it was a masterpiece.

When our voices were hoarse and our bellies sore from laughing, Iya Ayoola, Olatunji, Fagunwa and Olokun went to the guest house so they could rest up for the wedding. Fagunwa's family had arrived that evening and we were all one big happy family.

Darryl and I had one day together before we jumped over the broom into the land of marital bliss. Bad luck or not, I was jonesing for some of his special medicine. I needed to feel, smell and touch my man in a big way.

I ran us a hot bath. Added some *Nanina Ra* lavender and lemongrass salts to the water. Let that soothing fragrance caress our hearts and minds. Darryl stepped down into the hot, soothing water and exhaled. I sat in front of him, my back on his firm chest. He picked up a plate of fruit and fed me a few grapes, a slice of fresh pineapple and a sip of apple champagne.

"I still can't get over the fact that you dreamed about these people and they were real. How amazing is that?"

"Pretty damn amazing. Hell, I can't believe it and it happened to me. You know how much I love you brother man?" I asked, kissing him on the forehead.

"I love you more." Darryl answered, licking the sweet taste of the pineapple and champagne from my lips.

"I've decided something." Darryl announced.

"I know. You want to marry me."

"Woman, that was decided the day I met you."

We laughed in unison at his sweet humor.

"Violet, I've decided I want to learn about the Yoruba religion. I'm not saying I'm getting initiated and all that. I just want to learn more about it."

"It is a fascinating spirituality."

"I've been reading that book your teacher gave you. The Historical Origin of Christianity. It's an eye opener like a mofo."

"Reading that book changed my entire life. If Alfred—or Dr. Bones—hadn't walked through the park that day, none of this would've ever happened. He woke up a question in me and until that question was answered, I couldn't rest."

"And you tell *Baba Alfred* I said that he should've grabbed you when he had the chance."

"What are you talking about?"

"I'm a man. A man knows when another man is attracted to his woman."

"You have nothing to worry about. Not in this life anyway."

"I *know* I don't have anything to worry about. But you tell him what I said."

I splashed some water on him to lighten the moment. He splashed some back at me. We played like two children in an adult wading pool. I felt so happy and free.

I stood up and took two small steps to the left. I stepped over him and eased down on his lap. When I was seated, I started moving my hips in neat little circles until he was moaning for me to let his toy play inside my toybox.

"Damn...Violet. That feels good....real good. Been too... long. Way too long." Darryl said, closing his eyes and letting his head rest on the back of the tub.

After a few more minutes of my teasing, he picked me up out of the water and carried me to our bedroom.

He had me stretch out on the bed while he opened a jar of coconut-vanilla scented Nanina Ra body oil. He gently massaged it into my skin.

When he was done I returned the favor. Only I added a little dessert.

I took his chocolate in my hand and caressed it slowly. Slid it into my mouth and licked him where it counted.

"Shit, Violet. Damn....you better do that shit....ahhh....just like that baby. Feels so damn good...."

I didn't answer. Couldn't answer. I just stroked him with my mouth again. When he was almost ready to burst, I mounted him. Let him slip inside of me inch by inch.

He started grinding his body against my pearl. Pulled me as close as he could get me and built the intensity in long, sensuous strokes.

"Darryl, oh God....stop....I can't take it."

I moaned, held him tight around his neck. He pushed his chocolate deeper.

"Don't fight it, Violet. Tonight....tonight, you're going to let me love you the way I've always wanted to. Open your soul to me. Give me all of you."

I twirled my tongue around in his mouth like it was a searchlight looking for a criminal.

He blew his breath into my mouth, filled my lungs with his love. When our orgasm rocked through my body, I couldn't stop the tears. I could feel his spirit inside of me, bonding with my own, making itself at home in my soul.

"That's it baby. Let it go. Feel me, Violet. Feel what it feels like to be loved by a real man."

"Darryl....Oh God! I'm....don't stop...ahhhh. Please don't stop!"

Darryl's pace quickened a notch. He started grinding me faster and harder. We merged, then crashed, melted and burned.

"Damn. Violet. Shit…this is some good shit…."

I felt his warmth explode into my body. I felt something else too. At first, I couldn't put a name on it. My womb. It felt funny. Full like. Then the ancestors told me what it was.

"Darryl, I think….Baby, I think you just got me pregnant."

"Huh? Whatever. All I know is…that shit was good."

"Darryl, did you hear what I said? I'm pregnant."

"Baby, I know you're psychic and all but it's a little too soon to know if the sperm made it."

"Not for me it isn't. I'm pregnant, Darryl. I just know."

"If you were, it would make me the happiest man alive."

CHAPTER
Fifty-Nine

Our nuptials were held in Darryl's backyard amidst a sea of lavender bushes, white orchids and fragrant roses. Diane, Mrs. Jasper and I floated down the aisle toward our husbands-to-be. Each of us wore a stunning lavender gown. The men wore black tuxedos, white shirts and mauve accessories.

Bushels of lavender were in vases throughout the patio. The scent of the flower made the space feel calming and spiritual. The arch through which we'd travel to love's paradise was made of purple roses, white lilies and stargazers. Our garden was packed full of people from all over the world who were delighted to be a part of our celebration of love.

Hazel and her husband sat on the front row along with my African dream team which included Fagunwa, his wife and daughter Adina—who'd been freed with the Mefaeru—Iya Ayoola and Olatunji, and Oshunike. Behind them was Amy from the J.B.

Good show, Laqueeta and Trunisha, my friends from college and several of the lawyers and interns from the firm where I worked. My Uncle Jerry, who happened to be on parole, had driven up from Chicago. My best and oldest friend, Cassandra, stood by my side at the altar as my maid of honor.

Dr. Bones officiated our wedding along with the pastor of my childhood church, per Daddy's request. Daddy was still an old-fashioned, God-fearing, Christian man and he always would be. And that was a-okay by me.

After each of us exchanged our vows, Darryl and I jumped the broom to symbolize the joining of our ancestors. At the last minute, Daddy, Diane and their spouses decided to take a leap over the broom too.

Calling our reception multi-cultural would've been an understatement. The menu included African delicacies personally prepared by our distinguished West African guests. We also had a vegetarian gourmet buffet that was so good, it could've turned a meat-eater into a vegan. On the other side of the room there was T-bone steak, potatoes and steamed carrots for the bonafide Americans.

The entertainment went from traditional African drumming to old school R&B to the best of the 1950's swing. We partayed until our feet were humming.

Later on that night, when most of the guests had gone home, Iya Ayoola and Olatunji announced their engagement. They made Darryl and I promise to come to Ziberia to attend the ceremony.

"We'll plan the wedding during the time you'll complete your Iyawo year. You can complete your rites in Africa where the tradition comes from. Iya Ayoola said happily. That announcement started another round of African drumming and dancing.

Dr. Bones and Oshunike were held up in a corner talking until the last guest went home. When Dr. Bones came to give me my goodbyes, I saw Darryl watching us from the corner of his eye.

"Congratulations, Violet. Darryl is a good man.'

"Thanks but I could've told you that. Hey, is that a love connection I see between you and Oshunike?"

He tried to conceal the smile sneaking up on his face. "We have a lot in common. I'm trying to talk her into staying in the United States. We're gonna go have some coffee and talk about it. I'll bring her back in a couple of hours."

"I think she's the one."

"One of many." Baba Alfred said, cracking up.

"Go 'head then wit-cho bad self, brother."

After I walked Dr. Bones and Oshunike to the door, Iya Ayoola and Olokun followed me upstairs to my Spiritual room. Darryl, Fagunwa and Olatunji hung out in the media room while Iya Ayoola, Olokun and I talked. Fagunwa's family chillaxed in the guest house. They were still jet lagged from their flight.

I had special gifts for Olokun and her mother in honor of the reconnection of our family. I explained to Iya Ayoola how rare it was for African-Americans to discover their roots.

"Because of slavery, Black Americans were almost completely separated from their African heritage. We lost our names, our language, our culture and our religion—everything that kept us connected to our ancestors. It means so much to me to have found you."

I gifted Iya Ayoola with my mother's pearls. I wanted her to have them. Couldn't explain it, I just knew she was supposed to take them home. She was moved to tears and quite honored by my gesture.

Olokun followed me down the hall to our office, a space that was now full of presents for each of her birthdays I had missed. Darryl and I had gone on a shopping spree the day before. We bought Olokun a whole suitcase full of state of the art electronics. I also gave her a Blackberry and a Mac laptop so we could keep in touch via Skype and email no matter where she or I were in the world. We filled a second suitcase with as much GAP and Baby Phat as it would hold.

I made a commitment to help Iya Ayoola get her human rights project funded so that the movement would continue to grow.

Darryl and I gave her a check for twenty-five thousand dollars to help expedite the vision.

"This will help so many women. The fight is long over. There are other Mubosa's out there. This will help us stop them." Iya Ayoola said, tearfully.

"And that's not all. Darryl found a bank account your husband had stashed a good amount of money away in. He's getting the funds transferred to your name."

Tears filled her eyes. "Oh my God! That's amazing."

The next morning, a couple of hours before we were to take them to the airport, Olokun and Iya Ayoola pulled me to the side to talk to me about something they deemed *very important*. For a brief moment, I wished I were going home to Africa too.

Olokun took my hand. Her small, soft fingers laced with mine.

When she let go, I looked down at the palm of my hand and in it was the necklace with the sacred stones.

"Olokun....I can't accept this. What if something happens and you need...."

"We want you to have it. It is important that you preserve our traditions."

"But I can't...I don't know how to...."

Iya Ayoola intervened.

"Iya, you must take the necklace. We divined on it this morning and this is what Mamiwata wants. When you return to Africa, we will take you to the secret cave where your great, great, great grandmother was born. It is almost time to give birth to a new stone. Two more girl children must be born in order for us to access the power needed to consecrate the stones. There must be five descendents present in order to conduct the ritual. We are told they are coming into the world quite soon. Until then, you must be the keeper of our legacy."

"I don't know what to say."

"Right now, we need to perform the ritual of passing down the necklace. You have to say an oath of loyalty to our lineage. Are you ready?"

"Yes. I'm ready."

I repeated the words that had been passed down for hundreds of years.

"I vow to uphold the rites and rituals of the sacred lineage of my ancestors. I will dedicate my life to preserving the rights of a free humanity. Wherever I am, whatever I am doing, I will continue to stand for the return of our people to the traditions of the old ones. Ase. Ase-o. Ase."

"Now the ritual."

Iya Ayoola stepped forward, placed her hands over the stones to bless them and placed them under her left breast. After her heart beat over them, she put them to her lips and spit on them. She passed the stones to Olokun who prayed over them, placed them beneath her left breast and spit on them. When they were done, Iya Ayoola dried the stones with a white cloth and placed them in my hand. The stones seemed to pulsate with life.

"Violet, on this day we bestow upon you the power to change futures. We give you and all of your descendants our gift. The gift of the Seers. You must use this gift to help save people from their own destruction. You must never forsake or misuse the ase' we have placed on your Ori. We have saved you, now you must save the others. It is done." Iya Ayoola said, tying the necklace around my neck.

"There will be tribulation on your path. May the color of these stones remind you of your greatness, of the blood that runs through your veins, of the power that rest in your hands and your vision. In times of great struggle you must invoke the energy of the stones. We will come to you. You will be a great healer, my daughter."

I couldn't believe this day was really happening. I remembered witnessing the ceremony in my dreams with the Sacred Five on the morning Odu was born.

They'd entrusted me to preserve our family's legacy. It was their greatest honor.

"Long live Ziberia!" I shouted.

"Long live Ziberia!" They said in unison.

We said our final goodbyes, agreed to e-mail each other every day and talk over the phone once a week. Bit by bit, we would continue to share the fabric of our lives—past, present and future.

"Where's Oshunike? I didn't get a chance to tell her goodbye?"

"We think you will have a little longer to visit with Oshunike. She has decided to extend her stay in America to help Dr. Bones with his wellness clinic."

That made me smile.

Darryl's driver arrived to take all of us to the airport. They were going home to Africa. Darryl and I were taking a long overdue honeymoon vacation. Diane and Brandon had already left for their Jamaican retreat. Daddy, Mrs. Jasper-Brown and a nanny were stay-cationing at Darryl's house with the kids.

Darryl and I almost missed our flight. Once we were seated and sipping our first class champagne, we started to unwind. I was excited about spending two glorious weeks with the man I loved. I'd heard the Maldives were incredible. I imagined us strolling on the beach, drinking fresh juice out of coconut shells and making freaky, passionate love into the wee hours of the night.

Two glorious weeks later, tanned, toned and thoroughly relaxed, we reluctantly returned to the city from our fabulous honeymoon. Darryl went back to work that Monday. His schedule was long and hectic after being out so long but I didn't complain. While we were in Maldives I made him promise to give me one weekend every month that I could have him all to myself. No cell phones or laptops allowed. He agreed. I made him put it in writing like my father taught me.

The following Wednesday, I celebrated my first day as executive director in-training of the International League of Women United. I loved my new job from the moment I stepped foot in the office. Daddy was really happy I was finally putting my law degree to good use. Hazel was able to transition into her retirement knowing that someone who really cared about the people was taking over the helm.

Darryl and I celebrated three months of being married by renting a spacious cottage in Half Moon Bay. I woke up one morning during our vacation and noticed my pants were a little tight. When I commented on it, Darryl teased me about my putting on what he called "a few married pounds."

"That's my love on you. And you wear it well. You better start working out though. Somebody's gonna think you've got a little bun in the oven." Darryl said, laughing at his own joke.

I looked at him and he looked at me. The light bulb went on simultaneously and we remembered the words I had uttered in the heat of our passion.

Both of us got up, threw on sweats and t-shirts, went to the drugstore and got one of those home pregnancy tests. We made ourselves a cup of tea and sat waiting in the bathroom for the results.

When the timer went off, I chickened out.

"Darryl, you read it. I'm too scared to look."

Darryl got up off the edge of the tub and went to the counter. He picked the plastic strip that would determine our next eighteen years or more.

A big smile stretched across his face.

"I'm going to be a father and you, my love, are going to be my child's mother."

We met in the middle of the bathroom for a long embrace. I thought about my last pregnancy and for a minute, I felt afraid. Then I remembered that my past didn't dictate my future. Only love. Love was my only existence now.

"Darryl, I can't believe it. This is like a fairytale. I'm waiting for the wicked witch of the East to step in and put a dark cloud over our sun."

"She ain't coming, Violet. She ain't ever coming to this address."

"I'm kind of old to be having my first baby. What if something goes wrong?"

"You're a psychic, you'll know in time to do something about it."

That night, when we went to bed, I did something I hadn't done in a long time. I dreamed.

I dreamed about our daughter. Her cocoa-colored skin and curly hair. Her goo-goo ga-ga words. Her baby lotion scented cheeks. I dreamed of breast-feeding her and her taking her first steps. I saw nothing but happiness in my future.

At the end of my dream, Mamiwata came to me. She was sitting on that rock where she'd first shown herself to me. I walked up to her. Ran my fingers across her locks. Climbed up on the massive stone and laid my head on her lap.

She gently caressed my face, looked into my eyes and made me release her. I knew it was time but still, I didn't want her to go. She'd been with me so long. She'd been my comfort when I was at my lowest, when I had no one.

My work with you is done for now, beloved. I can finally rest. I've waited so long to rest, Violet. You must stay close to your new family as well as your old one. Your work in Africa is not finished. There will be many more battles to fight in that country and in yours. Use your gift whenever you are unsure. Your students are waiting for you, Violet. You mustn't forget your promise to Iya Ayoola.

Return the people to the tradition.

Your daughter's name is Heaven. That is where her soul comes from. She will be a great seer just like you. Olokun will bring the fifth wife to the sacred circle. Her womb is preparing itself. Your mother says to tell you that she loves you and that she is proud of you. You've accomplished everything she hoped you would and then some. Take care of your father. He is more fragile than he seems.

Always keep Ifa close to you. Follow the guidance of Dr. Bones and never forsake him. He is one of our special angels that is still able to be seen by the human eye.

Remember to laugh, Violet. Remember to play too. Most of te living take life way too serious. And most of all, remember to love. I will always be watching over you.

I jerked a time or two then summoned my spirit back into my body. The motion woke me up. I watched Darryl toss and turn a few times before settling on his left side facing me. I could tell he was awake even though his eyes were closed. His arm stretched across me and pulled me close.

"Heaven." I said out loud.

"Huh? What are you talking about woman? Good morning, by the way."

"Our daughter—her name is Heaven. And that's where she comes from."

"How do you know it's gonna be a girl? Isn't it too early to tell?"

"I just know. And her middle name is Danielle."

"Heaven Danielle Collins. I kind of like the sound of that."

"Me too, Darryl. I love Heaven already."

"You are my heaven, Violet. My heaven on earth."

"Only when you've survived hell, do you really understand what heaven is."

He put his hand on my stomach. "Welcome Heaven. I can't wait to meet you. I wonder if you're gonna be a seer like your mother?"

Other titles by
LOVE TA'SHIA ASANTI

* The Sacred Door: A Spiritual Path to Power Living (Noble Trinity Media)
* The Master Breakthrough: A 24 Hour Spiritual Revolution (Noble Trinity Media)
* Any Heart Open (Rainmaker Publishing)
* The Bones Do Talk (Glover Lane Press)
* Sheep & the Wolves (Noble Trinity Media)
* Tapestries of Faith-Anthology (Glover Lane Press)
* Letters to My Bully-Anthology (Glover Lane Press)

To book Love at your event, to speak to your book club visit:
www.officialtashiaasanti.com

ACKNOWLEDGMENTS

To D Pepper Massey. Thank you for your unwavering love and support through the rebirth of another of my literary babies! None of these books would be possible without you. I love and appreciate you so much! ETL

To Jacquelyn "Pinky" Kennedy. Thank you for listening to my creative utterings on highways, hotel rooms and plane rides and all the fab meals that kept me going while I was writing this book! I love you with all my heart! Puma

To my daughter, Danielle and my grandchildren, Khalil, Lavelle, Kaelan and Malcolm, remember you can be ANYTHING you want! Dream big.

To my spiritual teacher and warrior sister, Betty Henderson, thank you for believing in, encouraging and supporting me with this and all my goals and dreams. You are so amazing and I love you!

To my powerhouse publisher, Naja Hayward, thank for your love, patience and support and especially for your encouragement, faith and work on this project. Onward!

Thank you to my biological and the Massey family. I love you with all my heart. Especially to my brother, Francis and nieces Monique, Shawntel, Kaywanna and Toni and daughter Danielle, as well as all my brothers and sister, grandchildren, cousins, nieces and nephews. I am because you are....

To my dearest friends and spiritual family: Iya "Kaykay" Nanina Ra, Cleo Manago, Jeff Fard, Jeffrey King, Sharon Seigel, Stephanie Dakara Wynne, Oloye Ifa Karade, Iya Sokoya Karade, Geevani Singh, Jenenne Macklin, Jerome Woods thank you for going hard to support and show up for EVERYTHING I do. For always supporting my writing and for being my friends through thick and thin and for supporting my success in ways that made a huge difference. I love you!

To my chosen family and friends who are the wind beneath my wings, LaQuetta Shamblee, Naji Ali, Thomasina Jackson, Laurence Pinckney, James Saunders, Alexis McSween, Preston Vargas, Oshunike Ifadoyin, Sangotade Luis Diaz Figeroa, Senakhu Donald, Queen Oyade Hollins, Marci Acoma, Malaika Mason, Olorisha Osundara, Akilah Osunlade, Pat Munson, Awo Lou Florez, India Omiosun and JJ Kayode Harville-Omelagah, Rory McMahan, Iyalosa Olori, Nicole Smith Johnson, Brad Smith, Peter Stocke, Talon Ifakemi, Michael Nobleeza, Olorisha Ifasina, Oriade Harbor, Nauddy Meriweather, Sister Meisha, Almeta Corbin and all my Godchildren, too many to list. To my babies Zannie, Denise, Deborah, Crystal and Anne--thank you for your support and faith in me. To my teachers, Michael Datcher, Peter J. Harris, Dr. Haki Madhubuti, Amiri Baraka, Ayofemi Folayan (Ibae), Akilah Oliver (Ibae) and Sonia Sanchez--thank you for helping to birth the words in me. And to the entire World Stage Family, Conney Williams, V. Kali, Kamau Daood! Love you.

To all the book clubs, book reviewers, friends and family who will buy or have bought, read and reviewed my books--you are the reason I write. Thank you for affirming my life purpose.

Love TaShia Asanti is an award-winning fiction writer, journalist, filmmaker, poet and television personality. Love's essays, short stories and editorials have appeared in distinguished magazines, books, anthologies and newspapers such as Essence Magazine, Poets & Writers and Chicken Soup for the Soul.

The author of nine books, Love has studied with renowned fiction writers and poets including Michael Datcher, Sonia Sanchez, Peter J. Harris and Haki Madhubuti. Love is the recipient of the *Kathleen E. Morris Award for Best Contemporary Fiction* and the *Seed Scholarship Award* given by the *International Black Writers and Artists Organization* to a writer with exceptional promise. Love was named a Lambda Fellow and awarded a highly competitive scholarship award from the *Lambda Literary Foundation* to attend their distinguished UCLA Writer's Program. Love founded the *Read US Book Club* and *Read US Annual Book Awards* at the Urban Spectrum Newspaper where she was a Senior Book Reviewer and Managing Editor. Love's social media platforms and web site www.officialtashiaasanti.com attract thousands of visitors and viewers.

Made in the USA
Las Vegas, NV
11 April 2024

88541098R00222